Danny King was born in  rew up in the wilds of Ham nod carrier, a postman, a shelf an't honestly recommend any of them. *The Burglar Diaries* is his debut novel and the first in the Crime Diaries series. He moved to London in 1992 and currently lives in the pub.

The Burglar Diaries

Danny King

Library of Congress Catalog Card Number: 00–102188

A complete catalogue record for this book can be
obtained from the British Library on request

First published in 2001
by Serpent's Tail,
4 Blackstock Mews, London N4 2BT

website: www.serpentstail.com

Typeset by Intype London Ltd
Printed in Great Britain by Mackays of Chatham plc

10 9 8 7 6 5 4 3

For my Mum and Dad

Sorry about all that unfortunate business. Just tell the neighbours it was a phase I was going through (as well as their belongings).

Acknowledgements

First and foremost I'd like to thank John Williams for everything he's done for me. It's not an exaggeration to say that if it wasn't for John's backing and support you wouldn't be reading this book today. For that I am in his debt. I'd also like to thank Pete Ayrton and Serpent's Tail for publishing my book and proving Hod Carrier, Andy Shaw, wrong when he told me I'd never have a book published. That's been bugging me for the last fourteen years and I showed him (I wonder if he remembers who I am?). My thanks also go to my agent, Kerith Biggs, for investing her faith in me; to my mate Clive Andrews who read all of my manuscripts, even after I'd bored the shit out of him telling him all about them fifty times over; to my brother, Robin, who is a talented actor but sadly out of work at the moment (regardless of whenever you're reading this); to the lads, Simon Kempthorne and Cliff Harrington, for dressing up as burglars and robbing their own kitchen while I photographed them (nothing fruity); to my oldest mate, Brian McCann, for asking me if he can be thanked in this section; to my girlfriend, Claire Bull, for constantly telling me how awful I look in my favourite shirt; and finally to my old partner-in-crime, Darren Berry – take care, mate, and stay out of trouble wherever you are.

1. Fred sees red

'What?' says Ollie, shining the torch in my face for the umpteenth fucking time.

'Get the instructions.'

'What instructions?'

'For the video.'

Ollie swishes the torchlight around the room a couple of times as I struggle to disconnect the cables out the back of the machine, before bringing it back to rest in my face.

'Why?'

'Electric told me to get 'em while we was here.'

'Where are they?'

What a great question. Like I'd know any better than he would. Ollie's like that though, king of the stupid question. Ain't no question too pointless for him to ask. It's the same all the time, whenever we go anywhere together for the first time he becomes a real 'where's the bogs' or 'how much further is it' merchant. One time after I had a medical and I was telling him about it, he even asked me what blood type group he was. My standard answer to all of these questions, over the years, has invariably been 'How the fuck should I know?' You would have thought he'd got the message by now.

'How the fuck should I know? This ain't my house, I

don't live here do I? Have a look in those drawers over
there by the videos,' which he does, as I make a little more
room for my hand so I can finally yank out the last of the
cables. I pull the machine out from under the table and take
it through to the back door – our point of entry for this
evening – to put with the rest of the pile. A big telly, a
portable, a microwave, one of those miniature hi-fi systems,
an answerphone, a camera, a leather jacket, a three quarter's
full bottle of scotch (for personal consumption later) and
an alright looking set of graphite golf clubs. Some burglars
would take the furniture as well, but I'm not really in that
game. Too big and too much of an effort to be arsed with.
I'm strictly an electrical appliances man; they yield the most
amount of wedge for the least amount of bulk – not
counting jewellery of course, though there ain't an awful
lot of that about in reality. The image of some Milk Tray
man shinning up a drainpipe to steal Lady Fanshaw's
diamond tiara is nothing more than a product of Hollywood
and a romantic view of burglary. Let me assure you, if
Raffles had lived on this estate, he would've nicked videos
as well.

'These 'em?' says Ollie, holding out a manual with 'How
to use your new video recorder' written in big letters on
the front.

'Yeah, that's them,' I say.

'Well here'ya.'

'Don't give 'em to me, I don't want them. Stick 'em in
your pocket.'

'I ain't got the room, you take 'em.'

This is another of Ollie's little traits, filling his pocket
with crap. We ain't in most houses more than ten minutes
before he's stashed half a ton of junk we ain't ever going to
get a penny for away in his slacks. Calculators, pens, cheap
digital watches and anything else shiny that catches his eye.

We did this one job once where the geezer had a big bottle of coppers – you know, one and two pence pieces – and old Jackdaw here practically gives himself a hernia trying to clamber over the back fence in a hurry, a bit later on, with little more than £19 in his pocket. Cunt!

'What you got in there?' I ask.

'A chess set.'

'Chess?'

'Yeah, all nice carved pieces and a pucker board, it was all set up on the coffee table in the other room.'

'What the fuck do you know about chess?' I ask. This is rather patronising, I have to admit, I mean it's not something we've ever really discussed. So far as I know he could be the next Gary Kasparov or that four-eyed idiot that keeps losing on telly. I'm just naturally assuming that he's a thick bastard who knows fuck all about fuck all – though I'd always be prepared to back up that assumption with cash.

'Enough to know that I ain't got a set and I want one.'

'Fuck's sake, you'll nick any old shit won't you. Why don't you try and be a bit professional for a change?'

'Oh yeah, I don't see you slinging those CDs you slipped into your pocket earlier? Who died and made you the fucking boss? I don't go telling you what you can and cannot take now do I. It ain't your fucking stuff, so fuck off.' A good point, well made he no doubt thought.

'Give me those here then,' I concede and tuck the instructions inside my shirt. We don't normally bicker like this. Ordinarily, if you met us down the pub or ... or ... well anywhere else we might be, you couldn't wish to bump into two more agreeable blokes. It's just when we're doing a job, you know what it's like, it's a tense situation, the pressure's on, you want to get in and out of the place a bit lively, while all the time it seems like the other bloke is doing everything he possibly can to fuck about and get you nicked.

I'm sure Ollie thinks exactly the same about me, with the one little difference in that he ain't got half the ammunition to complain about me as I have on him, because I don't fuck about nowhere near as much as him. Coming up is a case in point.

'Come on then, that's the lot, let's get out of here,' I say, picking up the microwave, video and leather jacket (actually, if I put that on, that'll be one less thing to carry and I can then grab something else, the camera or something – leave the big telly for Ollie). 'Grab what you can and let's make the first trip to the van.' I lean the load on the corner of the work surface, fish the van keys out of my pocket and clamp them between me teeth. Better to do it now rather than stand on a street corner hunting through every pocket holding on to matey's stuff as his neighbours watch us from their bedroom windows. 'Ready?'

'Hold on a sec, just got to go and have a shit. Where's the bog?'

'Hey? Fuck off, come on let's get the stuff out to the van and get out of here.'

'In a minute man, I'm busting,' he says wearing that face all people wear when they're busting for a shit.

'Why didn't you go before we come here then?'

'Oh sorry Miss, but I didn't want to go then did I,' he says screwing his face up like a man having a rough time at customs. 'Look, I thought I could get through the job okay and have a dump after, but I was wrong.' He looks at me looking at him through the darkness of the living room. 'I'm absolutely fucking heaving, if I don't go now my arse is going to explode, alright?'

And with that, he wanders off in search of the bog.

'Upstairs, right?'

'I don't know, just hurry up,' I tell him. 'Wanker,' I mutter to myself.

'It's alright, no panic, we've got all night on this one.'
This, to a certain extent, was true. The owner of the house
was a fireman. One of the blokes who drank in his local
had put us on to him – for a small standard commission, of
course; well you can't expect anyone to sell out their mates
unless there's a good drink in it for them. Anyway, Fireman
Fred was on the night shift all this week giving us a more
than generous eight hours to get in and liberate his gear,
and we still had a good four hours to go yet. However, it
ain't always the house owner that catches you in the act.
No! It's more likely to be the next door neighbour, or her
across the road with the binoculars and the twitching
curtain. Oh yes, Neighbourhood Watch schemes, they call
them. Sitting round each other's house every other Wednesday evening, drinking tea and complaining about the
ballast from number 18's kitchen extension spilling on to
the street. Or Audrey's daughter Wendy, seen out round the
back of the shops, smoking with a couple of dispatch riders
(and her not even out of school yet). Or the new black
people in number 43 and how the house prices are going to
tumble. Neighbourhood Watch, bollocks, Snoopers'
Charter more like.

'And don't take your gloves off,' I call quietly after him.

'Why, what's the Old Bill going to do, dust my arse for
prints?' comes back Ollie's response.

I decide to take one last look around while Ollie's
upstairs. Always worth one last shift around, if you've got
a moment, just to be on the safe side. There's a picture of
Fred, or whatever his name is, on the sideboard, in his
uniform with a couple of old codgers (his parents no doubt).
He's a strapping big bloke and looks proud as punch, as do
his old folks, but I don't stare at the picture too long. It
doesn't pay to think too much about who you're doing

over, just in case it triggers a little bit of weakness inside you.

Just as I wouldn't want to spend a day working with Mr Sing in his corner shop, watching him working from the crack of dawn to last thing at night; filling his shelves, keeping an eye on his stock and counting out the pittance he's made from fourteen or fifteen hours' work. A pittance which has to go to pay his rent, feed his family and leave enough over aside to see his son through university in a few years' time. You don't want to know about all that do you. You don't care. All you want to know is that he charges 30p over the odds for a bottle of Head and Shoulders, and is he looking this way when you walk past the Jaffa Cakes.

'Bex, oi Bex,' Ollie calls quietly from upstairs; you know, one of those half-whispers, half-shouts that people who don't want to be heard do, when they want to be heard. Fairly pointless exercise really, you might as well just talk.

'What?' I call back in kind.

'I need some bog paper, there's no bog paper up here.'

'Hey?' I respond in a moment of denial hoping I've misheard him.

'Bog paper, I need some bog paper. Bring us up a roll will you.'

Oh for god's sake . . .

'Where is it?'

'How the fuck should I know, this ain't my fucking house is it,' he says.

I allow myself a couple of moments to grumble and curse in the darkness and consider the possibility of just loading up the van and leaving Ollie to it, but something inside me won't let me do that. I put it down to a childhood spent watching dodgy 1950s British war films; the enemy is relentlessly advancing, ammunition is all but gone and Kenneth

More is holding up the whole fucking platoon with his gammy leg. 'You never leave a man behind,' they all say, 'never.' However, I'm sure even Richard Todd would have given it some serious thought had the bastard kept stopping every five minutes for a shit or to fill his pockets with board games.

'Bex, Bex, have you got any?'

'Hang on, hang on, I'm looking, alright, give me a moment.'

I go through all the cupboards in the kitchen, at both knee and eye level and even have a look under the stairs – all the universally acceptable places spare bog rolls should be stored – but Fireman Fred's obviously got other ideas on the matter.

As I search, I'm suddenly aware that this job is just taking too long and that we should be out of this house now and driving down the road. I know this because I suddenly really want a fag. I always spark up after a job and my urgent craving for nicotine is my body's way of telling me that I should be in the van on the way home, not playing hunt the toilet roll in some Red Adare hopeful's two bed semi.

Don't get me wrong, this ain't some sort of sexual ritual of mine, savouring a well-earned cigarette after yet another orgasmic escapade by the master criminal. I just want a fag. I smoke in the course of my everyday life and, like anyone else, I enjoy one when I knock off work. I could, in theory, have one while I'm here doing the job, but I don't like to. It's a question of manners. Not everyone likes to have people smoking in their houses, and I know it sounds funny coming from someone like me, but you've got to have a little bit of consideration haven't you.

There ain't no bog paper so what's left of the kitchen roll and a tea towel will have to do.

I'm not even half way up the stairs and a wall of stench hits me full in the face. I back off a step and cover my nose with the tea towel, wiping the tears from my eyes as I do so. Something ain't right up Ollie's arse. Now I know, everyone's shit smells worse than our own, but this was beyond a joke. The stuff's too painful on the sinuses to even consider approaching the door at the top of the stairs. All I can think of is that he must've been eating shit in the first place for it to come out smelling that bad.

'Are you gonna give me the fucking stuff or what?' calls Ollie as he peers around the door and through a vale of his own poison, immune to its potent evil.

'Here,' I reply as I toss up the kitchen roll in the direction of the epicentre, only to watch the lot unravel on the way back down.

It was about this moment, just as I came to the conclusion that I really didn't want to be here, when I hear the key turn in the door behind me. Fred steps in after a hard night's work to discover two total strangers filling his house with new and exciting smells and unravelling his kitchen roll on the stairs.

His face must've been a picture.

I have to guess at that because I didn't hang about for a look. I leg it the only way I can, the moment he comes through the door – up the stairs. I almost knock Ollie sideways as I barge past him and into the bog, ramming home the bolt behind me. Only then did I see the error of my decision. The place fucking stank. And I mean, it fucking stank.

I drop to my knees to try and get at some of the cleaner air when the hammering starts on the bog door.

'Come out of there you dirty bastards, I'm going to bloody kill you.' I really didn't like the use of the plural.

Surely there's only one dirty bastard in here, but I don't suppose it would do any good to point this out.

'Quick, give me that to wipe me arse on,' says Ollie reaching for my tea towel come gas mask. Under normal circumstances he could've fucked off, but these weren't normal circumstances.

'Get out of there. Get out of there,' demands Fred, still banging on the door. It was only a matter of seconds before he was through it. I put my shoulder and all of my weight to the door to hold him off a few more moments, while Ollie wrestles with trousers.

'Fuck off,' is all I can think of to tell Fred. I'm sure if I was the poet laureate or Noel Coward or Michael Barrymore, I could've thought up something much more amusing to shout at the angry fireman on the other side of the door. But I'm not, so 'fuck off', would have to do. I repeat it a couple more times, knowing full well that he wasn't about to 'fuck off', and in fact, what he wanted to do was 'come in and punch my head in'.

. . . size of the geezer, I keep thinking.

. . . size of the geezer.

. . . size of the geezer.

. . . size of the geezer.

'How d'you open this window? Where's the key? How come he's home early?' Ollie jabbers as he struggles to wrench open the locked window.

'I'm going to count to three . . .' Fred was saying outside.

'Smash the fucking window.' I scream at Ollie. 'Put the bastard in.'

Ollie doesn't need to be told twice. He does the window with a heavy shaving mug and the bog brush and launches himself through it, before the last shard hits the ground. Fred outside wises up pretty quick as to what the plan is and charges downstairs in order to head us off at the pass.

I'm not exactly going to hang about either and quick as a flash I haul myself through the hole – tearing a chunk out of my leg as I go – and jump down into the darkness. It's only when I'm half way down that I suddenly wonder if Ollie's out of the way down below. I'm hoping that he hasn't fallen badly and knocked himself out and urgently in need of medical help, because that's not what's on its way.

My feet sink deep into a bed of daffs and the lawn rushes up to meet the rest of me. My knees, hands, nose and chin already hurt even before I feel the first boot in my side.

. . . size of the geezer . . . size of the geezer . . .

I frantically try and scramble to my feet but Fred's having none of it. Boot after boot smacks into me, as well as a couple of punches in the back of the head for good measure.

All my options exhausted, I curl up into the foetal position and resign myself to the inevitable kicking. Without warning though, Fred collapses on top of me and looks up in shock. Ollie doesn't even hesitate and brings the spade down on his nut again. All of a sudden, you can see it in his face, Fred's somewhere he doesn't want to be – the wrong end of a fucking good hiding.

Reinvigorated by this I drag myself up and wobble over Fred for a bit as Ollie gives him another whack with the shovel, then goes in hard with his feet.

'Let's do the bastard,' he says, encouraging me to join in, but I hurt too much. But before Ollie has a chance to get into his stride, I pull him off and drag him in the direction of the back gate.

'Fuck's sake Ollie, come on let's go.' And we leg it for the van.

I should've wanted to do the bastard as much as Ollie did, but sometimes you just have to cut your losses. A smash in the face and a bastard of a headache would have to do for him.

And you know the thing that really pissed me off about it all, as we ran off into the night, I knew that we'd get blamed for it.

2. It's a bit like squirrels

Stealing is wrong.

Oh yeah, says who?

Says God, and he should know.

Yeah well God says a lot of things, most of which we choose to ignore because they don't quite fit in with our plans.

It's one of the ten commandments, thou shall not steal.

People only ever seem to remember that one, don't they. That one, thou shall not kill and thou shall not commit adultery. None of the others ever get a look in nowadays do they, simply because it ain't convenient to follow them all. Most people, myself included, can't even remember more than five, so what does that say about the sanctity of the commandments, hey?

What about thou shall not commit blasphemy? That's one of the ten commandments isn't it, no more and no less important than stealing, killing and coveting thy neighbour's ass, or whatever else. But how many of us stick to that one, hey? Who hasn't, at some point during their life, said: 'Christ, you fucking stink' or 'God, you are such a cunt'? No one worries about that though do they. They might tell you to watch your language in front of your gran, but they don't point out how wrong it is for you to take the Lord's name in vain now, do they?

And what about adultery? Another one of the ten commandments and one that people generally do like to go around quoting. I don't know if anyone's forgotten about this, or conveniently overlooked it, but wasn't Mary already married, when God came along and got her up the lemon? No one said anything about that though, did they? No, God was God and Mary became the mother of Christianity. Yet when my sister found she had one in the oven, she become known as the town slag and the lad who collected the pools money every Thursday got the shit kicked out of him by an unknown brother-in-law.

Yes, but God can do that because he's God.

Right, and there you have it, God turns out to be just like every other fucking boss I've ever had. A 'do what I say, not what I do' merchant. So, that means then, if God was to burgle my house, that also wouldn't be wrong, because he's God, and I'd all be in schtuck because the Old Bill couldn't touch him because he's exempt from the laws that govern us. And you couldn't claim on the insurance, because acts of God aren't covered in your household policy.

Why would God burgle your house?

Well, he probably wouldn't, but I'm just saying that things aren't as clear cut as everyone likes to make out, if you're using the old ten commandments argument. And besides, I don't believe in God anyway so none of it applies to me. Those commandments were chiselled out for Christians to follow. Well I ain't a Christian, so I don't have to follow them. Why follow the club rules when you ain't even in the club. Same as I ain't Jewish, which is why I can enjoy a nice bacon sandwich with my cup of tea and the paper in the morning.

Yeah, but stealing is wrong. In a civilised society, whether you go to church or not, it is commonly accepted that stealing is wrong.

Oh yeah, if it's so fucking wrong, then how comes everyone does it?

No they don't.

Yes they do. To a greater or lesser extent, everyone nicks stuff. It doesn't matter whether it's a couple of paper clips from the office stationery cupboard, a bit of scrap wood from the building site skip or five and a half million quid in gold bullion. Everyone, at some point in their lives, takes something that don't belong to them, there's no difference.

No difference between nicking five and a half million quid and a couple of paper clips? There's a world of difference.

No there ain't, they're both nicking, it's just a matter of scale that makes them look different. Same as a sardine and a whale, they're both fish, they both swim in the sea, one's just a bit bigger than the other one that's all. I'm sure if you asked a bullion robber what he thought about someone who nicked videos, he'd probably say it was so small it weren't real nicking at all.

It's immoral.

Immoral is it, how? How can you attach morality to a video recorder? Let me ask you this, is it immoral when a wolf or something kills a zebra, and is just about to sit down and eat it, when along comes a lion and chases him away and has it for himself. After all the wolf has done all the hard work, the zebra is rightfully his, but that doesn't stop the lion from nicking it does it. No, because it's survival of the fittest, law of the jungle. The hyenas aren't looking over and calling the lion a cunt for nicking the wolf's lunch, are they? No, they're all lining up to chase away the lion and have some zebra for themselves.

It's the same with squirrels. If one squirrel stumbles across another squirrel's stash of nuts, he doesn't think: 'Blimey, what a fucking load of nuts. I wish I had all these, that way I wouldn't starve to death in the winter. Still, fair's fair, old Sammy did collect them all, they are his. I'll go and get me own if there's any left.' No, he has the lot away for himself and leaves Sammy to face the winter with an empty larder and a bleak outlook. But we don't judge the squirrel though do we? We don't call it immoral, yet it's no different from what I do, except that no one has ever died as a result of me nicking their video. In that respect actually, I'm one up on the squirrel.

No, burgling houses has got fuck all to do with morality. Morality is something else, something higher. It's to do with trust and betrayal and all that sort of stuff, not fucking videos and microwave ovens and leather jackets. You want to talk about morality, okay I'll tell you what's immoral. Immoral is risking your life, fighting for your country in Malaya, obeying the rules, taking it like a man, paying your taxes your whole fucking life, then being left to starve on a state pension when you're too old to be of any more use to anyone. That's immoral. That's a betrayal of trust, so don't go giving me that bullshit about what's right and wrong and what's immoral and what's not. I've seen what passes for morality in this 'civilised' country and it's a load of bollocks. You tell me, if I'm doing someone's house over, whose trust am I breaking? I don't know the home owners, so there's no trust to be broken. It would be immoral, I grant you, if I knew who lived there – if they were a mate or something – then that would be immoral. But I don't, so it ain't.

Saying that though, there was this one time, Ian Banks was his name. We were in the same class all the way through junior school and both went on to the same secondary modern. He only lived a short bike ride away from me, so

I used to take my Action Man over to his house and kill him in various horrible ways. The Action Man that is.

Ian always use to have more toys and stuff than me – Ghost of Captain Kidd, Tin Can Alley, Stretch Armstrong – he had more toys than fucking Hamleys. And one day, for no reason (it weren't his birthday or nothing), his mum buys him a Steve Austin, with bionic arms, bionic eye and bionic everything else. I was jealous as fuck. *The Six Million Dollar Man* was my favourite programme and he had a Steve Austin. What a cunt! He played with it in front of me and my Action Man for three afternoons running before I finally decided, that there was no two ways about it, I was having it; accompanying plastic car engine and all. So when he went to the bog, I stuffed Steve Austin up me shirt, shouted goodbye to him through the door and ran for home. It didn't exactly take Sherlock Holmes to figure out what had gone down and less than half hour later, Ian and his mum were knocking on my door asking for his bionic man back. Ian was in tears. I thought at the time it was because his favourite toy had gone for a Burton, but looking back, I reckon it was because his best mate had nicked his favourite toy, without so much as a second's thought. He felt betrayed and hurt and I repaid him by telling everyone in school how he stood on my doorstep and cried.

He never talked to me again after that. So now, if I ever nick off friends, I always make sure I take extra care not to get caught. I just couldn't handle feeling that bad again.

You think it's right then, taking things that don't belong to you. Things that other people have worked hard for?

I never said it was right, I just said it weren't wrong. I ain't the one attaching right and wrong to every little action.

But then what gives you the right to take from others what isn't yours to take?

I don't have the right.

Then why do you do it?

Fuck it, why not? I need money to survive as much as the next bloke. What am I meant to eat, thin air? I just don't want to have to get up and go to work for it, that's all. Don't get me wrong, I've got nothing against working in principle, working's fine if you don't mind doing it, it's just it's not really my cup of tea. Tried it once, can't say I really enjoyed it.

See, the problem I have with working is that you've got to deal with cunts all day, most of who are usually in positions above you and absolutely live for the day they get to catch you coming in late, nicking paper clips or sleeping at your desk/shovel/wheel. Fucking life's too short to be dealing with these idiots all day. I left school years ago, I don't need to be told to keep my head down and no talking, when I've got tattoos and hairy balls. Fuck that.

But like I say, I've got nothing against it in principle. If that's your thing, an honest day's work for an honest day's pay, then I couldn't be happier for you. Personally, I'd rather do a dishonest night's work for a nice little few quid. The hours are better, the pay's generally better (though you're never guaranteed a wage when you're self-employed), my boss ain't a wanker and the tax man can whistle.

So what's to stop everyone from just doing what they like?

Well nothing. Fear of the law I suppose. Yeah, that's it, fear of getting caught. The way I see it, the only reason most people don't go around doing what I do is because they're frightened of getting caught. And that's the only reason; anyone who says otherwise is a liar. And don't start giving me that old shit about right and wrong again, if there was a bank with half a million quid in it and all you had to do was stroll in and stroll out with it – absolute water tight guarantee that you'd get away with it and no one would get hurt – there ain't a bloke in the world who wouldn't do it; with the possible exception of The Sultan of Brunei, the Queen and Richard Branson and so on, but only because they already have a couple of billion and don't get out of bed for less than £30m.

And the reason they're frightened of getting caught is that they don't want to go down and 'lose their freedom'. But this is bollocks because what freedom has anyone got when you have to spend the best hours of the day somewhere you hate, paying off a shit load of money you couldn't afford to borrow in the first place, and won't get to enjoy when you finally have paid it off, because the government'll grab the lot back the moment you get ill or die. You want to talk about freedom, you've got to have a little bit of freedom in the first place before someone can take it away from you. Work is the sentence everyone has to do. It's imposed on you at birth and ticks down to the moment you retire. And by that time, most people are so institutionalised, they shit their pants at the prospect of not having to get up in the morning and curl up their toes at the first convenient opportunity.

Not for me, no thanks, I don't want to play.

It's a good job not everyone thinks like you then, isn't it?

I should say, there'd be no one left to rob if they did.

So how would you feel if you got burgled? That would be alright would it, you wouldn't mind?

Of course I'd fucking mind, I don't want all my stuff to go wandering off now do I, who does?

Isn't that a bit hypocritical then? How can you possibly have the nerve to go around robbing people, and then feel aggrieved when it happens to you?

How the fuck should I feel then? Why should being a burglar make me any more cheerful about getting turned over than the next bloke? You don't see the bank manager smiling when him and his family are turfed out on to the streets, after he loses his job and falls behind with the mortgage, just because he's done it to other families in the past do you? People do things to other people that they wouldn't want done to themselves every day, so why should I be any different?

When you take the cat in to the vet's to have its bollocks cut off, who's idea is that? It ain't the cat's that's for fucking sure. He'd probably be half way to Scotland if he knew what was going down. But that's okay, because of course you wouldn't mind if someone came along and yanked off your nuts, just because your having them was slightly inconveniencing them now would you? Hey? Or is that being a bit hypocritical?

How about then if you went off shagging behind your old girl's back. Would it be alright then if she went off and did the same? Would that be alright by you? You'd think that would be fair?

I wouldn't do that.

You might not but there's plenty of blokes, and birds, who would and do. D'you suppose they think it's only right that their other half goes out and get's fucked for every fuck that they've had? 'Well darling, this week I've had my secretary, my dentist, Alice from number 40, some old sort I got hold of at the Starlight Rooms and your sister. So that's five I owe you, which gives you the milkman, the postman, the paper boy – lot of early mornings I'm afraid – the dustman and Alan from number 17. Though I'm afraid your plan to fuck the window cleaner would take you one over and that wouldn't be fair. Not unless Alice has her daughter over again. I'll check and get back to you.' No man, people are fucking hypocrites. They hate having done to them what they go off and do to everyone else all the time.

Saddam Hussein doesn't go around sucking on mustard gas now does he, but he's only too happy to give everyone else a go.

Noisy neighbours. Noisy neighbours who throw all night parties till six in the morning are always the first to complain when your kids are playing a bit noisy in the paddling pool out back. People are cunts. What is it they used to say in Hill Street Blues? 'Go out and do it to them before they do it to you.' Fucking right. Spot on.

You know, you really are scum aren't you?

It's been said.

3. Get out of my house!

I get Ollie to drop me off at the top of the street and walk it back to the house. It's gone three in the morning and the whole street's asleep. The only lights to be seen are the few odd street lights that haven't been smashed by vandals or short circuited out by dog piss. I hurry along, keeping out of the orange glare where I can, case in hand.

I love this time of night, the small hours. All the good people of the world are tucked up in their beds, with their hands shoved down their pyjamas, dreaming of someone other than the person they're sleeping next to. The street looks empty but it's not. All around are dozens of people, snoring their heads off just inches from each other; separated by no more than a few bricks and some nasty wallpaper. Blissfully dormant in their breezeblock and plaster cocoons, as Gerry once put it. I liked that, I must say. I'm a right one for nature programmes – David Attenborough and all that – so any comparisons with bees, termites or killer whales are alright by me.

I get to the house and have one last quick look about. Nothing. The only thing I could hear was the main road half a mile away, still noisy with the odd car and lorry. The house was dark like all the others in the street, which I decide to take as a good sign. I walk round the corner to the alley which ran along the back gardens and creep the rest of the way to the back gate.

A shiny new padlock and a rusty old bolt guard the rotten, broken-down old gate from unwelcome intruders and force me to break even more of the crappy old wooden slats by going over the top. I throw my case over and I climb up with all the poise and grace of a pregnant heifer with its pockets stuffed full of lead. Every deafening crack and splinter sting my ears, and just when I think I'm over the worst of it, the top of the gate collapses under my weight and falls into the garden with me. Shit, I couldn't have made more fucking noise if I'd ram-raided the fucking place in an ice cream van.

I get to my feet and look up at the surrounding windows. No lights. No twitching curtains. No vigilant neighbours looking out for the fella in number 4.

Cunts! I just made enough noise to wake Elvis, yet no one could be arsed to get out of bed and have a look. It was obvious that someone was climbing over next door's fence but nobody gave a shit. Like the antelopes that stand around looking on as one of their mates is torn to bits by tigers, able to relax and take a little breather, safe in the knowledge that someone other than themselves is having an off day. Cunts!

Still, such is the way of the world.

I pick up my case and walk over the flaking back window, and check to see if the latch is off. No such luck. I open my case and take out the twelve-inch metal ruler I'd packed earlier. I slide the ruler between the upper and lower window frames and give the latch a couple of taps, knocking it free. The street turns over, closes its eyes and goes back to sleep as I haul myself through the window and into the living room, landing awkwardly on my wrist as I hit the well-worn shabby carpet.

'Bollocks. Fuck. Fuck, fuck, fuck,' I mutter, willing my wrist to stop throbbing. 'Fuck.' I don't know what it is but there's something about swearing when you hurt yourself that helps soothe the pain a little bit. It's like your body's own natural Savlon. 'Cunt, fucking dick fucking shitter, cunt, bitch.' It doesn't really work with major injuries, such as gunshot wounds or broken necks, but for little scrapes such as twisted limbs or stubbed toes it usually does the trick.

'Oooh f-f-f-uc-k-k-k,' I moan, then notice that I've also landed awkwardly on my fags, squashing them in my back pocket. 'Ooow fuck,' I mutter, again making full use of that fantastic all-purpose word.

Clambering to my feet, I pull the window shut and make my way over to the centre of the room, dumping my case in a tatty armchair on the way. I'm just kneeling down by the video, when the living room lights suddenly come on and I'm called a bastard.

The sudden fright made my heart jump into my throat. 'Fuck!!!' I say.

'You scum,' she shouts. 'You bloody scum.'

'What?' I reply taking up my well-practised denial stance.

'Where the bloody hell were you?'

'What you doing in my house?' I demand weakly.

'I've been waiting for you to show up scum. Where were you?'

'Did we arrange something for tonight then?'

'You bastard, don't give me that. I had dinner on the table at eight o'bloody clock.'

'Look, something came up, it was important.'

Mel stares at me and readies herself to dismiss, out-of-hand, the bullshit I'm about to spin her. 'What was so important you couldn't have dinner with me on my birthday?'

Birthday? Fuck! I knew there was some reason I was meant to go round to her place to see her tonight – last night. 'I had a job on. Big job, lot of money. Trouble was, it had to be done tonight. Couldn't be done any other time.'

'What was it, the bloody snooker hall?'

'No.'

'Well that's your cue case you've just come in with isn't it?' she says, pointing at the cue case I've just come in with.

'Yeah?' I phrase my reply as a question to try and confuse her, though I realise that I'm probably not going to wriggle my way out of this one.

'One night, you couldn't give up one night for me.'

'Look, I'm sorry, I forgot.' This is my favourite excuse and one I've been happily using since I was a kid. Where's your homework? – I forgot. Why didn't you turn up? – I forgot. How could you sleep with my sister? – I forgot. It never really works (for 'I forgot' read 'I didn't give a shit') but ironically, it's an easy excuse to remember.

'I forgot.'

'Don't give me that, you forgot. The only thing you forgot is your bloody keys around my flat,' she say, hurling the big silver bunch at me but missing. Girls, they just can't throw. 'That's why you're breaking into your own house, because you didn't want to come round and get them isn't it.' I have to admit she's got it spot on so far, but there's no way I'm going to tell her that, not unless admitting it'll go some way to knocking some off my sentence.

'No.'

'You know, I must need my bloody head examined, I really do, sitting in all night waiting for a no good bastard like you to show up. I do it every time, every time. You know, I just think I must be some sort of mug to allow you to do this to me.'

'Come on Mel, don't blame yourself.' I'll admit that this

probably weren't the brightest thing to say under the circumstances, but you know, I'd had a few beers and I was trying to play the considerate bloke bit.

I hadn't seen it sitting there on the side until she's picked it up in a fury and slung it at me, again missing, but not by much this time. Chicken, stuffing, peas, carrots, spuds and gravy, all cold and covered in tin foil. She must've brought it all the way over from her place. God knows what for? I mean, what's the point? Was she going to try and force feed me it or something? Birds do silly things like that though don't they.

The plate explodes on the wall behind me and splatters everything with china, Bisto, meat and three veg.

'What the fuck are you doing? Are you fucking mad or something?'

'Yes, I'm mad, I'm crazy bonkers mad and I ain't standing for it any more.'

'Get out of my house you fucking nutter, before you do any more damage.'

'I'll show you damage . . .' she says, picking up my turntable.

'Don't you fucking dare,' I shout, launching myself across the room before she has a chance to smash it on the floor. 'Give me that here, give me it,' I say, wrestling it off her and pushing her to the ground by the face.

'You bastard,' she replies, getting up for more.

You could bet your last fucking quid that all those neighbours who didn't want to know before would all have their glasses pressed up against the wall about now.

'Go on, out.' Mel lands a couple on me as I usher her towards the front door. 'You're a fucking headcase, out.'

'Don't you worry, I'm going. And I ain't coming back either. That's the last time you piss me about.'

'Good. Because that's the last time I want to,' I tell her in no uncertain terms.

'Arsehole!' she shouts as I slam the door behind her. I stand by the front door, ready and waiting for the rock to come through my window, but it never did. I walk back into the living room, make a half-hearted effort to get the bulk of yesterday's dinner off my carpet, before flopping down in front of the telly, rewinding Match of the Day and pulling the kebab from my jacket pocket.

4. Melancholy

There ain't no funny or interesting story as to how I met Mel or anything. She didn't disturb me while I was doing her drum over, wearing nothing but a lacy nightie, and beg me to ravish her – though that would've been good. And I didn't save her from drowning, or bump into her trolley at the supermarket or chat her up at a wedding or anything.

I met her in the pub. That's it.

She used to work in the Rose and Crown about four years ago, before it went all spangly and became *Wayne's*. I think she decided she liked me because I was about the only bloke in the pub who didn't use to pinch her arse (nice arse), all the time, when she went round collecting the glasses, which in truth, ain't really like me. I'm usually the first one to be doing that, but, I don't know what was up with me, I probably just hadn't got round to it. Anyway, I got chatting to her over the course of a couple of weeks, found out her favourite colour and all that other rubbish you think you need to know, before finally asking her if she'd like to go out with me one evening. 'Yeah, okay,' she says, 'where d'you want to go?'

Go?

Shit! When I asked her if she wanted to go out, I didn't

mean did she want to go *out*. I meant did she want to come back to my place and get undressed after the pub closed.

See, the thing about taking out women – especially when they're a few years younger than you (Mel was just twenty-one at the time) – is that you have to be inventive. They're not like blokes, they're not content with just going down the pub, having a drink, playing snooker or . . . or . . . or . . . going to the football, or to the pub or anything. They want to go out and do something 'fun'. And having a drink, or a game of cards, doesn't qualify. They expect you to take them to fun fairs, or to zoos or the theatre or some other big fucking yawn that who the hell can be arsed with. Admittedly, the zoo should be the sort of thing I'd like, but you know, animals just aren't the same without a voiceover.

In the end I played it safe and took her for a bit of grub at the local Chinese. It was all very nice, I watched my language, managed not to spill half my dinner down my shirt and didn't spend the whole evening staring at her tits (nice tits). The only awkward moment was when she asked me what I did for a living and, even though it's not something I'm ashamed of, some people can be a bit funny about that sort of thing. Anyway, I lied and told her I was a self-employed contractor, which is one of those vague job titles – like management consultant or civil servant – that people rarely question because it sounds so dull. At the end of the evening, two bottles of wine for the better, I suggested we went back to mine for a drink (sex), but she was having none of it.

'I've had a lovely evening,' she says, 'but I don't want to spoil it.'

Spoil it? What sense did that make?

'Look, I'm sorry if you got the wrong idea, but I'm

not the sort of girl who jumps into bed on the first date.'

Christ! How many more of these fucking god-awful evenings do I have to endure before I can get into your knickers? was the question I didn't ask. I had to make do with a kiss and a cuddle and a squeeze of her arse (nice arse) that first evening, before getting the shove off when I got too near her tits (nice).

I was in two minds about seeing her again after that, but the trouble was both of them fancied her like mad, so I bought her some candyfloss and a go on the dodgems, a lolly at Whipsnade and a packet of dry roasted at Les fucking Miserables (and I know how they felt), before she told me that she didn't like the theatre, fun fair or zoo, and only came along because she thought it was something I was in to. I was just about to kick her into touch when she suggested we went back to mine and have that drink (sex), which I have to say was fucking phenomenal.

I don't know what it was; maybe it was all the waiting, or all the build-up to the main event, but she'd somehow worked her way into my system to such an extent that I was just about ready to blow. And that was only after a few weeks. Christ knows what it must've been like for my old man and his generation who had to go round 'courting' for fucking donkey's years before getting a sniff. I'm surprised they didn't just explode the moment they glimpsed a bit of bush. No wonder they all went round having loads of wars all the time. I think I would've probably been ready to bayonet a couple of Chinks to death too, if Mel hadn't of come across with the goods when she did.

Anyway, like I said, it was fucking fantastic sex. Hot, sloppy and plenty of it. So we start seeing each other on the firm and everything is rosy for a couple or three months. We see each other as much as we can, whole weekends around each other's places and I'm all daft as a brush for her, taking her flowers and what not and have you. We even get on fairly well when we ain't in bed, which is a bit of an unexpected bonus.

After a while though, she starts to complain that she 'doesn't know anything about me' and such like birds usually start coming out with after the two or three month mark. I'm in two minds again, which isn't an uncommon state of affairs for me. I've already lied once, so I'm reluctant to try and back it up with another. Not out of principle (don't be silly), but because once you start down that road, it can so easily get out of hand and you can end up shoring up bullshit with more and more ridiculous bullshit, until eventually it all blows up in your face. This I've learnt from bitter experience. All the best lies contain a thread of truth to hold them together.

So I tell her that my contracts are supply contracts, and that not all of the materials I handle are strictly above board, some of them are not VAT registered, some of them may have even fallen off the back of a lorry. 'In my business secrecy becomes a bit of a habit and you can end up never talking about it to anyone,' I tell her.

She's heard, I'm sure, from blokes down the pub, that I'm a bit dodgy, though I doubt she's heard anything specific. So, because I'm her boyfriend and the blokes in the pub are . . . well, the blokes down the pub, she gives me the benefit of the doubt and I hear no more of it for another couple of months. All this is doing though is putting off the inevitable and sure enough, after a couple more months, she starts banging on the old drum again. 'What exactly do you mean not above board?' 'How dodgy is dodgy?' 'It isn't drugs is it? Blah blah blah . . .'

'No it isn't drugs. And dodgy is fairly dodgy but not really dodgy. And not exactly above board means that actually hardly any of it's above board. Alright none of it, but don't worry it's alright. It's nothing silly, it's just a bit of gear I knock out to a few reliable fellas. Don't worry, don't worry.'

But she did worry.

She starts talking to more and more people, who hadn't got a clue but were only too happy to have a guess, and other people who had never heard a thing, but were only too happy to listen, so before long, I had no choice, I had to tell her the truth.

Not the full truth (don't be silly), but another watered down, lame version of it, just to shut her up. I told her that occasionally, I went along with some lads who lifted a few bits and bobs, out of warehouses, factories and shops, and that her going around asking a load of stupid questions was stirring up trouble and sooner or later, going to land me in the dock.

She was none too happy, although funnily enough, not for the reasons I thought she'd be none too happy. It didn't matter to her – no that's not strictly true, it didn't matter to her as much – that I was out robbing, it was the fact that I had kept her in the dark about it; I had lied to her, which was bollocks of course. I hadn't lied to her, I just hadn't told her the truth and, as we all know, there's a world of difference, although she didn't seem to appreciate that at the time.

We had a good couple of weeks of fierce rows and didn't talk to each other for quite a time, which, if I'm going to be truthful here, didn't really bother me that much (if I wanted to talk about chocolate, Take That and her parents, I'm sure I could talk to any of the boys down the pub). No, I think it was more the sex that brought us back together, or at least, prompted me to pay her a visit one Saturday night, after the pub chucked out. I went round with a Madras, a few take-outs and a quarter of puff, and had me feet under the table again before you could say 'a cup of tea wouldn't go amiss please love'.

I told her that it was just the odd job here and a little deal there, just to supplement my dole, while I was looking for a job and that she shouldn't worry about me, not least of all because it was really starting to get boring. 'It's not something I'm planning on doing my whole life,' I told her, 'so just give me a chance. I'm only doing it out of necessity until something decent comes along.'

We came to an agreement after that. She wouldn't go on and on and on and on and on and on and on and on and on etc, nagging me about it, and I'd double my efforts to find a proper job and get out of all this 'seedy business'.

Needless to say, neither of us have even come close to keeping our side of the bargain.

It's been a rocky old four years and we've split up and got back together so many times I can't sometimes remember if we're still going out. So I won't worry too much about her little tantrum just now. I'll pop round, be charming and smooth it all over in the morning.

No problem.

As for tonight though, it looks like I'm on wank detail again.

5. Clever plans: number 1

There's nothing quite so beautiful as a clever criminal plan; it's an art form unto itself. When I hear of a well-thought-through, well-rehearsed and well-executed plan, it just makes the hairs on the back of my neck stand up. There's just something about it that doesn't compare with everyday life.

Sure, a good idea's a good idea, even a legal one, and I'm the first to take my hat off to any entrepreneur who can make a million quid out of a new way to screw the lid on a jar of jam, but it's not in the same league of brilliance as a good criminal idea. I think this because besides brains and imagination, which you need for any idea, you need one other vital ingredient for your criminal idea – balls, big balls. And that makes all the difference.

Take the Trains Robbers for example, what a fucking great idea that was. A train loaded with millions in used notes, being taken off to be burned, and just a couple of postmen to guard it. The sheer daring of that caper caught the imagination of the whole country and made heroes out of everyone who was associated with it. Shame they were all caught and got thirty years each, but still, it's a piece of history now; even the name, 'The *Great* Train Robbery' says it all. It was a fucking great idea.

Not all criminal ideas, though, have to be on such a grand scale. And you don't necessarily have to be clever to think up a clever idea. Some right doughnuts come up with potentially great ideas only to fuck them all up in the execution.

A case in point. A mate of mine – no that's not strictly true, I think he's a cunt – this bloke I know called Norris hit upon what could've been a good idea (oh and by the way, Norris isn't his real name, I've changed it just like I've changed all the names in this book to protect the guilty). Anyway he was knocking off this bird who worked in the local estate agent's, Wendy I think her name was, but for the purposes of this story I think we'll call her Pauline.

Pauline must've been fucking blind or foaming at the mouth to let something as nasty as Norris touch her, let alone agree to go along with the sort of disgusting and depraved things I imagine Norris would like to do. But this is neither here nor there, it's got nothing to do with the story, I just wanted to set the scene a little. Personally, if I was a bird, I wouldn't look at him if he was on fire on a dark night, but again . . . like I say.

Anyway, Norris was put up in a bed and breakfast by the council, after he got out of the nick and his old folks told him that they never wanted to see him again (which is a bit of a fucking cheek when you think about it. After all, what grounds have they got for complaint when it was them that brought him into the world in the first place). One of the rules at this B&B was that you weren't allowed to bring anyone back after ten, especially girls. Well heaven forbid. As for Pauline's place, that was out of bounds as well because she lived with her parents and they'd met Norris once; they only needed the once to fall into line with the rest of the world with regards Norris and his cuntiness.

So to get round this, Pauline use to swipe the keys to empty properties on the agency books and meet up with

Norris for horrible sex in the afternoons and evenings. This gave Norris the idea, that if he copied the keys, he could return to the house a few weeks later and do them over when the new occupants moved in.

This, potentially, was a good idea. If he had left a reasonable amount of time from when the new people moved in, to when he done his job, and faked a point of entry when he left, he could've been on to a right lucrative little number. He could've let himself in, had a bit of a scout about, loaded up the stuff and then broken in – which is always the most noisy and risky part of any job – and been away before the glass hit the deck.

But no, not Norris, not the fucking mastercriminal. He goes after these poor bastards after they've only been under their new roof a single night, figuring that everything would be easier to nick if it was still in the packing crates. Welcome to the neighbourhood.

And when this family come home after having a meal in the local pub to find half their worldly belongings gone and not so much as a cat flap ajar, it didn't exactly take DNA fingerprinting to point the suspicion at Pauline.

Thinking about, even if he'd been pushed for time, Norris could've left the back door open to make it look like the incoming family had been a bit careless in their new and unfamiliar gaff.

Norris does two of these jobs in a week and is picked up thirty minutes after Weasel of CID has his girlfriend blubbing her eyes out in the manager's office. They split up shortly after that.

Now this, admittedly, wasn't a brilliant plan born of pure genius, but it could've been a clever idea worth a few quid.

I've used the old estate agent's a couple of times myself, but in a different way. What you do is go along and arrange to view one of the houses in the window. The estate agent's will then take you on a guided tour of the place and you can decide whether you think it'll be worth robbing in a few months' time. The agent sometimes even tells you where the alarm is, how you can gain access through the back garden and whether or not the neighbours could give a shit if you were burgled, tied up, tortured and left for dead, etc. It's not as good as getting a key, but it can still be useful.

If you want to do a more immediate robbery, you can sometimes even call on spec and get shown around by the sellers themselves. This gives you the opportunity to wander round and make out a bit of a shopping list of all the stuff you might like to come back for in a day or two. All you've got to do is gain entry and load up the van while they're looking round someone else's house. And you don't have to worry about the next door neighbours, because they'll just think that the removal men have come early. Again, not a stroke of genius but useful if you're hard up for a job.

Norris had a good idea – and a good opportunity – what with his bird Pauline working at the estate agent's and willing to help out, but he fucked it all up. And if you fuck it all up, even a great plan becomes not worth the brain-cells it took to think it up.

The mark of a truly great plan (and this is where The Great Train Robbery falls short also) is that you have to get away with it.

Anything less and you might as well just walk into the Bank of England with a water pistol.

6. Roland, the jailbird

I see Roland in the pub the other day. He just strolls in and orders a pint like he's never been away, which is exactly where he had been of course. Comes in, gets his pint, clocks me and comes over.

'Alright Bex, how's you?'

'Well fuck me, who let you out?' I laugh.

'Oh, I escaped, tunnelled me way out. If anyone asks, you ain't seen me alright,' he says and sits down. This is a joke of course. Anyone who knows Roland knows this. He couldn't even escape the washing up if all the plates had got smashed. I ask him how long he's been out.

'Last Wednesday. I'm back round the old girl's again.'

'Oh yeah, she took you in again?' I ask.

'Yeah well, you know how it is.'

'Yeah, yeah, I know, I know.'

'Yeah.'

'That alright is it?'

'Yeah, 's alright, not bad, not bad. I've seen worse, you know.' I scratch my head for a bit, while he looks at the fruit machine.

'Yeah. I know.'

'You alright?' he asks.

'Yeah, I'm alright. Can't complain, you know. Can't complain. I do though, but I shouldn't, you know.' We chuckle good naturedly for a bit then stop. Now it's his turn to scratch his head, while I look at the fruit machine.

'Still seeing that Mel bird?' he asks.

'Yeah, still seeing her. You know.'

'Yeah, nice bird . . . nice bird.'

We now both scratch our heads and look at the fruit machine in no particular order.

'Hmm yeah . . . hmm.'

We spend a few more minutes asking after each other's families and promising to pass on a hello next time we see them, talking about the weather and stuff, but basically, that's it. That's all the conversation we can manage. I haven't seen him in two years, a few words pass between us and we're all up to date. Anything else that follows between us is forced. Things we've deliberately racked our brains to come up with to talk about just to break the god-awful silence. It's not that I don't like Roland, or that we haven't got a load of things to talk about, it's just that, well, who can really be arsed? I only came in to have a quiet pint and a read of the paper.

'What's the headline?' says Roland.

I lift the front page up for a moment and he reads something about some farmer's wife giving birth to a fish.

'Blimey, what next hey?'

'Hmm . . . yeah.'

He looks out of the window, around the pub and takes a big sup of his pint.

'What you up to, working?' I ask.

'No, probation service've got me doing one of those "improve your chances to get a shit job" courses down at the college.'

'Oh yeah.'

'Yeah,' he tells me.

'What's that like?'

'Shit.' I thought it would be somehow. It would've been quite a surprise if he'd said 'it's brilliant, a right laugh, and the birds on the course, Jesus, all of them are stunning!' but he didn't. He looks at me for a bit and nods slowly. 'Yep, shit.'

We sit for a bit longer. 'You want a game of pool?' he finally asks. I agree, realising that the only alternative is another half-hour of this fucking torture.

'How long you been out?' I ask again as I set up the balls.

'Since Wednesday. Yeah, Wednesday. Got out in the morning.'

'Yeah? Well, gives you the day I suppose, don't it.'

'Yeah, well . . . yeah.'

'Yeah.' I mutter to myself and break. I don't know what it is. I'm sure if Ollie came in I'd have had a good chat and a couple of laughs, paper or no paper. But with Roland, it's different. It's hard work, because I haven't seen him in a few years. I should talk to him. I feel obliged to be pleased to see him and ask him in every tiny detail all about his adventures in the big house. But I did that the last time he came out, and the time before that, and the time before that, and the time before that. And I can't imagine it's changed all that much since then. It wasn't even a very interesting story first time around.

I think if I'm honest though, the truth is that I just don't care. Not at all. Not one tiny little bit.

It's not that he's boring or a wanker or anything, he's a nice enough bloke, I just couldn't care less about him or anything he ever does, that's all. And I don't mean that in a nasty way. I'm glad he's out and back in town and all that. I'm glad for him. I just think that, if he happened to fall on to his cue while we were playing pool, and speared himself through the heart, I'd be hard pushed to give a fuck, because I just don't care. And I'm sure he probably wouldn't give a monkey's about me either. It's just the way it is.

See, the problem is that we had the bad luck to be in the same class at school together and feel that we have to put ourselves through this fucking ridiculous charade every time we see each other. And this will be the way it is for the rest of our lives.

'Last Wednesday?' I ask.

'Wednesday just gone, yeah.'

We play pool in near silence for a while, each of us taking a stupid amount of time over our shots. Every now and then one of us says 'unlucky' or 'good shot' or 'oh bollocks', but other than that we just smile idiotically at each other.

I'm tempted to ask him again about how he was arrested last time, just for conversation, but I've heard the story a couple of times from a few different people, and so I can't even be bothered with that.

Thinking about it though, I've never actually heard about any of Roland's arrests from Roland himself. I've always heard about them from other people. I guess Roland's just one of those people I'd rather talk about, than to. It's quite a funny story though, so I suppose I should ask Roland about it, but Roland might spoil it by not telling it in as funnily a way as it was told to me. So I drink my drink, take my shot and keep my mouth shut.

Basically, Roland's a burglar, but not a very good one. He's been caught more times than a rash in a whore house. The reason for this is simple, he's a fucking idiot. Almost all the times he's ever been caught have been of his own making.

He just doesn't think. He does things like rob houses and leave his snooker club membership card behind. Or drops his passport or his birth certificate or stuff. Straight up, this actually happened. Why on earth Roland felt he needed to take these things with him on a job in the first place is beyond me but, there you go, that's Roland. Like I say, he doesn't think.

Another time, him and Parky are turning this place over when they come across a fully stocked drinks cabinet. For reasons best known to themselves, they decided getting pissed and watching Sky was a really good idea. The bloke and his wife come back the next morning, from a lovely weekend in Devon, to find some scruffy sambo, sleeping off his scotch in the Parker-Knoll, the telly switched to the German porn channel, the fridge is open and the remains of a fry-up still burning away on the ceramic hob. Roland, meantime, was snoring away upstairs under the duvet in the main bedroom. They were especially impressed by the fact that he'd decided it was best all round if he left his boots on, despite the fact that he'd approached the house through the woods out the back. The geezer and his wife left it to the police to wake them up – and even they had a job. From what I heard, the wife refused to ever sleep in the bed again and the Sally Army carted it away that day.

Another, even more stupid time, was when Roland decided he should give ram raiding a go. He nicked this motor – his dad's motor – picked up Parky and headed off for Dixon's. He didn't use his old man's key, because he figured that if that key went missing, everyone would realise it had to be Roland or his dad behind the job. And seeing as his dad was a JP, that narrowed the field slightly. So Roland used one of his own keys. He had a huge bunch of them he used for nicking cars, all held together on a big fuck-off keyring. This keyring had been bought for him by a girlfriend he'd long since been chucked by and it said, printed on a bit of leather the size of an odour eater: ROLAND IS DUMBO IF HE LOSES HIS JUMBO. She bought it for him because he was always losing his keys and it got a big laugh down the pub when he showed it off to people. Well not that big a laugh, more of a 'huh'. Anyway, Roland didn't make it to Dixon's and ended up ram raiding a concrete bus shelter instead. Him and Parky legged it and, yes you've guessed it, he left his keyring there for the cops, his dad and everyone else in the world to find.

The last time was probably the best of all though. That's what I think anyway. Him and Animal (not Parky this time. I think Parky started to get pissed off at being nicked all the time) robbed this house together and did a real good job of it. In and out in under five or six minutes, a good stash, everything went smoothly and both of them got away clean. Beside the TV, video, microwave, jewellery and all the other stuff, Roland nicked a couple of videos as well – video cassettes – which ain't a bad idea, I often do the same myself. One of them the bloke has rented from a local Blockbusters. Roland watches it, enjoys it, good film, lovely, thanks very much and, without thinking, returns it when he goes down to get another video out. Anyway, the bloke he robbed goes in to Blockbusters a few days later, explains the situation to matey behind the counter, that his house was done over and the video he got out was nicked, and says sorry about that, here's a police statement blah blah blah. Matey checks the computer, the bloke checks his statement, the police check the security camera footage and Roland checks in for another long stay at Her Majesty's Pleasure. Still, he didn't grass on Animal so he's always got that in his favour.

'Shot!' says Roland as I pot my last stripe.

'Black, centre pocket,' I tell him and do just that. Roland still has six spots on the table.

'Good game,' he says, holding out a hand for me to shake. 'Good game.'

'Yeah, cheers, yeah.' Roland puts his cue back in the rack and drains the last of his pint.

'You say you were still seeing that Mel bird?'

'Yeah, you know, still there.'

'Hmm yeah . . . Hmm. Well give her one for me won't you.'

'Will do . . . you er . . .' I say.

'No I've got to shoot. Things to do places to be. We'll have to go out for a drink sometime yeah?' Roland says.

'Yeah, definitely, definitely.'

'Alright then, well, I've got to shoot. Say hello to Ollie for us next time you see him.'

'Will do.'

'Right, well, I've got to shoot,' he says checking his pockets for his wallet, keys and birth certificate. 'See ya then.'

'Yeah, mind how you go.'

'Yeah see ya,' he says and leaves. As he walks past outside the pub he gives me another wave and disappears. I get another pint and sit down with my paper.

After half-hour or so Ollie comes in and gets us another one in. We chat for a little bit about this, that and the other and I tell him I saw Roland.

'He out is he?'

'Yeah, got out last Wednesday,' I tell Ollie.

'Where's he staying then?' he asks.

'Back with his old lady.'

'She took him back? Fucking hell.'

'I know, that's what I said, I couldn't believe it,' I think I remember me saying. 'By the way, he says hello.'

'Oh right. What's he up to now?' Ollie asks.

'One of those courses, you know, "get a shit job for £2.50 an hour in ten easy lessons" down at the college.'

'You ask him about the video?'

'No, I was going to but I don't know, just didn't come up. Just had a game of pool and that, you know.' I finish the little bit of me last pint and start on me new one.

'You should've man. I was talking to Animal and he reckons that when the Old Bill came to get Roland he ...'

And for the next hour and a half, we talk about nothing else but Roland.

7. Short leash

The thing about being a burglar is that people think that you're always on the thieve, you can't give it a rest, not for a minute. In an ironic way, I guess the same can be said of policemen. People assume that they're always on duty and hardly ever invite them to parties in case they go and spoil it by checking the tread on everyone's tyres outside. People think that we don't know how to behave in polite society, and to be honest, by and large they're right. After all, opportunism is a burglar's best friend. But there are exceptions.

'What time do you call this?' nags Mel before I've even got both feet out of the van.

'Traffic, alright. I had a nightmare getting here. All the main road's blocked up and the lights are playing up on . . .'

'Save it for later, just come on. Everyone's already gone inside.' I lock the van up and try and straighten my tie in the wing mirror as Mel pulls on my arm. 'Here let me do it,' she says pulling me into tie-straightening position. I give in and let her, chin up, arms down. She's really overdone it on the perfume front. 'Keep still.'

'No, don't do up the top button, I don't like it like that,' I whinge as she slaps away my hand. My shirt, like the rest of the suit, is probably about two sizes too small for me by now, but I didn't realise until I tried it on this morning because I haven't been to court in ages.

'You are such a baby,' she tells me.

Yeah, and you smell like a whore, I don't tell her.

'There, that's it.' She grabs my arm and drags me off in the direction of the church, as I loosen my tie again with my free hand. As we squeeze past Mel's mum and dad to take our places, I realise that swimming in cheap perfume must be a family tradition for Johnson women. Mel leans forward and whispers a few words of encouragement into her brother's ear and he whispers something back. Probably 'What the fuck d'you bring that cunt for?' But I can't be sure of that.

She takes her place next to me, gives me a smile and prepares to well up.

'I don't believe you, I really don't.'

'What's a matter with it?' I ask as we drive to the reception. Mel looks at me as if I've just beaten up one of the bridesmaids. 'What?'

'You think it's funny don't you?'

'No,' I tell her.

'Yes you do. You think it's all a big joke don't you. Anything to spoil it, anything to show me up.'

'How does it show you up?' I ask looking down at Philip and Leslie's present on the seat between us. Philip and Leslie's present looks back up at me and gives a little bark. Well more of a yap really.

'I just don't believe you sometimes, I really don't.'

'I thought it would be a good present. New house, new start, new dog. It's the perfect present. Come on, they'll love it.' I try and gee her up. Honestly, women can be such fucking miseries sometimes.

'They don't want a dog. If they wanted a bloody dog they would've bought one themselves.'

'Maybe they just never thought about it?' I say. This could be true. After all, I'd never thought about it until Parky came in the pub last night with a box full of them.

'If they've never thought about it, then chances are they've never wanted one,' Mel says. What tosh. You've never thought about throwing a surprise party for yourself either but they're always good when they happen.

'Oh well too late now, they'll just have to lump it won't they,' I tell her.

'Oh no they won't. We ain't giving them that dog.'

'Yes we are.'

'No we are bloody not,' she shouts, giving me the old daggers. Personally, I reckon we should ask Philip and Leslie, let them decide if they want it or not, but there's no arguing with her when she's in this mood.

'Well, what the fuck are we going to give them?'

'Don't worry about that, I'll pick them up something next week. Just you keep your mouth shut about the dog.'

'And what we going to do with it then?' I ask as the dog starts yapping annoyingly. 'SHUT UP!' I shout at the dog, but he don't take any notice. That's if it is a he, might be a bitch for all I know. Everything else in the van seems to be.

'Well that's your problem isn't it. You bought the dog, you keep it.'

'What, you are joking aren't you? What the fuck do I want with a dog? I haven't got the room. I'm never in. I can't keep a fucking dog.'

'Well then you should've thought about that shouldn't you.'

'I'll throw it in the fucking river then,' I say, although if it actually came to it, I'm not sure I could.

'No you bloody won't. You harm one hair on that poor dog's head and I'll report you to the police.'

'Poor dog? A moment ago it was a bloody dog and you couldn't wait to be shot of it.' I pull into the community centre car park and circle, looking for a space. Most of the congregation is already here and I'm forced to park just about as far away as I can from the door.

'I'm warning you . . .'

'Alright, alright. Of course I ain't going to do it. I was only kidding. Christ!' We get out of the van and cross the car park to the hall.

'And you make sure you come out here and give that dog a drink and a walk after we've had the dinner.'

We all stand out in the hallway for a bit waiting to go in, as the wedding party line themselves up on the other side of the door so they can have their hands shook. The doors open and we go in shaking and congratulating as we go.

'Congratulations,' I say.

'Thanks for coming,' she says.

'Well done, how are you?' I say.

'Thanks for coming,' he says.

'Hello Joan,' I say.

'Thanks for coming,' she says.

'Alright Tony,' I say.

'Thanks for coming,' he says.

'Good luck with the speech,' I say.

'Thanks for coming,' he says.

'I like your dress,' I say.

'Thanks for coming,' she says.

'Congratulations Leslie,' I say.

'Thanks for coming,' she says.

'You want a dog Phil?' I say.

'No,' he says. 'Thanks for coming.'

Bastard!

Cold cuts. What a bunch of tight arses! Two families, their son and daughter's wedding, and they're too fucking tight to put their hands in their pockets and pay to have a bit of meat warmed up. Three new potatoes each, a spoonful of tinned veg and peaches for pudding. Lucky I made sure I stopped on the way over to the church for a bag of chips otherwise I'd be starving.

Me and Mel are sat half way from the front, on a large round table of assorted uncles and aunts. I saw this as a bit of a snub on Mel's old folks' part. I mean, it is Mel's only brother who's getting married, surely we should be higher up on the cast list, but I think they were worried about putting me too near the wedding presents. As if?

The aunts and uncles and Mel rabbit on about the bride and her dress over dinner, only looking over my way when I finish dinner ten minutes before everyone else and spark up.

'Oh isn't she just beautiful, she looks really lovely,' and such like comments. Personally, I reckon she looks fat and her hair's a fucking state, but nobody asks me my opinion. I look around the room as the rest of the table start on the groom and realise that today is going to be a long, and boring affair. I make the effort a couple of times to join in with the odd 'and the bride's mum's got a nice hat ain't she, I wonder how much it cost?' but no one bothers to have a guess. So I decide to give up and dodge the speeches by taking the dog for a piss.

I should've known how today was going to pan out the

moment we got out of the church and the photographer started taking the pictures. I stood on the sidelines with the other smokers, waiting to get in on the action for fuck knows how long, as the bride, the groom, vicar, best man, family of the bride, family of the groom, friends of the bride, friends of the groom, relatives of both sides and every other cunt had their picture took. I was still waiting for 'the scummy hangers-on we felt obliged to invite' and their spouses when the photographer started packing away his equipment. I think I should've been on one of the groom's family photos but Joan was having none of it and kept asking me politely to move off, telling me I'd be in the next one.

What, the next wedding?

It's just prejudice you know. Her old folks have had it in for me ever since I started going out with Mel. I used to drink in a few of the same boozers as Mel's old man, Tony, and I half-knew a few of the blokes he worked with on the dust (yes, he's a dustman, and he looks down on me). Now don't get me wrong, I don't go around making public announcements about what I do or anything like that, but whatever you're into, there's always a certain amount of rumour that follows you around, and I should imagine every bloke in the pub or on the cart was falling over themselves to tell Tony just what they'd heard about me. Most of it bullshit of course, but that's by the by. I've soiled his daughter with my no-good, scummy lifestyle and am threatening to do the same to his son's wedding. If it wasn't for Mel, I wouldn't even be here today. She's had some right old slanging matches with the old cunts, which, as it happens, almost always works in my favour with her, more than anything I've ever done to her – for her. She told them, 'If Bex doesn't come, I don't come.' Personally I wish she'd fucking let up just for once today.

I look down at the dog as it sniffs the lamppost.

'You having a piss or what?' I ask it.

The dog doesn't answer. It just starts off for the next one. I pull it back by the lead and push it towards the lamppost again.

'I don't care if we stand here all day, you are having a piss before you get back in my van whether you like it or not.' I light up another cigarette and look back at the hall. 'I've got all the time in the world.'

I figure two hours are about right. Speeches over, tables cleared away and the first drunks stepping out on to the dance floor. I finish my pint, buy another packet of fags on the way out of the pub and start to walk back up the road to the hall. The dog's happy as Larry, he's had half a pint of bitter in a bowl and a packet of beef crisps. No stopping him now as he pisses away up the side of the bus shelter like a garden sprinkler on full, right after I show him how to do it. Man and dog in perfect harmony. We get back to the centre car park and I stick the dog in the van thinking that I'll probably have to take him for another walk in about an hour's time.

The reception's in about as full a swing as it looks likely it's ever going to get. Most of the blokes are standing at the bar with one hand in their pockets, the old ladies are sitting around the edges finishing off the cake and three or four ugly kids are running backwards and forwards to the cloakroom. I buy a pint and get Mel a VAT.

'Where the hell have you been?' she asks.

'Dog slipped the lead. Been running all round the streets after him. I'm fucking knackered.'

'Is he alright?'

'The dog's fine, he's in the van.'

Mel's six-year-old cousin stops in mid-gallop. 'You've got a dog in your van?'

'Go away,' I tell the kid.

'Don't be horrible, take him out and show him the dog,' Mel says.

I look at him and wonder if they let kids in the pub I've just come from.

The evening's getting dark and me and half a dozen other little brats stand out in the car park as they squabble over who's going to stroke it. After a minute or so one of them asks what it's name is. I tell them it hasn't got a name and they all look at me as if I just told them the dog was for dinner.

'Why doesn't it have a name?'

'Because I haven't given it one.'

'Why not?'

'Because I haven't,' I say. I think they were waiting for a fuller explanation than that, but sod 'em.

'Why not?' This kid must be some sort of relative of Ollie or something.

'Can I give it a name?'

'No, can I?'

'Can I?' Blah, blah, blah.

'Listen, okay, listen. You can call the dog whatever you like, I don't care.' Immediately all the kids start shouting Rover, Rex, Woofer and Lassie at the poor bastard and stroking it harder than looks healthy.

'Of course,' I say as I light up a cigarette, 'the dog is for sale.'

Half a dozen pairs of eyes light up and plead for me to sell it to them.

'It costs £30 and it's a shame really,' I say, getting an idea, 'because if I don't sell it today, I'm going to have to sell it to a bad man who's going to kill it and eat it.'

'Noooo,' they all cry and run off back to the hall to their mums and dads.

Sorted.

Looks like I might not get lumbered with the dog after all.

8. Clever plans: number 2

I read about this one in one of the papers and laughed my bollocks off. They only gave a few details so I've had to fill in the blanks with a lot of guesswork, but it went something like this.

Some country nob, living in a big house up in Lovejoy country, decides that he's had enough of Britain and decides what him and the family need is a break for a few years in Kenya, whipping the houseboy and shooting rare animals. Of course, he's not going to sell his house as it's been in the family for generations and he's one of these cunts who can afford not to. So he decides to sack the housemaid, sling her out on to the street and mothball the place, leaving just the caretaker and his missus to look after the grounds and take care of general maintenance.

Now, he's not too keen on the idea of all the old savages coming round and leaning their spears up against his Chippendale grandfather clock while he's down in Ooga-Booga-Land, so he decides to stick all his stuff into storage over here while he's away, with the exception of the odd two or three paintings he can't do without. So he contacts this storage company – a reputable and above board firm – and they agree a price to come round and cart off his stuff.

It's about this point, I imagine, that the old burglars got wind of it. Don't really know how. Maybe they were watching the house already or planning to do the storage depot over, or perhaps they had someone working on the inside, or maybe even the housemaid decided to give her employers the same sort of parting surprise they'd given her. I don't know. What I do know is that they phoned up the storage company and cancelled the geezer's contract, and then the night before the company had been due to collect, the lads nick a lorry, stick a few 'Blogg's removals', or whatever they were called, stickers on the side, and drive round to see matey.

They spend the best part of the day cleaning this bloke out and make as many as three trips before finally clocking off for the night. Old matey wanted them to do another run but they were so fucked from a hard day's robbing that they just didn't have the energy, so he contents himself instead with giving them a lecture on the state of the British worker and why he was leaving this country and tells them that they'd better be back round first thing. I suppose they thought that would've been pushing their luck a bit because they didn't show the next morning, though you can just imagine how fucking tempted they must've been. Personally, if that had been me, I would've had the light bulbs out of the fittings, the carpet grippers, the lot. I wouldn't've left him so much as a curtain ring. But these lads were professional and they made sure they had all of the best stuff on the first couple of runs thanks to Clive of Africa. He spent the whole of the day giving them the Antiques Roadshow tour.

'Be careful with that, it's worth £4,000.'

'This table has been in the family since the twenties. If you scratch it, it'll be £12,000 out of your wages.'

'Stop that, stop that at once. Do you know how much

that cost? £20,000, that's how much. Get an ashtray from the kitchen if you want to smoke.'

I would've loved to have seen the cunt's face the next day when he rang the company to see where the hell the van was. The sudden, sickening realisation that he had literally waved good-bye to almost all his worldly goods as they disappeared down the drive. Knowing that he'd helped them load some of the more fragile stuff aboard. That he'd had his cook make them lunch. And that he'd paid the storage fee in full after they had insisted on cash up front. I would've given anything to be there. Anything.

There are so many great things about this job, not least of all the fact that the three-man gang was never caught and only one rug and a gold-leaf portrait frame – minus the oil painting of his old dead gran and her dogs – were ever recovered.

Lads, wherever you are, my hat is off to you.

9. Electric Avenue

'First things first, they drive you to the prison, unload you then give you a cup of tea,' Ollie tells me as I turn off the high street. I smile along, as he's told me this story before but it's always good to hear.

'Then they process you, give you a medical, assign you to a cell and give you some grub and a cup of tea, before locking you up for the night. In the morning, they unlock the cells, you all go down and get a cup of tea. Then you have a wash, breakfast, cereal or porridge, and toast usually, and another cup of tea. If you've got a job then you go off and do that, but you get to stop at eleven for a cup of tea.' This was Roland. Ollie had asked him once what prison was really like, expecting something between *Scum* and *Midnight Express*, but Roland's version weren't quite there.

'You go back to work and stop for lunch, when you can have chips, if you like, or something else if you don't want chips – I just stuck to chips really – and a cup of tea. You go to your cell or back to your job and work right through to three o'clock, when you can stop for a cup of tea.

'After work you go and have a shower after you've had a cup of tea, then go back to your cell for a little bit. You can take tea with you.'

'Sounds hard doesn't it,' I say.

'Ah yeah, but then they let you out for dinner, when you can have a bit of stew or a pork chop, with chips if you like, and a cup of tea. After that, you've got some recreation time when you can have as many cups of tea as you like, or even coffee, they've got both you know.'

'Drank a lot of tea then did he?' I say as I pull to a stop out the back of Electric's.

'Seems that way. Didn't say anything about stopping for a piss though. The amount of tea he reckon he poured down his throat he should've been gushing like a fucking water cannon for hours. I'm not joking, he went on for fucking ages. Cup of tea, then a cup of tea, then some chips, then a cup of tea, then two cups of tea, then another cup of tea. He must like tea.'

'And chips.'

'Yeah, and chips.' Ollie winds up his window and climbs out, slamming the door behind him. After a few moments' struggling, we finally get the washing machine out of the back and lug it over to the door. Electric comes out and squints at us then the washing machine.

'What's this?' he says.

'It's a washing machine,' Ollie says as if he was serious.

'I know that, but what do you want me to do with it?' he says in an old Jewish accent he's developed over the years, even though he's about as Jewish as the Ayatollah.

'Give us money for it, you old cunt,' I tell him.

'There's no call for washing machines, I wouldn't be able to sell it.' This is a load of old bollocks really. Whatever we bring round there's never any call for it. We could bring round boxes of free money and pictures of the Spice Girls having it off with each other and he'd still tell us there was no call for them.

'We've got a video as well,' Ollie says. 'And a calculator. Give us £120 for the lot.'

'£120. I'd be cutting my own throat for £120,' Electric whines.

I'd pay £120 to see that, tight old bastard. 'I'll give you £40.'

'Fuck's sake, £40. Don't be a cunt,' I tell him. 'Give us £120 for it, you're going to knock it out for double that anyway.' There's no way he's going to give us £120, me and Ollie both know that. But if we asked for £75, he'd offer us a fiver. 'Come on you tight bastard.'

'I'm afraid I can't do business at £120. Maybe next time, okay lads?' He goes to close the door, fully expecting one of us to block it with our foot – we have to, we've got nowhere else reliable to take the stuff. We can occasionally knock out a few odds and sods ourselves to 'blokes in pubs', cutting out the middle man, but in the main we need Electric and he knows it. Ollie jumps in.

'Alright, give us £70.' £70 – what a cunt. We'd already talked about this and decided that our second price would be £100 and he charges in with his size nines shouting £70. Electric bites as I knew he would.

'£55 and that's my final offer, take it or leave it.' I look at Ollie and give him a sneer but he misses it completely and just nods at me.

'Just give us the money,' he says.

'Okay, bring it inside and I'll sort you out,' Electric says, walking back into the shop. I'm tempted to have it out with Ollie, but this ain't the place. I'll put him straight in the pub later.

We haul in the washing machine and I go back and get the video out of the van as Electric disappears upstairs to wring some blood out of a stone. I put the video on top of the washing machine and Ollie fishes the calculator out of his pocket and puts it on top of that.

'Is that all you got?' Electric asks, reappearing with the dosh.

'They had nothing else worth nicking,' Ollie says. 'Few ornaments, shitty old gramophone, toaster, not worth the effort.'

'What about the telly?' says Electric stuffing the bundle of notes in to my top pocket. I pull them back out and count them, just in case he's made another one of his famous 'counting errors'.

'He dropped the fucking thing,' says Ollie, pointing at me as if I'm halfway across the room.

'I didn't drop the fucking thing, it slipped out of my hand. You were meant to have unplugged it.'

'When?' asks Ollie blankly.

Electric opens the washing machine door. 'No washing?'

'You joking. This thing weighed a fucking ton as it was without being full of water. We had to flood the kitchen just to be able to pick the bastard up. Left the washing behind.'

'Could've given you a couple of quid for jeans and things if you'd brought them along.'

'Well we'll remember that for next time,' I say.

'What about the video, did you get the instructions for it like I said?' Electric asks.

'Huh. Oh yeah, I've got those,' I say and pull them from my back pocket. 'What d'you want those for anyway?'

'Do you know how to work the seven-day timer on this model?' Electric asks. I shrug, Ollie doesn't care. He's off checking out some of the old man's stock. 'Well neither do I. Can't sell it if I can't work it. People want to know how to use what they're buying. Right now, what's this?' he says picking up the calculator. 'This ain't a calculator.'

Ollie puts down the camcorder he's been looking at and comes back. 'Yes it is.'

'No it isn't, it's one of those personal organisers.'

'Personal organiser? Well what's that when it's not being a calculator?'

'You know, it's an organiser, like an electronic diary. Tells you what time you've got to be where and who you've got to see at whatever time. That sort of thing.'

'What a load of rubbish,' Ollie says. 'What sort of idiot needs to add up what time he's got to be at the pub.' I don't always agree with what Ollie says, but occasionally he does make a lot of sense. I mean, what sort of idiot does need to add up what time he's got to be at the pub?

'How much do they cost then?' I ask.

'Less than calculators,' Electric tells us.

'Here, you ain't having any money back, a deal's a deal,' Ollie says, jabbing his finger a few inches from the old bastard's face. Yeah, quite right. He ain't stitching us up again.

'A deal's a deal,' Electric agrees.

We'd been coming here for some time now, me and Ollie. Animal introduced us to the old bastard about six years ago and we've done pretty much most of our business through him since. Like I say, we've managed to offload a few bits and bobs ourselves but that's a lot of hassle, unless you're stealing to order. Even then, a lot of blokes who give it the large in the pubs about taking 'X' 'Y' and 'Z' off your hands 'no problem', turn out to be bullshitters the moment you take them out to the boot of your car and show them the 'X' 'Y' and 'Z' you just stole for them. Electric's not like that. He might be a tight old bastard who'd short-change a bob-a-job scout, but he's always there to take the gear off your hands. And there's something to be said for the value of cash on the hip.

'When you coming by next then?' Electric asks.

'Well, we're going to be working again this weekend,' I

tell him. 'We've got a couple of places already lined up, and hopefully we'll have a better score with those, so we'll probably be by Monday . . . Monday lunch-time. Alright?'

'Can you make it in the morning?' Electric asks.

'Huh, if we could make it in the morning, we'd probably be able to stick real jobs,' I tell him. 'We'll see you at lunch-time.' Fair's fair, what's the point of being your own guv'nor if you can't lie-in in the morning. It's not just that though, Electric's shop is more than forty-odd miles from mine and Ollie's, which is probably why he's been in business so long. It's one of his rules, he doesn't handle any stuff nicked from his local area, and local area for Electric means within thirty miles.

'No later than two, then. I've got to go out in the afternoon, see a man about a dog.'

'Shame I didn't see you a couple of weeks ago, I could've sorted you out there,' I say for a joke.

'What?' says Electric not realising it was one.

As I'm explaining that it was just a joke and why, there's a knock at the back door and Electric excuses himself. Ollie gives me a 'come on, let's go to the pub' look and I nod and we both head for the back door. When we get there, we see Electric standing to one side to let this bloke in. He looks at us, heads up the short hallway and stops. Electric gives him a pat on the back to reassure him. 'It's alright. They're alright, come on, come in.' The man gives me and Ollie a serious once over and steps inside and squeezes past us. 'You off then lads?' Electric says holding open the door.

'Yeah. We'll see you Monday alright?' I tell Electric as we leave.

'Okay, see you Monday,' he says and shuts the door.

Ollie and me look at each other as we climb into the van. I've never seen the bloke before, but I've seen his type. I don't know what he was into, or what he had in the sports bag he was carrying, but I do know this; he was a serious geezer, way out of our league.

10. Down the chimney

I love Christmas, there's just so much stuff to nick. It's like harvest time. A time of plenty. With me and Ollie out and about, filling our little pockets as much as possible, for the long, hard, cold months ahead.

And it's not just that there's plenty to nick, there's also plenty of buyers to sell to, so we don't have to fuck about and get stiffed by Electric. See, most of the stuff we nick around then is new and still in the box, and blokes around this way are only too happy to do most of their Christmas shopping off a bloke in the pub, rather than fight their way through the crowds down the shops. It's great as well because, as most of the stuff is still in the box, people naturally assume that it's been nicked from a shop or factory and don't feel as bad about handing over cash for stuff that's 'fallen off the back of a lorry'. Me and Ollie, of course, don't get the stuff off a lorry, we get it straight from under the tree. But after a few pints, who cares.

The other thing is that there are so many more opportunities to go out nicking. Everyone's out. The pubs are full of once-a-year drinkers, trying to find Slade on the juke box and walking in front of you when you're playing pool. And if they're not down the pubs, they're round each other's houses, wearing paper hats and trying it on with each other's wives.

All you have to do is drive round the streets and look for a party. Once you find one, burgle the house next door. People are funny when it comes to parties and always invite the people next door, even if they don't like them. They do this mainly so that next door can't complain about the music being too loud. And next door feel a neighbourly obligation to go, so you can nip in and rob them blind while they're drinking too much wine and flirting with people they don't really like. And yet another advantage of this is that any noise you might make breaking into next door gets drowned out by Wizard, Band Aid and Cliff fucking Richard.

God I love Christmas.

'Yo ho ho, there's one,' says Ollie spotting a bash in full swing. 'What d'you reckon?' Drunken laughter, Christmas crackers and Noddy Holder blaring out from behind a pair of middle terrace curtains. Balloons, fake plastic holly and fairy lights in the evergreen out the front; I just knew the man of the house would be inside wearing a fluffy Santa hat and organising charades later.

It was December 23rd and a Saturday to boot, so there was going to be no shortage of parties. We'd only been driving five minutes when we'd come across this one and things already looked promising. Both houses either side of the party were in near darkness.

'Which one you fancy?' I ask Ollie. He votes for the fella with spray-on snow in his windows.

'Very festive,' says Ollie. 'He's bound to be in there.' We park just around the corner and walk back to the house, looking out for twitching curtains as we go. There were none. With the exception of Captain Christmas in number 13, the street was pretty quiet. Hardly any traffic about and too cold for people to be wandering around in the night. Conditions were as perfect as you could get them.

We walk up the path of number 15, Ollie tucks the crowbar down the back of his jeans and I give the bell a ring. Ollie keeps an eye on the windows next door to make sure no one looks out, and no one does. Twenty seconds pass and Ollie's already off round the back, when the lights in the hall come on and the door opens. A four-eyed baldy in a cardy stares at us in a way which suggests we've rung in the last ten minutes of the Ruth Rendell Christmas special.

'What?' he says all urgently. Me and Ollie look at each other then start up at near enough the same time.

'We wish you a Merry Christmas, we wish you a Merry Christmas, we wish you a Merry Christmas and a Happy . . .'

'Clear off,' he snaps and slams the door.

'Well that's very nice isn't it!' says Ollie ready to bang on the door and get him out again.

'Full of the Christmas spirit isn't he,' shouts a voice from next door. We look over to the old dolly bird, with a glass in her hand, smiling over at us.

'Yeah, a right miserable cunt,' Ollie replies.

'Well would you like to come in and sing for us?' she says. 'Be a glass of wine and a couple of mince pies in it for you both.'

'No thanks,' Ollie shouts back. 'Come on let's go.' I grab him by the arm and stop him from walking off.

'Hang on, slow down a minute, look a bit suspicious won't it, couple of Carol singers turning down a gig just like that. Let's just give 'em a quick ten second blast then split.'

I shout back at the mutton: 'It's alright, we don't need to

come inside, we'll just give you a quick sing on the lawn.'
I turn to Ollie. 'Right, ready? We wish you . . .'

'Wait, wait, just wait a minute.' She turns and runs back
in to the house. 'Everyone, come on out here, we've got
Carol singers.'

'Owww fuck this Bex, let's go,' Ollie says to me, but it's
too late, half a dozen people in paper hats are already milling
around on the front lawn. Last to come out is her old man
– wait for it – in his fluffy Santa hat. Me and Ollie go over
and stand in front of them, wearing a couple of smacked
arses for faces.

'Right, what are you going to sing for us? How about
Silent Night?' says Santa hat.

'Don't know that one,' I tell him.

'Away in the Manger?' suggests someone else.

'No,' I reply.

'Well,' Santa hat says, 'why don't you just do what you
want to do then.'

Me and Ollie give them a nod and start. 'We wish you a
Merry Christmas, we wish you a Merry Christmas, we wish
you a Merry Christmas and a Happy New Year. Good
tidings we bring for you and a king, we wish you a Merry
Christmas and a Happy New Year.'

They stare at us in silence, for a moment, before Santa
hat states the obvious.

'You're not very good are you?'

'Well what the fuck do you know about singing anyway,'
Ollie says back.

They give us a couple of mince pies in a cellophane bag
and two plastic cups of red wine and shut the door before
the Carol singers turn ugly. Me and Ollie walk back to the
van and drive off in search of the next party.

*

'How come he weren't at the party?' Ollie asks as we head over to the other side of town.

'How the fuck should I know,' I reply. 'Maybe they don't like him. Maybe he don't like them. Maybe I don't give a shit.' All I knew was that old four-eyes badly needed burgling, but it wouldn't be today.

We drive past three more parties and finally decide the house next to last one looked the best of the bunch. A large four bedroom semi, set back a little from the road, with a nice dark garden surrounded by a couple of tall hedges and several trees. Next door sounded like a much more upmarket bash than Santa hat's, but the only real difference would be more expensive grub, more expensive booze and more expensive crumpet on the menu. The people inside would still be making the same old cunts of themselves.

I park up on the curb by a dozen other motors and get out. We crunch our way up the gravel drive, keeping our eyes peeled and Ollie gives the bell a ring.

'Any sign of an alarm?' he asks. I've already had a quick peek up on the wall when we first got out the van, but didn't see a box. I shake my head.

'Any sign of an alarm?' he asks again.

'No! I just fucking said.'

'When?'

'I just shook me head.' I shake my head again to demonstrate.

'Oh, I weren't looking,' he says, looking away again. No lights come on in the hall and Ollie's all keyed up to get cracking, but after the last fright, I want to give anyone in there another chance to get to the door, so I ring the bell again and give it a good thirty seconds before agreeing with Ollie that nobody's home.

We have a look round the back and find a decent point of entry; a small, thin top window above the kitchen sink.

Ollie pulls the crowbar from his back pocket and wrenches it open. I give it a count of five to see if anyone's heard anything, before climbing up and through.

Several things fall off the draining board, and the bastards have left a nice lot of washing up soaking in the sink for me to step into, but I eventually find a decent footing and slide through. I open the larger side window for Ollie and he knocks even more metal and china on to the floor as he clambers in.

Straight away I clock a microwave and a portable telly. I unplug them and set them down on the floor by the back door, as Ollie gets his torch out and heads off for the living room. Normally it's telly, video, stereo, then upstairs, but Christmas is a special time of the year. Ollie's already on his belly under the tree unwrapping the presents, by the time I get down and join him. Torch in mouth, feet kicking in the air, we go through and see what Santa has brought us. Nintendo, Chanel No. 5, Rotary watch, remote control sand buggy, hair dryer, Action Man frog man and a Hornby train set all get the nod, while the slippers, tie, novelty oven gloves, X-Files board game, golfing umbrella and half a dozen books (books for Christmas?) are left for whoever else wants them. We pack them away and see what else we can bag.

Ollie's drinking a glass of sherry left out for Santa and looking at the collection of china cats on the sideboard, wondering if he can fit them all in his pockets, as I take the telly out to the back door. 'Leave those alone,' I tell him, 'and give me a hand upstairs.'

We've only been in the place about four or five minutes but most of it's done. I ain't exactly keen to hang about when the owners are so close. It would only take one of them to decide to nip back for five minutes and set the video for Morecambe and Wise, for us to be in big trouble.

I start with the main bedroom, Ollie takes next door. The patron saint of burglary is smiling on us tonight because the geezer has left his wallet on the bedside cabinet with £70 in cash and two credit cards, probably deciding he wasn't going to need it at next door's bash. It'll be a different story with the wife's purse though. She'll have it with her in her handbag, along with her war paint, tampons and half her belongings.

I'm just going through the drawers when Ollie comes in and shines the torch in my face.

'I think we've got trouble.'

My heart thumps heavily in my chest and my bladder goes to battle stations.

'What is it?' I say, rushing to look out the window. I can't see anyone coming but they might already be in. I didn't hear a thing.

'This way,' Ollie says as I look at him. 'Come on, this way.'

I follow him through the hallway to the third bedroom on the right, where he stops in the doorway and stands to one side. I wait for him to say something but he doesn't. He just stands there and shines the torch in. I squeeze past him and look for myself at where he's shining the torch.

'Jesus,' is all I can say. The boy looks about seven while the girl is no more than five. Tears stream down both of their faces as they look at us, paralysed in sheer terror. They were both down on the floor, curled up together, in their pyjamas. They'd tried to hide at the end of the bed, but hadn't really given it much serious thought. I knelt down in front of them. 'Get that light out of their faces,' I tell Ollie.

'It's alright, it's okay, we're not going to hurt you, we're just ... we're not going to do anything. Okay? Are you okay?' I can see them both trembling like leaves. 'It's alright, you're alright. We're . . .'

'Your mum and dad sent us over, alright,' Ollie says in a less than sympathetic voice.

'Yeah, your mum and dad told us to come over from the party and make sure you were okay. They were worried about you.' The boy makes his first sound, a sort of whimpery sniff. 'They told us to come over and check that you were still asleep, so that we could let Father Christmas know it was time to come and drop his presents off.'

'Oi, uncle Bex,' Ollie says, 'let's move.'

'Go and stick the telly in the van,' I tell him. 'I'll stay with them, make sure they're alright. Go on.' Ollie goes without arguing, which in itself was a fucking Christmas miracle. 'Oi,' I call after him as he gallops off down the stairs. 'Leave the Action Man and the train set.'

After five minutes, I manage to get them back into bed and find out, through sobs and gulps, that their names are Ashley and Sara. Ashley's favourite toy was his Jurassic Park Tyrannosaurus Rex, and what he wanted was a bike, and Sara's favourite toy was her dolly and what she really wanted was a Wendy House. Ollie comes back up and gives me a nod.

'All done, come on.'

'Me and uncle . . . Roger here, have to go now okay, but don't worry because your mum and dad . . .'

'Are a couple of bastards and you can tell 'em that from us,' Ollie snaps. 'Now come on Bex, for fuck's sake.'

'Watch your fucking language,' I snap back. 'Not in front of the kids.'

'Well come on then.' Ollie pulls me to my feet by the jacket and through the door.

'Got to go,' I whisper at the kids. 'Got to go.'

We both run down the stairs, out the back door, tip-toe up the gravel, into the van and drive off.

'Fucking bastards, hey,' says Ollie. 'Leaving their kids like that. What a couple of bastards. We could've been anyone, child molesters, murderers, anyone.'

I totally agree. What a couple of bastards. Ollie's all up for going into the party next door, dragging them outside and giving them the fucking good hiding they both richly deserved. He eventually agrees that this weren't a good idea, but neither of us want to leave it there. Twenty minutes later, from a phone box outside town, we ring 999 and give it the old hanky over the mouth routine. Plod turns up ten minutes after that, force an entry and get the kids. Just about now, the party next door starts to notice all the commotion outside and the concerned parents stroll out with a glass in their hands.

It made the local paper. BURGLARS TIP-OFF LEADS TO HOME ALONE ARREST. They were fined £500 and the kids put on the 'at risk register'. As for me and Ollie, we were congratulated in the paper for grassing on the Osgoods.

Funny old world ain't it.

The Osgoods.

What a couple of bastards.

11. Somebody's home

Of course, the Osgoods isn't the only place where I've run into someone I didn't expect to. I was doing this place over a few years back, on that new estate out by the river. Me and Ollie'd had it lined up for a few months. One of our mates had worked on it when it was a building site, took a copy of a front door key and sold it to us for a few quid. All we had to do was wait until the estate was finished and someone moved in.

About five months later, I spot lights and some curtains one evening when I'm making a pass and see that we've got the green light. Only trouble is, by this time, Ollie – the fucking sap – is all loved up with some old slapper and doing his usual bit about giving up nicking and going straight; he's even got his old job back on the door at *Glitzy's* turning away any blokes who want to get in and bouncing drunks down the stairs. I tell him that his bird is probably shagging every geezer in town while he's working nights, but he doesn't listen and tells me, point blank, that he's out for good.

So that's me, lumbered with doing the job on me jack, which I don't really like, but I've got no choice, because I need the money and every other cunt I ask don't fancy it.

The only bloke I don't bother asking is Roland, but fuck that, I'm in no hurry to join him for a cup of tea.

It doesn't matter though, I've done jobs by myself before, but like I say, I prefer not to.

Anyway, I take a drive down there in the evening and check it out. It's one of those small one-bedroom back-to-back starter homes. This pisses me off a little bit because it's bang-smack in the middle of a load of four- and five-bedroom houses, which are much more likely to have stuff in them worth a nick. The one-bedroom first-time buyer, about now, is probably finding a jar of decent coffee outside his price range.

I give it a few minutes and watch the front of the house. It's nice and dark and there aren't any lights on in the house. No cars outside either. In and out, I tell myself. In and out, five minutes max. I walk across the road, calm as you like, give the door a quick knock, take the key out of my pocket and enter the house in one smooth move. When I close the door behind me I give a little call to doubly make sure that no one's in, before closing the curtains, getting out my torch and going to work. There's a small telly, no video, a very old and very weak hi-fi, a microwave and a bike (a girl's racer), which – get this – is chained up to the radiator. It's about the only decent thing in the whole place and it's chained up. Why would you do that? Why wouldn't you think that simply shutting the door and locking it behind you wouldn't be good enough? Some people are just so fucking paranoid.

Anyway, I figure I'll load up what I can after I have a quick look through the drawers upstairs and be away. I find a jewellery box, a camera, a radio alarm and pair of hair things, which I don't understand but I've seen Mel use before. I'm just about done when I hear the front door go downstairs and the light comes on.

Shit! I think. Fuck!

I go to the window but the bastard's got window locks on it and it won't open. And of course, because I had a key for this job, I left the crowbar in the van, so I can't prise it open. I can't just slip out downstairs either, because it's all open plan down there. So I'm a bit stuck. I'm wondering whether I should just make a run for it, when I hear footsteps on the stairs coming up. I decide the best option for the moment is to hide, so I tuck myself down the wall-facing side of the bed and hope it all goes away.

It doesn't.

She comes into the bedroom, kicks off her brogues and starts to get out of her nurse's uniform. At this point I'd like to tell you that she was tall blonde and gorgeous and that she was pleasantly surprised to find me lurking in her bedroom, but this ain't *Razzle*. She was a big, fat, wobbling porker of a bird, who needed a good scrub with soap and water, and who freaked out the moment she saw my feet sticking out the end of the bed.

I launch myself over the bed and down the stairs as she breaks down in hysterics up in the bedroom. My heart's already pounding like a fucking Zulu on the warpath by the time I get to the front door, but it goes into overdrive when I find that she's double locked the door from the inside. I tear at the latch and try and force open the door but the bastard won't budge. I run for the back door, but soon remember there isn't one.

'Shit,' I swear. 'Fucking shit.' This is probably freaking her out even more, but it needed to be said. 'Have you got the keys for the front door?' I shout up the stairs. No answer, just hysterics. 'I'd really like to leave now, but I can't get out because you've locked the front door. Have you got the keys?' She still doesn't answer. I really don't want to have to go up there, but things are looking like I'm going have to. It's about this time that I remember the phone on the bedside table.

I charge up to the bedroom and find her curled up into a ball whispering either 'cheese curry' or 'please hurry' into the phone. I don't really catch it so I can't be sure, but under the circumstances I'd say it was the second one. I snatch the phone out of her hands and hang up, but the damage is done.

'Don't hurt me, please don't hurt me,' she says, sobbing and crying and stuff. 'Please don't hurt me,' over and over again. I have to say, seeing her in this state, and knowing that it was me that put her in to it, I feel fucking awful. Her face all red and puffy and looking at me like I was Jack the Ripper with a hard-on. I feel like a right cunt.

'Look, I'm not going to hurt you okay,' I say kneeling down a safe distance from her.

'Don't . . . don't . . . touch me, please,' she sobs.

'I'm not going to, honest. I don't want to. I'm not here for that okay. I'm just a burglar, that's all. I'm just a burglar,' I try and reassure her. 'Now look, I'd really like to leave now. I really want to go, you've frightened me away. But I can't because you've locked the door and I need the keys to get out.' I reach for her handbag which she has dumped on the bed. 'I promise you alright, I ain't going to hurt you. I just want to go.' I pull the handbag to me and start searching through it. This in itself is enough to send most birds right over the edge – even the ones you're going out with – let alone when it's some strange geezer holding them prisoner in their bedroom. Not that I was holding her prisoner you understand. If anything it's the other way round. I'm being held captive by some big, fat, horrible nurse, but I don't suppose anyone gives a shit about that, do they.

I'm getting to the point now when I'm starting to make

stupid deals with old Nurse Gladys Emanuelle as I'm rum-
maging through her bag.

'Look, I tell you this, when I'm out of here, when I'm
gone, I won't come back, that's it. Your gaff will be off
limits for me.'

Still I rummage, deeper and deeper, with no sign of those
fucking keys.

'Me and all my mates. None of us will come back. That's
our lot.'

Hairbrush, hair spray, under-arm, clips, bands and
pins . . .

'You'll have a burglar-free house, guaranteed.'

. . . tissues, lip-stick, mirror, cigarettes, lighter, pens and
pencils . . .

'All I want is to go. Go home and see my little son.'

. . . postcards, scissors, lolly sticks covered in sand-paper,
Tic-Tacs, tampons, cat's flea collar, broken bits of
jewellery . . .

'Who is ill!'

. . . address book, more sprays, pair of tights, more pens,
cotton pads, purse – ooh, there's £20 in there – stamps, gas
bill, undeveloped 35mm film . . .

'Whooping cough, we're all really worried actually.'

. . . torch, paperback, perfume, watch strap, assorted
toffees, plastic bags, twisties . . .

'WHERE ARE YOUR FUCKING KEYS?' I yell at her,
finally losing it. She makes a sort of 'urhh' sound of fear
and throws me a bunch of keys which she's had behind her
back all this time. I grab them and toss her the bag.

'Thank you,' I say, trying to hide my anger at her holding
out on me. I'm almost tempted to say: 'Now that I have
these, I can kill you,' just for a laugh, but I'm not that much
of a bastard.

I hold up a silver Yale key. 'Is it this one?' She doesn't

answer. Instead she pulls something out of her bag really quickly and sprays white-hot pain into my face. I can't even begin to describe how much this hurts my eyes and my nose and my mouth and my ... well, everything really. Everything hurts. My face burns like a bastard and suddenly knows how my arse feels after a vindaloo. I scream in agony, stumble blindly to the bog and stick my head under the cold tap. It takes several seconds for the water to put out the fire in my eyes, and even then, there's still a decent amount of sting left over.

'Enough fucking about!!!!!!!' I shout at her at the top of my voice as I stagger back out of the bog. She reacts by wailing with fright again and curling up even tighter.

'Don't hurt me, please don't hurt me,' she begs.

Hurt her? I want to throttle the ugly, fat fucker, but there isn't time. The clock is ticking. I throw myself downstairs, pick up the microwave out of the kitchen and sling it through the living room window, diving after it before it even hits the deck.

I'm halfway across the other side of the estate, driving like a trucker on a promise, through a waterfall of tears, when the Old Bill screech to a halt by a smashed up microwave and charge in to *her* rescue.

Which just goes to show, there are certain times when you should never try and resort to reason when violence will do just as well.

It's never very nice to bump into the house owner while you're filling your pockets with his stuff, and I'm sure it can't really be that pleasant for him either, but that's neither here nor there really.

At least when you're caught by the filth, it's just business. Householders take it all so personally. What's up with them?

The most common complaint I've heard from people

who've been burgled – especially women – is that it ain't
the stuff that's been nicked that upsets them, it's the thought
that someone's been through their stuff. Well what sort of
sense does this make? It's not as if me and Ollie are holding
up their pants to the light looking for skid marks is it.
Personally, if I was going to be upset by anything it would
be not having a video any more, not that someone's been
through my wardrobe and looked at my shirts. Fuck's sake!
And anyway, what have they got to hide?

Besides, I do know how it feels. Four times now I've had
Plod round turning my drum upside down looking for
nicked gear, but I'm sure no one's crying into their beer
over that are they.

Saying that though, not all close encounters turn out this
way.

Parky was doing over this house one time right, place
over in Nutmeg Glade, and actually turned out to be the
hero of the day. See, he knew, for a fact, that this couple
had gone away on holiday for the fortnight, because he was
slipping one to Denise in the travel agent's at the time. This
was a nice little variation on Norris's estate agent plan except
that Denise didn't know about Parky's line of work. She'd
just mentioned it by-the-by, that this lucky couple had
managed to wangle a half-price last minute cancellation to
Jamaica and were in the air fifteen hours after leaving the
shop. Parky's a right smooth bastard when it comes to a
good tip and bombarded her with two dozen questions
about the deal in order to disguise the one he really wanted
to know. Where do they live? Loose lips sink ships.

Anyway, two days later he's jemmying open their French
doors and going through the silver. He's just about to go
upstairs when he notices – well, actually he almost steps on
– this old geezer lying at the bottom of the stairs holding a
light bulb. Parky takes a good look at him and comes to

the conclusion that, even though he ain't dead, he ain't that far off it. So, he tucks a pillow under the geezer's head, dials 999 and leaves the front door open as he legs it. The ambulance gets there fifteen minutes later and takes the old fella, and his fractured skull, to hospital for an operation. According to the paper the next week, he was jet-set Johnny's old man, who'd been draughted in at the last minute to house-sit the Yukkas and goldfish. Daft old idiot was trying to change the landing light bulb when the kitchen chair he was standing on decided to go for a walk without telling him. Everything turned out alright in the end, the doctors got to him just in time, the geezer made almost a full recovery and his son and daughter-in-law had to cut their dream holiday short after only three days and fly back to Britain.

Oh, and two of their goldfish were eaten by a cat that got in when Parky left the door open.

Now I'm not saying here that burglars are the fourth emergency service or anything, but without Parky that geezer would've still been there to welcome his kids home. All the blokes in the pub reckoned Parky had done the right thing and gave him a pat on the back for saving matey's life. Only Norris said he would've cleaned out the place first then phoned the Blues and Twos. But then, Norris would say that now then, wouldn't he. The cunt.

Unusual as Parky's day off from being the villain was, the most bizarre encounter happened to me and Ollie about three years ago.

We didn't have anything lined up one particular weekend. Actually we hadn't had anything for a little while, so we was having to go through a period of going out on spec, which to be honest, I fucking hate. Salesmen call it cold calling.

I'd much rather have an address, a key and a guaranteed forty-eight-hour window to do the place over, but you don't always get what you want do you. Needs must as the Devil pisses in your tea, as they say.

The way we do it is, we drive about all evening (usually a Friday or Saturday night because most normal people are in the pub getting drunk) and look for houses with the lights off (yes, the old leaving the front room light on does actually work). When we find somewhere, we park up nearby, walk round and knock on the door.

If no one answers, we go around the back and do the place over.

If someone does answer however, we ask if Alan or Frank or whoever is there. They say no, we say sorry to bother you and leave them alone.

If however, someone does answer and Alan, Frank or whoever, turns out to be there, we ask him if he's the Alan or Frank who wants his fence creosoted. 'We were given this address.' He says no, we say sorry to bother you and leave them alone.

If, in the extreme, it turns out that, yes, Alan or Frank is home and, yes, he does want his fence creosoted, then we quote him a price of £4,000 for the job. That usually does the trick. He says no, we say sorry to bother you and leave them alone.

Alan and Frank have occasionally turned out to be home, but me and Ollie have yet to run into an Alan or Frank who wanted his fence creosoted for £4,000. I don't know what we'd do if we ever did – probably do it. I mean, you can't really turn your nose up at four grand for creosoting a fence now can you?

Anyway, we were out and about one Friday night and find this place that looks fairly promising. End terrace, nice and dark, street light nearby not working and *Terminator 2* on BBC1 for all the sad bastards stuck at home. Conditions were perfect. We park up round the back by an alley and wander round the front. Alan's not home. Neither's Frank, Bob, Dave, Neil or anyone else. So me and Ollie nip back round the back alley, over the fence and in. Old Alan has even left open the back window for us so we climb in without a sound.

We have a quick look around and, on first inspection, there is fuck all, and I mean fuck all, worth nicking. On second inspection there's even less.

Occasionally this happens. We come across a fully furnished drum where we find ourselves hard pushed to nick anything; no video, no telly (no telly?), no hi-fi, no nothing. Nothing. We go upstairs to the bedrooms and there's books and a bed and clothes and stuff, but nothing we can nick. No jewellery, no money, no antique clocks. Not-a-thing!

This really winds up Ollie every time.

'Those fucking wankers,' he says. 'They ain't got anything, fucking nothing.' I start going through the drawers with a fine-tooth comb in case I've missed some valuable socks while Ollie flips out a bit and starts turning over the bed looking for that never-present shoebox full of cash. 'Cunts,' he says when he doesn't find it. 'Fucking cunts. Where's their video? Why ain't they got nothing? What's up with them, hey? Wasting my fucking time like I ain't got nothing better to be doing. Wankers!'

Personally I feel almost sorry for them. I'm almost tempted to go out to the van and get the colour portable we liberated from Ashley Gardens and leave it with a note and some luncheon vouchers, but Ollie's ready to beat them up.

'Come on let's go,' I say and we both trot downstairs. We walk into the living room and suddenly there's a torch in me face and someone that isn't me or Ollie shouts 'shit'.

We both turn and bolt, but something stops me. It's like I'm looking in to a mirror or something, because whoever was just waving the torch about was now trying to follow someone else through the back window. This isn't normal behaviour for house owners.

'Oi,' I shout. 'Oi, oi. Hold up. Who are you?' The lad slows for a moment, as he clambers over the windowsill. He stops and looks back at me. 'What you doing?'

Matey's confused enough to take a moment longer to give me the once over.

'What are you doing?' he asks me back.

'Nothing,' I say, which is such a bollocks answer because it's obvious I'm doing something, but this is a time for treading carefully.

'I saw the window open,' the lad says. 'I was just checking to make sure everything was alright.'

'You lying bastard,' I say back. 'You've come in to rob the place.' At this moment, his mate appears at the window behind him with an expression of 'What the fuck are you doing?' on his face.

'Gerry, what the fuck are you doing?' he says.

The penny drops and suddenly Gerry gets it.

'Me, robbing this place? I like that,' he says to me. 'What are you doing in here then, sleep walking I suppose?'

Ollie reappears behind me. 'Bex, what the fuck are you doing?'

'I think we can all relax,' I tell everyone. 'We're all friends here.' There's a couple more moments of tension, then we all breathe a sigh of relief. I take a step forward and hold out my fags to Gerry and (as I later found out) Pete. 'Smoke?'

Gerry takes one, Pete doesn't, and we both spark up together. 'Anything nice?' asks Gerry.

'Joking int'cha. There's fuck all in here, nothing. Just furniture and clothes and stuff.'

'Any nice pieces of furniture?' he asks.

'What? Nice pieces?'

Ollie wanders over. 'What are you fucking doing in here?' he says aggressively.

'I think we've covered this ground already,' Gerry says back. This stumps Ollie a bit, because he still hasn't fully got it yet, while we're all on to the next conversation.

'You want a smack in the mouth?' is all he can think to reply.

'No,' says Gerry matter-of-fact, as if Ollie's just asked him if he wants a cup of coffee. 'Not really.' Now this really stumps Ollie, who is used to people responding 'fuck off' or 'come on then' or 'who's gonna give it to me then, you, you big wanker?' But Gerry's cool and all it takes is the offer of a fag to defuse a punch-up in the middle of a job.

'Furniture?' I ask Gerry.

'Yes furniture, it's worth money believe it or not,' he says, flicking his ash outside the window.

'Who can be arsed with all that?' I say.

'Well, we can,' Gerry says back. 'Do you mind?'

I look at Ollie as he flicks his ash all over the tablecloth. 'What?' he says.

'You want anything in here?' I ask Ollie. 'Or d'you mind if these boys have a go?'

'Huh, help your fucking selves,' shrugs Ollie. 'Good luck, you won't find anything, 'cos there's fuck all in here to find.'

Pete climbs back through the window and him and Gerry go to work.

Before me and Ollie leave, I get Gerry's number and tell him I'll give him a bell. I do this a couple of days later and we meet up for a few beers in town to exchange war stories, useful tips, and such like. Since then we've become pretty good mates, although Ollie still doesn't like him much. But then, Ollie doesn't really like anyone.

Oh, and at the end of the evening, I asked him if he'd gotten anything decent out of the house after we left and you know what he said?

Well you're wrong, he didn't, because there was absolutely fuck all there to nick?

12. Clever plans: number 3

Usually, the clever plans I like to concentrate on are burglary plans, which is my particular field of interest. But I'm going to make an exception here and tell you about these bank robbers that came up with an absolutely brilliant plan. Again, I read this in one of the papers and so, I don't know the full ins and outs of it, just what little was written.

But what happened was, these bank robbers, in France, burst into a big bank in the middle of Paris, waving machine guns about and making a lot of noise. This in itself might not seem that brilliant and original, but bear with me. They shoot out the cameras, empty the cash tills and frighten all the customers, before dragging the manager off his knees and ordering him to take them to the vault. The manager says something about his wife and kids and cries a bit, but eventually he gets himself together enough and takes them out back to the safe.

Around about now, some young bank employee, on about five francs a day, decides he fancies staying the night, barricaded in his place of work, in the company of half a dozen desperate nutters with machine guns, so he trips the silent alarm. The local Gendarme are there in a matter of minutes, taking up position outside, sealing off the street and shouting at the bank robbers, through loud speakers, to come out with their hands up, that sort of thing.

Well, the bank robbers, they don't fancy that in the slightest and tell the police to fuck off, telling them that they've got hostages and that they'll kill them if the police try anything. This old business goes on for a while, with le Old Bill trying to talk the robbers out and the robbers asking for helicopters and speedboats and that sort of stuff, but eventually it all becomes a bit of a stand-off. The robbers don't want to come out and the police don't really fancy going in. They've got the only exit covered and they know that it's only a matter of time before the robbers realise that the game is up.

A couple of hours later, the robbers ask to speak to a brief, and not just any old legal aid plea bargainer, but the top man in Paris, monsieur Rumpole dans le Bailey, or whatever his name was. The police track him down, get him to the bank and sit him in the command centre, where he and the robbers chat about their chances, and what they're likely to get, what they can do to help themselves, and so on and so forth.

The robbers let half the hostages go as a sign of good faith and the police breathe a sigh of relief as they see this thing coming to a peaceful conclusion fairly shortly.

A little while later, the bank robbers ring the command centre, all sounding a bit fucked off and defeated and asking for a little more time to talk it through amongst themselves and the police agree. The robbers ask one last favour, as a sign of good faith, dinner for them and the rest of the hostages, because they haven't eaten all day and that's a long time for a Frog. The police agree and go out and get two dozen plate loads of grub and deliver them to the bank. Another half-hour goes by and the police give the robbers a ring to ask them if they're ready to come out now, but there's no answer. They try again, but still no answer. The police look at each other and suddenly worry that something serious has happened inside the bank and they prepare to move in.

They try ringing one last time and when, once more, they get no answer, it's all hands to the pumps and they go in full steam, stun grenades, tear gas and everything.

The robbers are gone though.

All they find is the hostages tied up in an empty vault, two dozen untouched portions of snails and a big fuck off hole in the floor. The hole leads on to a tunnel, and the tunnel leads on to a small rented flat on the other side of the road.

Now I know what you're thinking, you're thinking that the robbers couldn't possibly have tunnelled all the way across the road in just a few hours. They didn't. What they did was, they dug the tunnel before they went in to the bank. Spent weeks digging it, leaving themselves about a foot or so to break through on the bank's side. And this is what they were doing while they were asking for helicopters and lawyers and dinner and garlic bread, buying themselves enough time to finish the tunnel and scarper with the entire contents of the vault.

What a great plan!

13. Insulated

Men and women have different ways of defrosting the fridge. Women go about it by taking out all the food, opening the door, turning off the plug and leaving the fridge to it. Blokes differ in that they turn off the plug, get a hairdryer, a screwdriver and a hammer and knock big lumps of ice off, toss them in the sink and pour boiling water over them. This was what I was doing a few weeks back. It's how I've always defrosted the fridge, it's how it should be done. The man's way.

I'm not usually given to household chores, I don't normally stand around in a pinny, ironing my pants or nothing. It's just that all four walls of the icebox had finally touched and I had a packet of Microchips in there somewhere. It was also a Sunday afternoon and there was fuck all on the telly except for *James and the Giant Peach* and some mincer of a chef.

So there I am, just getting into it, giving it all I've got with a heavy duty flat-head, when all of a sudden ... *Pschshshshshshshshshsh* ... straight in my face. The wall goes and fucking splits and all the gas comes out, and that's that fucked. There's no way to fix it, the fridge is finished, knackered, only fit for the scrap heap now. I know this to be true because it's the third time I've done this. I'm so pissed off with myself that I accidentally smash up the hairdryer I was using to defrost the fridge, having a tantrum.

A joint, two cans of lager and *The Antiques Roadshow* later and I've calmed down enough to give Ollie a bell and tell him what I did.

And you know what, the fucker laughs.

That night we're in a house over on Hersham Park Road, ex-girlfriend of a bloke we drink with. We do a lot of ex's, it's good reliable work. The relationship goes wrong, one wants the other out of their life. Maybe a bit of hanky-panky's gone on or there's been ten beers and one slap too many or something. It doesn't really matter because at the end of the day, the result's always the same – there's a lot of bitterness, a lot of spite and a lot of will to see some horrible harm happen to the other half. People have real trouble letting go and just walking away, they feel a real need for revenge. And I ain't just talking about blokes either, half of our tips come from birds. One old sort even asked me to kill her old man once. But fuck that big time! I absolutely did not want to know, which was just as well because three months later they got back together and have now got a kid. Fucking nutters hey!

Anyway, just for the record, this was a bird's house we were doing over – well, it was her mum and dad's – but that didn't matter to me and Ollie, we ain't fussy. Not quite sure what she was supposed to have done, chucked her bloke over for someone better-looking probably. That's usually the case.

So, for this unforgivable smacking of his ego, her ex provides us with a time his bird and her parents are all out, the best access point and a full shopping list. In return, we give him £30 or £40 for the tip and the revenge he wants, plus any particular little mementos he might want us to pick up for him – all part of the service (although nothing too personal like photos or stuff otherwise it wouldn't take too many man-hours of police work to figure out it was an inside job).

Anyway, we're already piled up by the back door and all set to go, just as soon as Ollie finds her Pentax. Apparently, that's her favourite possession in the whole world and Justin – the ex – thinks she might even have the last ever pictures of her late nan on the film. What a charmer! Still who am I to criticise.

Ollie finds it and rejoins me in the kitchen.

'Smile,' he says and there's a flash.

'Don't take my fucking picture you stupid cunt!' I say, holding my hand up to my face too late.

'I'm only having a laugh,' Ollie says.

'Fucking laugh. What if we drop that and the Old Bill finds it, hey? They won't need to take fingerprints to work out who nicked it will they, they'll have your fucking photographic essay. Give me that here.'

'What are you doing?'

'I'm opening the back to expose the film,' I tell him.

'But it's pitch black.'

'Well I'll shine the torch in it then.'

'Well hang on,' he says. 'Take one of me before you do the film.' I stare at him for a moment to see if he's serious then realise he is. At this point I can't even be arsed to argue with him so I do as he says and take the shot, but he says: 'Here wait up, the flash didn't go off.'

'Does it matter?'

'Oi come on, play the game, you got your photo done, fucking take mine.' So I did, and through the flash I could see the big dozy fucker grinning into the camera like a schoolboy on a daytrip to the zoo. At this point the camera gives a click and starts to whirl. 'What's happened?' says the brain donor.

'End of the film, the fucking thing's rewinding.' When it stops, I open the back and the film pops out.

'Don't leave that on the side,' Ollie says quite unnecessarily.

'Oh yeah right,' I say. 'Thanks for telling me. Don't worry I'm taking it with us. Now come on Kate Moss, give me a hand getting this stuff in the van.'

As we load up, I tell Ollie to leave a bit of room in the back of the van and meet me back in the kitchen, as there was something else I wanted to get.

We stash most of the stuff in the lock-up for the night and head back to mine. Another ten minutes of huffing and puffing and I plug in my new fridge/freezer.

'Not bad is she,' I say as I push it back into the gap where my old fridge used to be.

'Yeah, better than your other one,' agrees Ollie. 'Got anything to eat?'

'Don't know,' I say. 'I'll just see what I've got in shall I.' I open the fridge part of the fridge/freezer and see what grub we've got. I threw out most of the milk, orange juice and other drinks back at Justin's bird's but kept all the food to save me a shop. 'Steak, chicken, prawns, fancy a prawn sandwich? I've got real butter.'

'Yeah, I'll have some of that, and look, a bottle of wine,' says Ollie pulling a bottle of white from my in-built wine rack.

'Cushty. You crack it open, I'll make the sarnies. Cork-screw on my Swiss army knife on the living room table.'

'What's insulin?' asks Ollie holding up a couple of tiny little bottles.

'What? Where?'

'Here, look, there's loads of them. About half a dozen or so little squeezy bottles.' He fishes around in the mess at the bottom of the fridge and pulls out another four or five of them and what looks like a little medical kit.

'It's a sort of drug isn't it. You inject it. Dyslexics use it or something.' Ollie holds up one of the bottles and gives it a squeeze.

'Is it worth anything?'

'Shouldn't think so. To a dyslexic it probably is, but it ain't worth anything to us,' I tell him.

'What about Rodney, he might have it.'

'Nah, Rodney. He ain't gonna want to buy it, he deals in Charlie and puff, not fucking medicine. This stuff ain't worth nothing. Sling it,' I tell him. 'Any mayonnaise in there?'

The insulin belonged to Justin's bird's mum. She's got a little problem with her blood sugar levels or something. She had just the one portion of it with her in her handbag, but the stuff in the fridge was her month's supply. So not only did she come home from the bingo to find her house done over, she also had to spend half the night up at the hospital, while they sorted her out with some more. Justin was so chuffed he gave us back the £30.

Ollie took the film into Boots and got it done on the one hour service. They came out really well, but if you ask me, Justin's bird's nan doesn't look too well.

14. A nice little chat

I don't know why they always have to take my fucking boots. The floor is freezing and my socks have got big holes in the bottom. I must remember to pick up a few pairs next time I do over someone with the same size feet as me. On second thoughts maybe I won't, last time I did that I got a verruca. All the cops have given me is a crappy little tan blanket that, when I pull it up to my chin, only reaches down as far as my knees.

Cunts!

I go over to the bell and give it a push. After a while I give it another, then another, then another, and then eventually Sergeant Atwell appears at the catflap. 'What d'you want?'

'Me boots, this floor's fucking freezing,' I tell him.

'You know the rules.'

'Ohh fuck the rules, come on give me me boots. I'm freezing. I'll see you alright. There'll be a drink in it for you.' He slams the trap shut and walks back to finish his crossword. Bastard. I don't know what this boots rule is anyway. I swear they're making it up. Maybe they're frightened I'm going to slip justice by stringing myself up with the laces. This is rubbish, because in the first place I'm a self-serving cunt of a coward who would never do anything to harm himself and in the second, my boots are slip-ons.

Thinking about this for a second though, if I was an Indian, would they take my turban? No, of course they wouldn't. They couldn't. They'd have to let me keep it on religious grounds. Yet I could still top myself with that couldn't I? So that means this is racial discrimination.

I ring the bell again.

Sergeant Atwell appears at the flap.

'What now?'

'If I was an Indian, you wouldn't take away my turban would you hey?' I tell him.

'Fine, you can keep your turban, but I don't care if you're Mahatma fucking Gandhi, you ain't getting your shoes back.' And that's it, he's gone again.

I shouldn't even be in here really. I came down the station of my own free will. Weasel came round in the morning asking questions about the job me and Ollie done last night and tried to frighten me by giving it the old, 'We can either do this here or down the station.'

Fine, let's go down the station, I don't care. I'll go down the station all you want mate, I still ain't putting my hands up to nothing though.

What's so bad about going down the station anyway? I'd rather go 'down the station' for a few hours than 'give you a full confession' any day of the week. Go on, do your worst. The villains on *The Bill* are always shitting them-selves about 'going down the station'. They usually crack the moment Tosh Lines says 'Right then, in the cell, and you can stay in there until you're ready to talk.' Two minutes later they're banging on the door and grassing up the Jackson brothers from the Jasmin Allen Estate. Come on, let's get real.

Fact – the Old Bill can only hold you in the cells pending enquiries for a maximum of twenty-four hours, unless they get a special extension order, but this is rare. Fact – the longer they keep you in the cells, the less they know. If they had it all figured out, they wouldn't need to keep you in the cells half the night, while they try and talk your friends and family into making statements against you. Give me twenty-four hours in the cell over six months in the nick any day. I could do it on my head.

I'm only in here, anyway, while we wait for my brief to get here. Charlie Taylor, known to one and all as The Tailor (it's a pun, something to do with being stitched up that doesn't quite work). Everyone likes Charlie because the first thing he gets you to do is fill in the forms for legal aid. It wouldn't matter if you walked into his office wearing an Armani suit and had a Porsche outside, he'd still reach straight for the legal aid pad. And when I say, he gets you to fill it in, I mean, of course, he gets you to sign it after he's filled it in. 'Savings? None. Assets? None. Outgoings? Oooh, what shall we make that . . .' First time I ever dealt with him I read through after he'd done the business and couldn't figure out how I was making ends meet, but Charlie told me not to worry about it, just sign at the bottom. According to the form, I was one step away from refugee status. But still, if it meant me not having to put my hand in my pocket for his fee, then fuck it, crack on. I mean, what do I pay my taxes for?

I give the bell another ring.

'What?'

'Can I have some dinner?' I ask.

'You've only been in here an hour,' Atwell tells me.

'So? What's that got to do with it? It ain't how long I've been in here is it, it's how long it is since I've eaten. And I usually have dinner about now.'

'It's 3 o'clock in the afternoon,' says Atwell, theatrically checking his cheapo watch. God I would love to nick that.

'Well, I work funny hours don't I.'

'If you touch that bell again, me and a few of the boys'll come in there and test out our new batons on your head. Got it?' Slam.

'Charming. Don't hear that sort of talk from Bob Cryer now, do you?' I shout after him and am rewarded with a bit of solidarity from someone in the opposite cell when they shout 'fat wanker' at him as he walks off. I just fancied some overcooked turkey steaks with tinned peas as well.

I sit back down and bite my nails for a bit, then see if I can reach my toe-nails. I can't.

I spend the next hour of so going over the graffiti scribbled all over the walls. There's all the usual stuff here; swearing, nicknames, 'Man Utd' (obviously had some scrumpers in), stuff about Weasel, and what he gets up to with his mum, and a short poem:

Weasel's men came over the hill
like a troop of Monty's tankers
one in ten were righteous men
the rest were fucking wankers.

Pam Ayres would've been proud. There's also a pretty good drawing of a couple of coppers pissing on top of Weasel's head with a speech bubble coming from it that's left blank. Obviously the geezer's given it too much thought as to what Weasel should be saying and was chucked out before he could finish. I use my belt buckle to scratch in the word 'LOVELY', in the vacant bubble, then sign it off 'BEX'.

The flap is pulled down, Atwell looks in, opens the door and then steps aside for Weasel.

'Ah, Mr Haynes, I was just reading about you,' I say. Weasel looks around the cell and screws up his face.

'On your feet. Your brief's here, come on,' he says, all

efficient like. I pull myself to my feet when he spots the picture. 'Oi,' he says pointing to it. 'Have you done that?'

'Not lately,' I say looking at the rivers of cartoon piss running off his face. 'Why, are you interested?' Weasel's just about to grab me by the collar and tell me what a cunt I am when Sergeant Atwell interrupts and tells him that it was already done before I was put in.

'What's that then?' he says pointing to where I'd written 'BEX'.

'What?' I say.

'That, there, your name. Where did that come from then?' Weasel insists.

'What?' I say.

'Oh come on,' Weasel says shoving me towards the door. 'And you,' he says to Atwell, 'get this cell painted.'

'It was painted only last week. This stuff's all fresh.'

I have a quick five minutes alone with Charlie while he gets me to fill in a few forms and tells me the score, such as what was on telly the night of the job. He's got copies of the *Radio Times* going back more than seven years, just in case I ever 'forget' what I was at home all night watching. I have no idea if this is legal. Probably not, but that's hardly the sort of thing that's going to put me off a good idea now is it.

Charlie also tells me Weasel's had a word with Ollie but hasn't brought him in, because his one and only witness only remembers seeing me – 'or someone like you', Charlie corrects himself – and the van. Still, that was enough for Weasel to get the go-ahead to set up the ID parade waiting for me next door.

'Don't say anything until we see how Blind Date goes,' he says, like I need telling.

*

Weasel leads us both through to the parade and tells me I can stand anywhere I like. I look around at all the idiots they have assembled and frankly I'm offended.

'Are they meant to look like me?' I complain. 'They look nothing like me.'

'Just pick a number and no talking,' Weasel says.

'My client objects to the quality of the line-up and thinks that this will cast great doubts upon the validity of the witness testimony,' Charlie says for me.

'Look at him, he's bald, how am I meant to look like him?'

'You will all put on the hats you find at your feet,' Weasel tells the line-up. 'That goes for you too,' he says looking at me. I pick up a black woolly hat and try and find the geezer that looks most like me, so I can stand next to him.

'Fuck me,' I say, clocking one face-ache. 'Look at the state of him for the price of school dinners.'

'Just take your place, Bex,' Weasel says, losing his rag a little. Fountains of imaginary piss covering his face as I look at him.

'Yeah, but fuck's sake, how ugly does he want to be? Come on play the game, get some people in that at least look human.' Matey's looking at me all nervous. Student probably, throwback definitely, only in here for the £10 fee. He doesn't know what I'm in for. Could be anything, rape, robbery, violence. Reckon I could have him anyway if he fancies a pop. I finally pluck to stand behind the number seven on the floor.

As they wheel the old witness in, I tell number six next to me that there's another £10 in it for him if he winks at the old lady as she goes by – create a bit of confusion in her mind – he says nothing back. Weasel gives this old housewife the usual bollocks about taking her time, having a good look and only picking out a number if she's absolutely sure. She nods nervously and clutches her handbag to her tits. Then she begins.

Up the line, ever so slowly, giving each of the suspects the full once over, plenty of thought. By the time she gets to me, she really looks like she wants a cup of tea and five minutes in a comfy chair. As she checks me over I try and slightly stretch each of my facial muscles to distort my face a bit. Drop the jaw, suck in the cheeks, narrow the eyes. I'm tempted – what with her being so close and everything – to give her a good punch in the mouth, but I think that'll give her a bit of a clue as to tonight's mystery guest, so I don't. She moves on to number eight, and then starts back down the line, before stopping and turning to Weasel.

'It's number four. I'm sure of it. Number four.' Charlie gives me a smile, but personally I don't feel too happy about the decision. Cheeky bitch has only gone and picked the throwback.

'I think that was fairly conclusive, Sergeant Haynes, I trust you'll not be needing my client any more,' Charlie says to Weasel and DC Ross across the interview table.

'Not so fast Mr Taylor, I'd still like to ask your client a few questions, if that's alright with you?' Weasel sneers.

'What evidence do you have to hold my client?' Charlie asks, lighting up one of his thin smelly cigars. I do likewise with my fags. Fags are a great tension reliever, but this isn't the main reason we both spark up in unison. This is a little tactical ploy Charlie came up with a few years ago. You see, Weasel doesn't smoke, so me and Charlie sit a couple of feet away from him chaining it until the bastard chokes. At the very least, this should prompt Weasel to hurry things along, so he can get out of it and breathe, and at the very best he'll develop cancer from passive smoking and die.

'We still have a statement from two separate witnesses,

who both say they saw your client's blue transit van parked on the driveway at the time of the break-in.'

'My client's blue van?' Charlie looks at me and lifts a well-worn eyebrow.

'Not my van,' I say.

'My client informs me that it wasn't his van your witnesses saw parked at the time in question. He thinks that your witnesses must be mistaken. Mrs Baker, earlier on at the identity parade, seemed to have been mistaken. Perhaps the rest of your witnesses are of a similar quality.' That's another thing I love about Charlie, he knows exactly what I meant to say and says it properly for me.

'Get the plate did they?' I ask.

'Were your witnesses able to recall the registration number of the vehicle, Sergeant Haynes?' Charlie asks.

'The number plates were stolen from a red Escort that evening,' says Weasel.

Weasel, I'd better just explain, is how Detective Sergeant Haynes is better known to the boys. Weasel thinks he's been given this nickname because of the real-life weasel's reputation for tracking down its prey, but he's wrong. We call him Weasel because he's got big teeth, a pointy nose and one of those horrible, thin, greasy moustaches. Basically, he looks like a weasel.

I take one of Charlie's cigars and light it with the end of my fag.

'Really?' says Charlie. 'And did you find these licence plates on my client's van? Hmm? I believe not,' Charlie says as I practise blowing a couple of smoke rings in Weasel's face.

'Witnesses saw your van at the scene,' Weasel shouts. 'Explain that.'

'Not my van,' I say again. 'Not my van.'

'I think my client has answered all of your questions Sergeant, if there's nothing else?'

'Your van,' Weasel says jabbing a finger at me. 'Your job.'

'Prove it,' I tell him and flop back in my chair, smug in the knowledge that he can't, and I know it. See, I don't owe him any explanation. I'm not going to sit here and make up some load of old bollocks about me lending it to some geezer in the pub I've never met before because I don't have to. We live in a democracy where you are innocent until proven guilty, and that's very important, remember that. At this very moment, as I sit here, I am innocent of this job. It doesn't matter that I actually did it – that's neither here nor there – I am innocent because it hasn't been *proved* that I'm guilty. Just as I'm innocent of every job I've ever got away with. And I don't have to prove it, that's taken as read. It's all up to Weasel to prove that I'm not innocent. And if he can't, well then that's just tough shit on him with a big stick in it. All I have to do is sit back and not give him anything he hasn't already got. Which in this case, is quite a fucking bit. I know, I know, it sounds daft doesn't it, but they ain't my rules, I just abuse them.

'Perhaps your client would like to go back to the cells and think about it a little longer. We can still keep him for another twenty hours you know.'

'Bang me up then, I don't care,' I tell Weasel before Charlie can say anything. 'Maybe I'll get some fucking dinner at last. Go on.'

'My client is merely making the point that it doesn't matter how long you put him in the cells for, any answers he may give will remain the same.'

'Yeah,' I say, and am tempted to add a 'so there', but that would be immature.

After a long silent pause Weasel says 'interview terminated' and switches off the tape recorder.

'That it? Can I go then?' Weasel doesn't answer me. He just asks DC Ross to see me and Mr Taylor out. I pick up one of the tapes off the table (my copy of the interview), which I'll play to Ollie later. We always play each other our interviews. Couple of beers, couple of joints and stick on the old tape. It's a laugh if anything else.

'Well thank god for that, I'm fucking starving, no dinner all day,' I say to Weasel. 'Didn't even get a cup of tea Charlie, can you believe that? What you got to do to get a cup of tea around here?' I ask.

'Confess,' DC Ross says, the first word I've heard him speak all day.

'Oh yeah, that seems like a fair deal don't it. Two sugars and the stuff's under the floorboards.'

'Come on,' says Charlie, 'let's go.'

'You're getting careless Bex,' Weasel says as we leave. 'You're long overdue for a nice little stretch and I'm going to be there when you get it.'

'Oh do me a favour will you. It wasn't me and that's the truth,' I tell him.

'I'll tell you something off the record shall I?' I say and look at Charlie. 'Off the record, you're running down the wrong rabbit hole with this one Haynes. It wasn't me.'

Off the record, what a load of shit that is. Nothing is ever off the record with coppers. It's just another trick they come up with to get you to spill your guts. They do it on *The Bill* all the time, Tosh only has to say 'Off the record' once and Doug McHard can't tell him about Mr Big and the shipment of hijacked fags quick enough. Well, I ain't painting pictures for nobody. If someone says to me 'Off the record, did you do it?', I'll tell him back 'off the record, no, I didn't.' I couldn't give a monkey's about off the record or on the record or whatever. If I'm going to lie, I'm going to lie, it's as simple as that. I ain't going to sit here wasting everyone's time denying everything, only to shoot myself in the foot and throw away several hours of perfectly good lies the moment someone mentions we should talk off the record.

Yeah sure they can't use it in court, but if you're going to speak off the record, you might as well say to him: 'You haven't got any evidence, but you're on the right track, keep looking.' Personally, I'd rather they hadn't got any evidence and didn't know what fucking track to look up.

It's my number one rule – deny everything.

Which is why I'm giving Weasel the old 'off the record' bollocks at this moment. I don't believe it, but maybe he does.

'I don't think you should say any more,' Charlie advises me.

'You're full of shit,' Weasel tells me. 'You did it, I know it.'

'Oh come on, use your loaf, it ain't even my style.' Ain't even my style, that's a great one. What is my style, someone's house was broken in to and stuff got nicked. How, what, where and when don't matter. Burglars who have styles always go down for a long time. Some even have calling cards. Not literally, but they do certain things to let the police know that this job has been done by the same geezer as the last eight other jobs in town. Bit of infamy, you know. One bloke I heard about (but never met) always used to do a big shit in the middle of the bed in the main bedroom. Another one used to plug the bath in and leave the taps running. These blokes were morons, the sort of geezers who give burglars a bad name. They probably gave themselves nicknames, like the phantom or the shadow or the panther or whatever. Both are inside now because they were more interested in making a name for themselves than earning a living, and making a name for yourself in this business is a one-way ticket to the nick. I've got no time for blokes like that. See, blokes who leave a trademark calling card seem to forget that if they get caught for the one job, they get caught for them all. And standing in front of the beak for eight jobs is a lot worse than standing in front of the beak for one.

But again, Weasel don't know this does he!

'Not my style.'

'Your van was seen,' Weasel says again.

'You know me,' I say. 'I ain't a grass.' Weasel looks at me funnily.

'What's that supposed to mean?'

'I ain't a grass.' And I give him a nod. Weasel's about to say something else when Charlie ushers me out and through to custody, where I check out. By the way, a little tip, always count your money carefully when the custody sergeant gives it back to you. Not because any might be missing, but because it winds them up a bit. Sometimes lose count and start again.

Anyway, I get all my stuff back and I sign on the dotted line and all of a sudden I'm a free man again. I turn to leave and as I do so I see Norris being brought through the back door by some spotty copper younger than me. Under his arm the copper carries a three-foot blind boy reading Braille with a money slot in the top of his head. I don't even want to know. Norris sees me as I'm leaving.

'Watcha Bex, how's tricks?'

'How's tricks? How's tricks? That's the last time I lend you my fucking van you cunt,' I say and leave Weasel and Norris to it, while I go and have some dinner.

15. A lesson in lying

Lying is a skill. Everyone can lie, but very few people can lie well. Like most skills there are a few basic principles you need to master and the rest is practice. I lie a lot, especially to Mel, over silly little things, just to keep myself sharp, so that when I do need to lie big time, I can do it convincingly.

About ten or twelve years ago, just a year or two after I'd left school, I had a job in this sales office. Yeah, I've had a few jobs in my time (none of which lasted longer than a month or two). I remember this one though, because it was particularly shit, selling advertising space in a car magazine over the phone, for about two quid an hour. I hated it, and it was enough to put me off working in an office ever again.

While I was there though, me and this other salesman – whose name I can't remember, but I'll call him Gary – were sent to this car show at the NEC, up in Brum, for the weekend. It weren't exactly hard work. All we had to do was sit behind a table, sell the magazine to any idiot who wanted it and get pissed with the advertisers. Then at night, we'd go back to the hotel, run up a big tab at the bar and put it all on expenses.

After one of these sessions though, Saturday night I think it was, the bloke behind the bar prints us off two receipts by mistake. Seeing as we're both claiming for our hotel room and petrol and everything else separately anyway, we grab one each and decide to both put in for it. It was only for about £50 and it was a big company we was working for, lots of expense accounts flying about. It was worth a go.

Monday afternoon, I'm summoned into the ad manager's office and asked if I thought he was a wanker. I did, but it weren't something I was about to share with him. When I ask why he shows me the two receipts and demands an explanation. I tell him it was all a big mistake and as far as I knew, it was me putting in for dinner. Five minutes later, Gary tells him the same. We both apologise, act all innocent and incompetent and tear up one of the receipts.

We'd lied, got found out, had a back-up lie to cover ourselves and, more or less, got away with it.

This should've been the end of this story, but Gary had other ideas and tells several people at lunch-time (including the editor of the magazine) what had really gone on. Why he wanted to do this is anybody's guess, but all of a sudden we're on the front page again. This information goes round the office faster than a dose of flu and it ain't long before the ad manager calls us back in to his office. We both deny it again but the wanker ain't convinced. We get a written warning and told that it would've been the sack if he had hard proof that we'd been on the diddle.

This pisses me off because we'd already gotten away with it when old big mouth decided to drop us both back into the shit for no good reason. And believe it or not, he still ain't content and while I'm telling people it was all just a silly mix-up, he's slowly working his way around the office bragging about the scam him and good old Bex tried to pull. Even after I tell him to shut his fucking mouth or I'll shut it for him, he's still yakking away. This is really fucking off the ad manager too, because, to everyone around the office, he's starting to look like a right cunt for not taking stronger action against a couple of self-confessed thieves. And Gary's giving it the large, is really starting to rub his nose in it.

There's nothing else for it. I've stuck to my story the whole time, didn't tell a single soul the full score, not even my best mate, but I've still been dropped in it. So after a week of having the world know my business, I start doing a little talking of my own in the pub. I tell a few people that I reckon I've been fitted up, that as far as I know Gary's tried to pull a fast one somehow and covered us both in shit. I tell my best mate that I'm going to get the sack all because that little wanker tried to fiddle the expenses. He, in turn, angry for me, tells someone else, who, in turn, tells someone else, who, in turn, tells someone else, who, well you get the picture, and before long, I'm not starting to look so guilty after all. Gary's finding himself in more and more arguments as he tries to convince people that we were both in it together. My best mate threatens to chin him, two of the secretaries threaten to quit if any action is taken against me and the ad manager buys me a pint in the pub on Friday lunch-time.

The following week, Gary is sacked. Three weeks after that, I quit and go and work as a window cleaner.

I sometimes bump into people from the office and they still go on about what a cunt Gary was for stitching me up like that and how they always blank him whenever they see him. I haven't really got the heart to shatter their illusions and tell them that, in fact, we were both in it together and if anything, it was me who ended up stitching him up – with their help. I don't feel particularly big about using them like that – especially my former best mate – but I had to save my own skin. No one would've argued my corner like they did if I'd told them what the real score was.

The basic rule of lying is, if you're going to lie, lie to everyone. If not, then don't bother.

As for Gary, he left town and got a job in the City – driving a bus around it.

You know what – and this goes back to what I was saying earlier – I swear if the wanker ad manager had said to him in the pub over a pint: 'So come on Gary, off the record, was it all really a genuine mistake or what?' Gary would've said back: 'Off the record? No, of course not. We were just trying to rip you off, ha ha ha.'

At the end of the day, Gary was sacked because he wasn't a very good liar, and I kept my job – be it for only another three weeks – because I was.

16. What, the real Terry Butcher?

I went to school with Terry Butcher, not the ex-England and Rangers captain, but a little short cunt who used to bullshit more than any bloke I've ever known.

People used to ask him – you know, just humorously – if he was the England captain Terry Butcher, and Terry would tell them that he was his brother. This doesn't make sense at all, I mean, why would Mrs Butcher call two of her sons Terry? She wouldn't, as far as I can see, but this minor detail never used to worry Terry.

See, Terry was a bullshitter, I never said he was a good one.

The way I see it, bullshitting and lying are completely different. When I lie, it's for a reason, usually to get me out of the shit. My lies are always about me trying to cover up by pretending I haven't done something when I have. When a bullshitter bullshits, it's purely just for the sake of bullshitting. Terry bullshits that he has done something when he really hasn't. See how it works?

The earliest bollocks I can remember him talking was at school. He told everyone that his dad had had all his organs transplanted (that's not some of them, but all of them) after a car crash and was only kept alive by a life-support machine.

However, he did get every Saturday off to take Terry up to see West Ham.

A lot of Terry's bullshit was to do with football. He told me that he played for a Sunday league team and how he never made it pro I'll never know, because every time I saw him he had scored a hat-trick at the weekend, usually in the 89th minute, and usually after coming off the bench as sub when the team were two-nil down. He sometimes even played in goal and saved every penalty that was shot at him, even though he was shorter than one of Ollie's rounds of drinks. Counting back eighteen odd years that's more than 2000 goals scored and about 500 saved. That's a better record than the last eighteen Division 1 Championship-winning teams put together.

When he went out on the pull, he use to tell the birds he was a session drummer for Level 42 and that he shared a flat with Mark Knopfler. This was when he was seventeen years old. All I can say is that Terry must've been a YTS session drummer, because he only took home £25 a week and in a certain light, Mark Knopfler didn't half look like his mum.

I never once saw this line work. I saw Terry storm off in a boo after none of the lads would ever back him up with anything except impressions of Jimmy Hill, but I've never, ever, ever seen this line work. Still, that hasn't stopped Terry shagging literally hundreds of birds, most of which were models or masseurs or high class prostitutes – Terry was so good they would refund his money in exchange for another fuck (and I'm not making this up).

The thing about Terry is, as well, that he gets really fucked off with you if you don't believe him. But he makes it fucking absolutely impossible to believe him. Like the time he joined the RAF as a fighter pilot. He didn't really of course, he just went around telling people he had and expected everyone to believe him. To become a fighter pilot, you have to have a degree in aeronautical physics or something; you have to be at the peak of physical fitness; and you have to have the sort of background where the RAF are going to be able to trust you with a £20 million piece of state-of-the-art warfare technology. Not two convictions for drink driving, a 40-a-day fag habit, an exclusive beer and curry diet and close family ties with the provisional IRA (although this last one could've been another bullshit as well). I put this to him and you know what he said back?

'No, straight up, I've already had the medical Bex, I'm in. I've passed. They said I've got 40–40 vision.'

Now I thought it only went up to 20–20 and that was perfect, but apparently there's another category set aside for blokes like Terry who've got better than perfect vision. I don't know quite what he could do, see through walls or into the future or something, he never demonstrated, but it explained why the RAF took Terry on. See if ever there was another war and all the radar were bombed out, then Terry could see home all the planes by himself. Run him up with the wind sock and let him get on with it.

There are thousands of other bullshits he's come out with, like Crystal Palace Athletics Club wanting him to race for them after the coach saw him running for a bus, or the Thomas à Becket Gym wanting him to represent them in the ABA after the coach saw him in a fight in a pub.

I don't know why he feels he needs to tell me all this. Maybe he can't help it? Maybe he's just a bullshitter and that's what bullshitters do. My guess though is that he's spent his whole life trying to live up to his brothers' reputations. Five of them. All older, harder, smarter, and all doing very nicely for themselves. If I was up against these sort of odds, I'd probably tell everyone that I'd invented Chicken Kiev as well.

Well, actually, probably not.

See that's what it was all about, impressing people, getting them to say: 'Wow Terry, that's fantastic. You're great. I wish I was like you.'

A year or so ago, I remember being in the newsagent's getting my lottery ticket and seeing Terry in there as well. 'Look at those for numbers Bex,' he says showing me his ticket.

'Just numbers. Got as much chance to come out as any other fucking numbers,' I tell him.

'No, no, but look, look at them. See, pretty good aren't they? Well thought out. Look.' Let's face it, your life's got to be a bit crap if you find yourself in the middle of a newsagent's trying to impress someone with six random numbers.

A couple of years ago I was having a drink with him and Ollie in the Dog and Parrot down Mill Lane. This is about the same time I almost got done over by that nurse in her house, because Ollie was still seeing that old boiler of his at the time and not wanting to know. Oh, and just out of interest, she did dump him a month later for someone else and I made fucking sure I told him that I'd told him so.

Anyway, Ollie goes to work about 7 o'clock and leaves me with Walter Mitty, who starts telling me about the time he got stuck in a lift with Eddie Murphy and before I know it, just to shut the cunt up, I start moaning on about Ollie. Now believe me, I ain't usually so stupid as to go yakking to a wanker like Terry, but I must've been having trouble with my brain or something because I started telling him about this job we had lined up.

Now Terry's not one of the boys, he never has been, he just hangs around. You get a lot of blokes like that, totally straight themselves, but love rubbing shoulders with the local faces, hoping that maybe a bit of the reputation'll rub off on them without them ever having to do anything to earn it. No one ever tells them anything, they usually just hang around, buy you a couple of drinks and laugh at all of your jokes. Not that Terry ever bought anyone a drink, even though he had a £200,000 inheritance in the bank and all.

'It's this bird of his see, she's got him wrapped round her little finger and he can't even see it,' I tell Terry. 'I said to him, I says "she's probably shagging every other fucking geezer in town while you're out all night working" but he just don't fucking listen.'

'I've shagged her,' says Terry but I pretend not to hear.

'With a bird you see, you've got your classic power struggle. You've got to show them who wears the trousers and who irons them.'

'Fucking right,' he says.

'Now I ain't the sort of bloke who goes on about a woman's place is in the kitchen and all that old shit. My argument is just that, if you don't take hold of the reins, she fucking well will. And then suddenly you've got the tail wagging the dog.'

'My old girl knows that I . . .' he starts to say but I can't be bothered to listen to how he gets some figment of his imagination to cook him dinner every night, so I just start talking again, over him.

'Fine, go round there, give her one and be all lovey dovey with her. There's nothing wrong with that. But don't go running to her for her permission every time you want to go out with your mates, who you've known a fuck of a lot longer than some old fucking slapper, who's agreed to suck your knob.' I take a big sip of my beer as Terry tells me what a wanker Ollie is for losing his bottle. I snap Terry shut and tell him to watch what he says.

'I've been through a lot with Ollie,' I say. 'I've got the right to call him a wanker, not you. Okay? Don't go jangling your spurs before you've earned them.' Terry nods and shrinks back down to size. Now I can go on slagging off Ollie.

'Five minutes, that's all it'll take. Five minutes. Ten at the outside,' I tell Terry.

'Fuck it Bex, I'll do it with you,' he says back.

'It's not like it's even a big job or nothing, bread and butter sort of stuff you know?'

'I'll do it with you Bex.'

'He don't even have to tell the old bitch if he doesn't want to.'

'I'll do it with you Bex.'

'Couple of hundred quid in his top pocket. How many nights is he going to have to work down *Glitzy's* to earn that, hey?'

'Bex, I'll do it with you.'

I look at Terry making a stupid puppy dog face at me and take another big sip of my beer.

'I mean what a cunt. Ten minutes.'

'Bex?' says Terry.

'Look Terry, this ain't no bullshit alright, this is a real job. I don't need my pisser pulled by . . .'

'No, I'll do it Bex, fucking no problem. Go on. I'm always up for doing a job, you should've said before. I know my onions, I've done jobs before, fucking hell, Bex.'

I take a good long, hard look at Terry, then lose my ability for rational thought and agree he can do the job with me. Even now, when I look back, I still don't know what the fuck was going through my brain at that moment in time. I just can't imagine what sort of dire straits I would have to have been in to think that letting Terry come on a job with me was a good career move. I think I just must've been sick of him lying all the time and I wanted to show him what it was really all about. I don't know, maybe if he did this score and did it well, I was probably thinking, he might grow out of his bullshit. He ain't a bad bloke really, it's just his bullshit. I guess I just thought I'd give him a chance.

I must've been fucking mad.

'Ready?' I ask him. He nods. 'Alright then, let's go.'

As we're leaving the pub we see a couple of blokes Terry knows in the car park getting out of their motor.

'You off then Terry?' one of them shouts over.

'Yeah, I've got a job on with Bex,' Terry shouts back and they nod and walk in to the pub.

'What the fuck d'you just say that for?' I shout at the cunt.

'What, oh he's alright,' Terry says.

'Alright! alright! what the fuck makes him alright? The cunt works in a fucking dry-cleaners, how does that make him alright?'

'He knows the score . . .' he tries to say.

'He don't know the fucking score because he's a cunt,' I tell him.

'No, he's alright, really.'

'When you're doing a job with me, everyone in the world is a cunt except me. And you don't go talking to cunts about me, you got it?'

'Yeah, alright, alright.' The smart move would've been to kick him out of the van then and there, but I wasn't feeling particularly smart. One little talking to and the leopard supposed to change his spots.

'You don't go grassing me up again,' I say.

'I wasn't,' he says back.

The only plus point about it was that everyone knows Terry as a bullshitter. No one ever believes a word he says.

We get in the van and drive to the house.

The job goes relatively smoothly. Terry is practically wetting himself as we get nearer the house, to the point that he can only answer yes and no when I ask him questions.

We get in and start rounding up stuff and, for a while, he behaves himself. For the most of it, I only get him to stand look-out by the back door and stack up stuff I point out. That's all he's good for. But it's quite a big house and once I've done the living room and kitchen, I've still got the upstairs to do. So I give Terry a shout and tell him to take one of the bedrooms while I take the rest. I've already given him a briefing on what to look for, no junk, just good jewellery, appliances, money, plastic and leather, and I leave him to get on with it.

After a couple of minutes or so I'm all but done, so I go in to check on how Terry is doing. I walk in the room and catch him pissing all over one of the beds. He looks up at me and laughs, but I ain't in no laughing mood.

'You dirty bastard,' I say. 'What the fuck d'you do that for?'

'Oh come on, it's just a laugh,' he says back.

I'm two seconds away from punching his fucking head in and leaving him face down in his own piss for the house owners to deal with when they get home, but that would drag me in to this mess and I want no part of it. I'm a burglar, I nick for a living, I ain't no fucking animal. I might be robbing from someone but you still got to have a little bit of basic respect. That's the sort of thing kids do. It really fucked me off.

I slap him hard to the floor and tell him he's in for a

fucking good hiding if I find he's left any other little surprises for these poor bastards. We collect the stuff and leave.

And I swear never to work with wankers again.

Of course Terry's all hyper the next day when I see him to give him his share of the cash (actually, I give him about a quarter of what I got from Electric but he's happy enough with it). He's all buying me a drink and talking about the next job and raving about how fucking sweet it was and did I see him when he slipped through the window and when he found that necklace and stuff like that.

He reminded me of how I was at fourteen when I did my first job. I don't get any sort of buzz from it at all any more. I used to like I say, but not now, I've done too many, it's just work. If I do a job and find a whole big shoe box full of money under the bed (still hoping), then yeah, I'll be chuffed to bits, but I don't get the same adrenaline pumping through my veins as I used to. I'd need to do something bigger to get back the buzz. Rob a bank, or bust Roland out of the nick next time he goes down or something, but who can be arsed with all that. I'm happy (enough) doing what I'm doing.

I leave Terry after two sips of lager because I can't stand being near him any more and fuck off home. I've told him what a fucking slap he'll get if he goes around shooting his mouth off about me, but I don't think that's going to stop him.

I sit at home, have a couple of joints and wait for Plod to knock on my door.

They come three days later. Weasel asking about the house on Pemberton Avenue. I tell him I don't know a thing. He says we can either do it here or down at the station.

I get my coat.

*

I've since heard several different versions of what happened. But from what I can piece together, Terry was in some boozer giving it the large to whoever would listen, when suddenly someone took him seriously and gives him the hiding he'd been fucking begging for. This person, as it turns out, was the best friend of the cousin of the person whose house it was, or something like that. I might've got them in the wrong order there but it's not important. Basically, this geezer rearranges Terry's face and frog-marches him down to the nick.

Suddenly Terry ain't so talkative. So Weasel drives him back to his house and searches his bedroom, where he doesn't find any trace of Mark Knopfler, but he does find a calculator, a brass horse and several other shitting little souvenirs Terry had kept from his little adventure. He gets charged with burglary and drops me in it.

Charlie points out to Weasel, after he fails to find anything at my place, that it is just Mr Butcher's word against mine, and seeing as Mr Butcher was a known liar, a fact to which he could produce a dozen reliable witnesses to testify to, that didn't make him a very credible informant. Me and Charlie are walking out of the station an hour later.

According to Sergeant Atwell, who I bumped in to in the pub a month or two later, when they shut the cell door behind Terry, he cried all night.

He got two hundred hours' community service and ordered to pay £250 compensation when his case came to court. Those are the facts. Though ask Terry and you'll probably hear a different story.

17. My favourite telly

I watch a lot of telly. I'm like anyone else really, I love it. I like to get out and about as much as the next bloke, have a drink down the pub and a laugh with the boys, but you can't beat putting your feet up with a cup of tea or a couple of beers and a packet of biscuits and sticking on the box.

I've only got the normal telly, you know, your five channels, I haven't got satellite or nothing. I wouldn't mind it, I've even got the dish, the box and everything, I just haven't figured out a way of nicking the monthly subscription yet. Be good though wouldn't it, twenty-four hour football, porn and nature documentaries.

This last one, as I think I've said before, is a particular favourite of mine. *Wildlife on One*, *The Natural World*, *Survival Special*, I love them all. I don't know what it is about nature programmes, it doesn't matter whether it's on the African plain, the Arctic Ocean or a British churchyard, they're all just fantastic. Maybe it's because it reminds me just how lucky I am being human, that I ain't in danger of being eaten alive every time I leave the house. Ollie sometimes comes over and watches a bit of telly with me and he always cheers on the lions or the tarantulas or the sharks. Me, I'm personally on the side of the antelopes and when the pack's closing in, I can't help but get a bit carried away shouting 'run, fucking faster, look out, not that way,' and stuff like that, while Ollie's jumping around on the sofa next to me willing on the lions to do the poor little bastard. He even came up with the idea that we should have bets on whether or not the prey gets away. That can be quite good, although, if you take my advice, never bet on a caterpillar.

Caught on Camera, and all those other silly programmes starring robbers and car thieves getting caught on security cameras, gets the same sort of enthusiasm from me and Ollie, except that this time we're both on the same side, cheering on the boys to run faster and get away. It pains me to see one of my own getting bundled to the floor and stuck in the cuffs, regardless of whether or not he's endangered countless lives by driving through Dixon's front window at 80mph on Saturday afternoon. It sends a shiver down my spine. Very, very occasionally, one of the boys 'caught on camera' manages to get away and that's great, a real victory. One up for the boys.

And then there's football. I love football, I absolutely love it. I could've been a professional footballer if I hadn't been really crap at it. Trouble is, most football is on Sky now, so you have to go to the pub if you want to watch a first division – sorry, I mean a Premiership, match. No great hardship really, but sometimes it's just nice to sit in your own armchair and hear the commentary without having a whole load of fucking idiots spouting statistics in your fucking ear all match. Or some trendy 'rah-rah' birds going on about how much they like football, then spending the whole ninety minutes jabbering on at each other about work, some wanker called Darren or their sister's wedding. And you can't really skin up in the pub either very easily, without the landlord getting shirty or every cunt in the pub wanting a drag.

About all you've got on normal telly is *Match of the Day*

– which is great, although it could be a bit longer – and the European games. And when they're on, you always get some old fucking miserable bitch writing in to *Points of View* to complain about how much football is on the telly, and *Coro*-fucking-*nation Street* wasn't on until 10 o'clock.

Oh boo-hoo.

Compared with soaps, there's hardly any football on the telly at all, but you don't get QPR fans all writing in to Barry Took, to go on about how much valuable telly time is taken up by bollocks like *Emmerdale Farm* and the like, now do you? I've sat down and worked this out right, and if you add up just the four main popular soaps – *Emmerdale*, *Coronation Street*, *Brookside* and fucking *EastEnders* (including omnibuses) – it comes to over nine and a half hours of mind-numbing pap a week. And that's not even counting *Neighbours*, *Home and Away*, *Prisoner Cell Block H* (now there's an argument for going straight if ever I saw one) and all the rest of them. That's every week, including Christmas.

And the worse thing about it is that they're all the fucking same. I feel very strongly about this.

Mind you, one three times weekly regular I don't mind is *The Bill*. It's great. Again, I'm always on the side of the villains and every now and then, very rarely, one of them gets away and old Tony Stamp is left looking like a man who's just remembered he's got diarrhoea, two seconds after farting.

Getting back to sport quickly, I do like *A Question of Sport*, although I always record it and then watch it, so I can fast forward through all the boring rowing and horse jumping questions. What bollocks they are; I mean, who the fuck cares? David Coleman should stick to football, boxing and Grand Prix questions. It's all anyone's interested in anyway.

Antiques Roadshow is a good programme as well. Gerry put me on to it and I've got quite hooked. It's good for a couple of reasons; firstly, if you watch it regularly you can pick up a thing or two about antiques and get an idea of what to look out for. I've never found anything yet that looked like it was worth anything, but there's always the possibility I might. And if I know what to look out for in the first place, I'll know when to nick it. Gerry's found one or two pieces – as he calls them, ornaments they are really – so you can make some money on them.

The second reason I watch it is because for the old punters, its great. They take along their old junk in the hope that Hugh Skully'll tell them it's worth half a million and look really gutted when it turns out it ain't worth the bus fare it cost to bring it along. Even when he does tell someone that they can expect to get about £200 for a crappy old teapot, you can see the disappointment plastered all over their face at not being able to jack in work and fuck off on a good holiday.

See, people don't watch *Antiques Roadshow* because they're interested in antiques, they watch it to see the punters – they're the stars of the show – who go along and act as if they give a fuck while some old expert's giving them a lecture on the history of their thimble. Just once, I'd like to see a bit of honesty on there.

'Well, Mr Roberts, this is quite the loveliest set of shaving mugs I think I've ever seen. Would you like to know a bit about them?'

'No, just tell me how much it's worth and I'll be off.'

When they do have some old carriage clock on there which turns out to be worth a few hundred grand, how long do you suppose it is before it turns up at Sotherby's?

I quite like *Through the Keyhole* as well. Me and Ollie usually watch it together and have a little competition with each other to price up the contents of matey's house. The winner is whoever gets the best job-lot price after Loyd's shown us round. There are strict rules we've got to abide by in the pricing, videos are a hundred (unless they're a really good make), microwaves are fifty, stereo depends on the make, and so on. I usually win because I count things like clothes and booze and stuff, whereas Ollie just sticks to the usual. So far, I think the best house has been Des O'Connor's, while the worst has to be Vinnie Jones – he ain't got anything decent. The only problem I've got with *Through the Keyhole* is that they don't review the house's security system and give you the address. Other than that, it's good.

While we're on the subject of quiz shows I must just mention *Family Fortunes*, which is the best quiz show on the box. And when I say best, I of course mean it has the stupidist contestants. And the families that appear on the telly are the families that were considered the cream at the selection process. Just imagine how fucking thick and ugly the families that didn't make it must've been. But still, it's for this reason that I love this programme and even set my video to record it when I'm out. You just can't beat it. In an industry full of supermodels, pin-up stars and glamour, *Family Fortunes* is one of the few things on telly that actually makes me feel good about myself. And as for Les Dennis, when the next comedy awards come around, if your name is one of those nominated, I'll give you the money myself.

Crimewatch is a must, I think it's hilarious, their reconstructions are so shit, I don't know where they get their villains from, but most of them are straight out of *The Sweeney*. I mean come on, I'm a villain and I know plenty of villains, and none of them speak like the fucking idiots they have on there.

Crimewatch is great as well, because you can get some really good ideas for jobs. We've never done one yet, because they're mostly robbery and stuff like that, but if ever we fancied jumping up a league, I've got a couple of great plans. A good tip, if you're a burglar, with *Crimewatch*, *Crimestoppers* and even local neighbourhood schemes and stuff, is to send off for the free leaflets or information packs that they produced to give you some sort of idea as to what you might find yourself up against.

Ollie mostly likes sit-coms, *Blackadder*, *Fawlty Towers*, *Only Fools and Horses* and stuff like that. I like these as well, but there's hardly any good sit-coms on the telly any more. All the good ones are repeats from the seventies, *Steptoe and Son*, *Dad's Army* and *Porridge*. Some of the ones on nowadays are just so shit. You think, there must actually be someone at the BBC who gets the scripts for these tired old shows and wets themselves laughing. There must be, otherwise how else do they get made.

How can anyone be that shit at their job?

Either that, or the whole of the BBC is just totally out of touch with the rest of the world. Don't they read any of the letters sent in to *Points of View*? Take *Last of the* fucking *Summer Wine* for instance, what an argument for euthanasia that is. I bet the canned laughter machine operator earns his money on that one. Makes me glad I don't pay my licence fee. I mean, if there's nothing on the telly I want to watch, why should I?

One of the few exceptions, though, is *One Foot in the Grave*, great programme, great actors. Apparently they bought the idea in America and got Bill Cosby to play a black Victor Meldrew and gave him a rebellious teenage daughter – bet that's funny! My favourite episode was when he got the phone call from the burglars who done his house over, asking how they set the timer on his video.

'As you can appreciate,' he said, 'we're out a lot in the evenings and miss a lot of our favourite programmes.' Fucking class.

I would love to have the nerve to do that.

18. Clever plans: number 4

Gerry's probably the cleverest burglar I've ever met. Where I treat house breaking as just a job, a way to earn money, he treats it as a career. He sits down and studies new techniques, new methods of entry, market prices and so on, so that he can become a better burglar. He takes time out to talk to others in the trade, he learns from them, passes on knowledge, improves his game. And he's got ambition, he ain't just satisfied with nicking the junk I thieve any more, he goes for bigger and better jobs; shops, warehouses, offices.

He's the sort of bloke who, if he had a big job coming up, he'd probably get little model buildings and cars and things, and have inch-high figures in black masks shinning up tiny plastic drainpipes, as preparation.

Basically, if there was a qualification in burglary, he could pass it no problem. Me, I'd probably just break in to the classroom and steal the exam papers, which I imagine would count as a pass as well.

One thing Gerry always wanted to be able to do was crack alarms. Actually, I wouldn't mind being able to do that either – be smart wouldn't it, like on the telly. Have a load of expensive drills and a laptop computer and grappling hooks and stuff. Yeah, I could do with some of that. I could see myself all blacked up, dodging laser beams, looping video tape and reprogramming access codes to break into the Queen's palace and run off with her video recorder.

But then, who can be arsed with all of that?

Gerry, that's who. Even though I can't be bothered myself, I can still admire someone who has got the gumption to get up off their arse and be all they can in their chosen field.

So what Gerry did was, he set out to find out everything there was to know about alarms. He rented a house in Dane Lane and got estimates from a dozen different alarm companies. When he'd read all the brochures he was sent, he phoned them all up and, one by one, got them to come round and fit their alarm systems. He had the lot, window alarms, pressure pads, heat sensors, those bright front garden lights that come on when you walk past, whatever they're called, the lot.

And as the chap was fitting the system, there would be Gerry, asking all sorts of questions.

'What sort of range has that got? Where's the emergency override button? What if the burglar hits it with a hammer, about here?' That sort of thing.

Then next day, he'd rip the whole lot out and get the next lot round. Six days and five alarms later, he packed his bags and went home. When the alarm people and the landlord called round to ask why their cheques had bounced, he was gone. So was the beard he'd grown and the dye he'd used in his hair.

Fuck hey, disguises, plans, pseudonyms – that's what it's all about.

But Gerry had only really learned a fraction of what he wanted to learn, so (and this is clever) he got a job – as an alarm fitter's apprentice. I don't know quite how he managed it, sent out begging letters and lied about his qualifications or something, but he got a job, holding ladders and carrying stuff, for a fully qualified fitter, earning about eight peanuts a week. But that was okay, because Gerry wasn't there for the money, he was there for the knowledge.

He took in absolutely everything – asked all the right questions and swiped the odd tool – so that after a couple of months or so, when he jacked, he knew as much about alarms as the fitter himself. Apparently the fitter nagged on at Gerry to stay, said he'd been such a good little worker, but Gerry told him he saw his future in another direction.

Now, if ever I've got any questions, I just go straight to Gerry.

He's tried to show me some of the stuff he's learned but it's like old money to me, no matter how many times I have it explained to me I still don't get it. I can never remember if it's the green wire, red wire or the whole fucking lot I'm suppose to cut. Gerry always says, if in doubt, black the whole street out. But I don't like fucking about with electricity. As far as I'm concerned, that's a quick way to a short life. There see, me and Gerry both have our little sayings.

He's now talking about getting a job as a locksmith. That would be smart wouldn't it, skeleton keys, expensive drills, bottles of acid. Be like on the telly wouldn't it.

Yeah, now I could do with some of that.

19. The Guns are never home

Every thief has at least one job they spend their whole life dreaming of doing. It don't matter if you're a burglar or an armed robber or a mugger or whatever. Everyone has one particular job they plan in the pub every Saturday night.

My particular fantasy job was this big house on Beechbrook Avenue. It belonged to a Mr and Mrs Gun. I know this because I nicked their paper early one Saturday morning. It was a big old place set back from the road in its own grounds and it was stacked full of brilliant stuff to nick.

See, the Guns ran their own business from home – I don't quite know what it was they did, faxed people for a living or something – and they had computers, printers, mobile phones, fax machines and all sorts, besides the usual videos, tellies and what not (all top of the range). And they must've been doing well, because they both had matching Range Rovers with personalised plates. They also had expensive leather furniture that even I could see the point of stealing.

The other alluring quality was the fact that they didn't have any kids and that they were almost always out in the evenings. So many dinner parties, so little time, you know how it is. I suppose people who work from home during the day are like that. Staying at home for them must've been a bit like spending the weekends sitting in the drainage ditch they'd been digging out all week.

I used to find myself driving past their house on the way home from the pub, even though their house isn't on the way home from the pub. I'd stop the van sometimes, get out and just stand there staring at the house, memorising every window, every brick and every drainpipe. I'd only ever leave when I'd try and get a bit too close and the big bright light would come on to chase me away.

I'd spent the better part of nine or ten years dreaming about this job, then suddenly, one evening last October, things were brought to a bit of a head, when a FOR SALE sign appeared on the driveway outside their house.

'I'm going do it,' I tell Ollie. 'I'm going to fucking do it.'

'Another pint?' Ollie asks. It's Saturday night by the way.

'I know I've been saying it for years but this time I really mean it. I'm going to do it. No bullshit.'

'I'm going to get some peanuts, want some?'

'No. Tuesday night, I'll do it then.' I mull this over as Ollie gets the beers in. It would be a tough old nut to crack but one well worth the effort.

Effort – the effort.

Would effort be enough? Surely if effort was all that was needed I would've done the place over years ago and have designs on some other poor cunt's drum. Replace effort with risk. Was it worth the risk?

Ollie carefully places the pints on the table, then knocks the top inch out of both as he jogs the table when he sits down.

'All we've got to do is get in without setting the alarm off.' I knew that this part of the job was way beyond me and Ollie. 'I might ask Gerry if he'll take a look.' Ollie drinks his beer and eats his nuts without saying anything.

He's heard all this before – going back nine or ten years – and is just humouring me with his silence, the same way people humour Terry. Either that or he hasn't had any dinner tonight.

'What do you reckon then?' I ask him.

'Mmm? Oh yeah, cracking,' he says in between mouthfuls of nuts.

Yeah, he's humouring me.

'I'm serious this time. We'll do the place on Tuesday.'

'You want a game of darts?' Ollie asks.

'No I don't want a game of fucking darts, I want to know what you think about doing the place on Tuesday?'

'I don't know,' he says. 'If you're serious . . .'

'I am serious,' I tell him.

'If you're serious, then I think you're a fucking idiot.' He takes a big sip of beer. 'Fucking asking to get caught doing over that place ain't ya.'

'No, no. Not if we do it right.' It suddenly occurs to me that Ollie must've been humouring me for the last nine or ten years. I put him straight that this job will be a fucking real good'un and that we'll be quids in and give him a little speech about it's not what you do in life that you regret, but it's what you don't do, the missed opportunities, the wasted chances and so on. Ollie's still not convinced but he eventually agrees to come along for the ride. Peer pressure wins through again.

We better not get nicked for this, I think. Old Ollie'll never forgive us if we are.

Gerry looks at the house from the passenger side window.

'Ollie, do me a favour,' he says. 'Go and step on the drive and set the light off.' Ollie gets out of the back of the van and walks towards the house. Two steps past the gate, the big light comes on above the drive lighting up the whole of the front garden. (There's also a second problem here, more of which later.) Gerry gives Ollie a whistle and Ollie gets back in the van. We wait for about five minutes and the light goes off again. Gerry pokes the air rifle out of the window, lines up his shot and fires. He shoots three more times before he is eventually rewarded with the tinkle of glass on driveway.

'Come on,' he says. 'Let's go get a quick half. Come back in about half an hour.' I start up the van and drive to the Red Lion round the corner.

Phase one complete.

A pint and a half later we come back and all is quiet.

'Keep your eyes peeled,' says Gerry as he climbs out and runs across the road and up the drive. The lights stay off but our second problem of the night is just as alert. I don't know what his name is but, if he doesn't shut up soon, his barking'll get the attention of all the neighbours.

Fucking dogs! They can be a right pain in the arse. And they don't have to be huge great Dobermans either – this one in here's small and yappy – it's the noise they make when you're trying to break in. It can be enough to put you right off – but not today. I've waited too long for this to let some little Snoopy spoil it for me. Gerry drops a couple of cubes of beef through the letterbox and sprints back.

'Anyone want a chewing gum?' he says climbing back into the van. We both take one.

Sleeping tablets in the beef should knock the dog out for the night, Gerry reckoned. He told us that he'd already experimented on next door's Labrador and it worked fine. It also gave me an idea about Mel. I told Gerry it might be worth trying it out on her next time she starts getting in one of her little strops, or if she's around when the football's on. Gerry agreed in theory, but warned me that she might start to get a bit suspicious if she finds she passes out every time Arsenal are on the box. I mean, even dogs will start turning their nose up at a fresh bit of steak if every time they eat it, they wake up eight hours later with a stinking headache.

'Most birds'll forgive you most things,' Gerry told me, 'but I don't think drugging them just so you can get a bit of peace is one of them.' He's probably right. Still, once or twice won't hurt her.

'Should only take about quarter of an hour or so,' Gerry says.

'Shall we go back to the pub again then?' I ask.

'No, let's do this one sober,' Gerry says a little bit too sarcastically for my liking, but I don't say anything back.

'Last time we come across a dog, it was a right big fucker, weren't it Bex?' Ollie says.

'Yeah, nasty bastard,' I say as Ollie tells Gerry about the time this Alsatian kept us penned in this little upstairs bedroom for about five minutes and the only way we were able to get out was to smash a bedside lamp and electrocute the fucker.

'Didn't kill it, just gave it a bit of a shock,' Ollie tells him. What Ollie didn't mention however, is what he said to me at the time. Just after he gave the dog a mouthful of AC he looks at me and goes: 'That's the way to do it. You should treat your dog like you do your bird.' Now, I know for a fact that Ollie didn't know what he was talking about. That little pearl was probably something he'd heard in the pub and tried repeating without fully understanding, or getting right.

I don't know though, maybe he does think that next time Mel goes disagreeing with me, I should give her a taste of the cattle-prod.

Gerry checks his watch and tells us it's time to go. I get out and Ollie slides over to the driver's seat. Gerry gives Ollie his walkie-talkie and tells him to give us a shout if anyone comes.

Fucking smart ain't it? Guns, walkie-talkies, we've got all the gear. They're only kids' walkie-talkies though, from the local toy shop, but Gerry swears by them.

I get his ladder out the back of the van and we take a wander up the drive. Gerry gives me a little smile halfway along when the light doesn't come on. We get to the side of the house and so far so good. The place is surrounded by big old evergreens, so we're pretty much out of sight to everyone around except Ollie in the van. I extend the ladder and rest it on the side of the wall by the alarm box.

'We all clear Ollie?' Gerry says into his radio.

'Roger,' Ollie answers back. We look at each other and Gerry shakes his head.

'Always the same,' he says. 'Give someone a walkie-talkie and they think they're Starsky and Hutch.' He hands me the radio and climbs up the ladder to the alarm. He reaches in to his pocket and gets out a little cordless drill. He's about to start drilling when he gives a yell, drops his drill and comes charging back halfway down the ladder again.

'Jesus, fuck, shit, fuck,' he panics.

'What is it?' I say getting ready to run for the van.

'Spider.'

'What?'

'Spider. It ran across my hand.' I look at him as if he's about to tell me the punchline.

'So?' I say.

'I hate spiders. They're horrible.'

'They're horrible? What d'you want me to do about it, go next door for a rolled-up newspaper?'

'No, I was just saying...'

'Hurry up for fuck's sake before someone sees us.'

Gerry takes the drill from me, climbs the ladder nervously and starts drilling at the alarm's red plastic cover.

'Alpha One to Bravo Zero, what's your ten-four, over,' Ollie says over the radio.

'Shut the fuck up you stupid cunt and keep your fucking eyes open,' I tell him back, hoping that answers his question.

Gerry pulls the drill and slips it back in his pocket, then pulls a little can of something out and sprays it in the hole. He does this for a minute or so, filling the box up, then pulls out another can – this one paint – and sprays the flashing light next to the box black.

'All done? Alarm off?' I ask after he climbs back down.

'I don't know. Let's break in and find out.'

We fold the ladder back up and hide it in the hedgerow by the side of the drive for collection later. At the back of the house Gerry sizes up our third hurdle – Double Glazing.

I hate double glazing, I've always steered clear of it, it's a right old turn off. Aluminium frames you can't easily lever open and two panes of glass that are a bastard to pick your way through. It's the housing equivalent of a chastity belt. But me and Gerry are right up for this one and nothing's going to stop us gaining entry. Gerry feels the window for a little bit and gives it a slight tap with his knuckle.

'What you reckon?' I ask. He takes a step back and looks up at the upstairs windows. I look as well, but can't see what he's looking at. He takes a few more steps back until he's standing in the middle of the garden. 'What you reckon?' I ask again.

'Give me the radio?' he says. I hand it over. 'Ollie?' Gerry says into it.

'What?'

'Can you see the roof from the road if you pass by?'

'What the front or the back?' Ollie asks. Gerry looks at me as if to ask if he's serious. He is.

'The front,' replies Gerry, pulling a spastic face at me as he does.

'Hold on, I'll have a look. No, you can't. It's up there somewhere but it's practically pitch black?'

'Thank you. Just keep looking out for us alright, and tell us if we start making too much noise?'

'How will I know if it's too much?' Ollie asks.

'If you can hear it, it's too much?' Gerry tells him. He hands me the radio and tells me to come on round the front. I ask him where we're going and he fills me in on the way round.

'I don't like the look of the downstairs windows. We can't get the frames open and I think we'll make too much noise breaking them. The upstairs windows look just as bad, sometimes they're easier, but it doesn't look like it here. What I did notice earlier though, was an old skylight on the roof. It looks like the only window that isn't double glazed. That's our entry point.'

'On the roof?' I say.

'Shhhush, for crying out loud. Yes, on the roof. It'll be a doddle, no problem?'

'How do we get up there, your ladder ain't big enough and I've left my fucking helicopter at home.' We stop by the front door and he points up the side of the house.

'Look, the ladder will go up a good half way, probably almost three quarters of the way up. The rest of the climb you've got ivy and guttering and quion brickwork to cling on to?'

'What's all this "you" business all of a sudden, it was "we" a minute ago. Where've "you" gone?'

'Fuck's sake, we don't both need to go up there. It only

needs one of us to get in and let the other one in by the front door?'

'Why don't you go then?' I say.

'This is your fucking job Bex, you only asked me to disable the alarm for you. Your job, your climb?'

'I'll break my fucking neck?'

'We can go home if you want, I don't care?' What a cunt! Of course he cares, he wants to get in there as much as I do. I have to do this and he fucking knows it, otherwise I get called bottler for the rest of my life and he never lets me forget the time we called off a job because I didn't want to do my part. What a cunt! what a cunt! This is how peer pressure feels from the other end.

'Is there any other way we can get in?' I ask.

'None that won't wake up the neighbours?' I think about that for another ten seconds while Gerry sets up the ladder before taking my first steps up towards the roof.

'Oi, take these?' says Gerry, giving me the radio and some small flat tool. 'I'll be in the van keeping a look out with Ollie?'

'What's this?' I say, holding out the tool.

'It's a glass cutter?' he shouts back. So that's what one of those looks like, I always wondered.

I climb up the ladder and get to the top and it's longer than I expected, more than halfway up. It's only about five foot short of the guttering. I climb up as many steps as I can until I'm standing on the second from the last. Reaching up, I can easily get my hands to the guttering – which, I find, is full of something soft and nasty. Pulling myself up over it though, is another matter all together. It's really only at times like this when you realise just how fit you were when you was a kid and how much heavier you've gotten since then. I used to love climbing about in trees when I was a nipper, jumping about like a little monkey without a fear in my head. But here, now, today, it's all very different. With a face full of ivy and a handhold that wouldn't support a sparrow, I'm seriously worried about spilling my brains on the pavement downstairs. I lift my left leg up and find the overflow pipe Gerry pointed out, but there's no way this flimsy little plastic tube is going to support twelve stone of me, so I lower my leg again. I fumble around for something more solid to hold on to but the only solid thing around is big and flat and eighteen feet below me. I try me right leg this time and try and reach the quion bricks sticking out on the corner, but they're more than five feet away and I give up after the ladder gives a quick wobble. After several more deep breaths I fumble about again but there's nothing more steady than ivy to hold on to. I'm so close, all I need is one or two footholds and I'm there, but this is just fucking silly.

'Hurry up?' says the radio in me pocket. I daren't let go to pull it out and tell it to fuck off so I just mumble to myself.

After a while I decide to have a go and try pulling myself up by the guttering. My feet scramble about desperately searching for something to take my weight and finally find several thick ivy knots that just about seem to be willing to help out. There's a couple of horrible cracks and the ivy sags several inches, but I'm almost there. I'm just hauling my stomach over the guttering and on to the roof when I feel the radio and the glass cutter fall out of my pocket.

'Ohh, fuckkkkk,' I grunt, which is all I can do in this position. There was no going back down for them though, I'd passed the point of no return. There was no way I'd be able to lower myself and find all the footholds and the ladder again and not fall. And more to the point, there was no way I wanted to. This was it. If I didn't do it first time, I weren't going to try a second.

I pull the rest of my body up on to the roof and breathe. Only then, at this moment of silence, do I realise what a fucking racket I must've been making. Getting up was hard enough, getting up in silence would've been impossible. The other thing I realise is that I am now busting for a piss. That pint and a half a little while ago, coupled with white knuckle fear, has really caught up with me. I pull myself up a bit further and, lying on my side on the sloping tiles, pull my dick out and have a piss. Halfway through I suddenly notice my right leg getting very warm, until it suddenly occurs to me that the piss is running downhill on to my jeans. As annoying as this is, there's nothing I can do about it as that leg's supporting most of my weight, and if I move, I fall. I have no choice but to continue to piss all over myself until I'm done, which just typically turns out to be about eight gallons later.

I pull myself over to the skylight (the other side of the piss of course) and have a good look round with my little penlight torch. The putty is old and cracked and covered in moss. I grip the torch between my teeth, pull out my pocket knife and start to chip it away. The putty turns out to be harder than it looks and after a couple of seconds I start using both hands to get a bit more strength behind the knife.

Hindsight is a wonderful thing and if I'd stopped to think about it I probably wouldn't've done it, but then you can say that about most accidents; 'if only I'd slowed down before I'd got to that bend – if only I'd listened to air traffic control before I'd started my approach – if only I'd checked to see if the power was off before I had a go at cleaning the blender – etc!'

The first I knew about it was the crack. Suddenly I realised I was leaning all my weight on the window. I try to get off, but of course, the only way to push yourself off something is to put even more pressure on it. I go straight through the glass and land on the attic beams. It's probably just as well that I don't have the radio with me, because the last thing I need is for Ollie to be giving me a call to tell me how much noise I'm making.

The initial shock of it all wears off pretty quick and leaves me with pain. My legs are cut to shreds where they've caught on the window frame on the way down and a big bit of glass had buried itself in my left hand. As for the rest of me, that has plenty to hurt about after falling on to a grid of fucking hard wooden beams. I pull myself up towards the window and look out to see if the van is still there. It is – fucking amazing.

I pick up my little torch, shine it down at my jeans and shit my pants when I see how much blood is covering my legs.

'Fuck, fuck, fuck, fuck, fuck, fuck, fuck!' I fuck.

I pull off my left glove and look at some more blood. The only thing that's going through my brain is: 'I wish I hadn't done that' and 'I want to be home'. But I had and I wasn't, and so it was tough shit all round. I hang the torch out of the window and wave it over at the van a couple of times in a 'come and get me, I'm bleeding to death' kind of signal before turning to look for the loft hatch.

I find it after a little look in the middle of the attic and try pulling it up before noticing the hinges that open it downwards. This is bad news, as it means that there is a catch on the other side, which I can't get to. I have to bust through.

Sitting on the rafters at the side of the hatch, I start stamping on the hatch, but the bastard don't move. I give it another, then another, then gradually more and more. This does my legs no favours at all and before I know it I'm standing on the hatch, jumping up and down on it for all I'm worth, until the first couple of splinter cracks makes me realise that this just isn't my day for common sense. Proof positive that I don't learn by my mistakes.

I really want to be out of this attic and with my hand and my legs the way they are, there's no way I'm getting out the way I came in. More than anything else, I don't want to be getting a bunk down out of here from Weasel.

I turn away from the hatch and pull some of the fibreglass foam out from between the rafters. Below that there's the plastered ceiling, which is slightly easier to hack through than the hatch. I give it a stamp and straight away my foot disappears to the ankle. I bring it out and do it again.

After a couple of minutes I've cleared a hole big enough for me to drop through. Before I do this though, I shine the torch down through it. I've had enough surprises for one day and really could do without chucking myself through a hole I've just opened up over the stairwell.

Carpet – I lower myself through, scratching the fuck out of my back as I go. More pain.

I open the front door and Gerry sprints from the van and in.

'What the fuck happened to you?' he says.

'What the fuck d'you think, I fell through the fucking roof.'

'Your legs, look at them.'

Yeah I know, thank you doctor.

'Come on, give me a hand, I want to get to the bathroom and see what I've done.'

Gerry helps me pull my jeans off and wash the worst off my legs with the shower attachment. Most of the cuts are nothing more than scratches but a couple aren't. He finds some Dettol and a couple of bandages in the bathroom cabinet and patches me up as best he can. He digs out the lump of glass in my hand with his pocket knife and wraps that one up too, then makes some crack about me crying, which I'm not. It's more like yelling or squirming or something, it definitely isn't crying. But it doesn't really matter, by the time he's finished with this story, he'll have me fainting and calling him Mum and all sorts.

It seems like I've been in here hours, but it's actually only been twenty minutes. Still, that's far too fucking long as it is, we have to crack on. I pull my jeans on and stagger outside, grab the radio and the glass cutter out of the flower bed and tell Ollie to keep them peeled. We're not going to be any more than ten more minutes. 'Right, let's just fucking do this,' I tell Gerry. 'Come on.'

We go and start in the living room but Gerry stops me when he sees a little green light flashing away in the corner of the room. I shine my torch at it but it's only an answerphone.

'Could've been a motion sensor,' he says by way of explanation. 'You've got to be careful in these big old places, they've got alarms everywhere.' I nod as if I know what the fuck he's talking about.

We walk in and give the place the once over but there's nothing here, the place is half empty. There's chairs and carpet and tables and books, but no stereo, no telly, no video, just wires where they look like they used to be. The kitchen is the same, microwave gone, crockery still present. We look upstairs and it's all the same story. Someone's already come in and cleared the place out.

One door, however, is locked. All the other upstairs rooms are bedrooms, so this one must be the office.

'Want to knock it in?' I say. Gerry feels at the lock.

'No, I think we've made enough noise already don't you. Got a credit card?' he says.

'What company's going to give me an American Express?' I say back. 'I've got a cashpoint card, will that do?'

'Yeah that'll do. I'm not buying anything,' he says. 'Give it here and watch this. A mate of mine showed me how to do it.' He takes my card, slides it between the door and the frame and wiggles it about. There's a click a moment later and Gerry hands me back the two halves of my cashpoint card. 'Sorry,' he says.

'Get the fuck out of the way, I've had enough of this.' I give the door a couple of whacks and a moment later we're in. But again, everything's gone, no computer, no fax, no nothing.

Gerry looks at me. I look at Gerry. And we both look at fuck all. Specifically the fuck all that was meant to be in the back of the van about now.

'This way,' Gerry says and heads back down to the living room. He stops by the answerphone and presses the play button.

'Robert,' a woman's voice says. 'Just to let you know, I've been by the house and collected what's mine. You'll be hearing from my solicitors over the next couple of days, and I've told them that I want my own separate evaluation done on the house. I hope she was worth it.' Click, tape rewinds.

'She's taken all the stuff,' I say but Gerry's already on his way back to the van. 'What a bitch!'

As far as the Old Bill and the local papers were concerned, Mrs Gun had some thug break in and get her stuff for her. They didn't care that she said she had a key and let herself in the front. Nothing else except the stuff she took was missing. It was all just a bit of a coincidence wasn't it. Besides, it didn't matter, it was her drum, her stuff, she could do what she liked with it. So despite Mr Gun's protests, there was no prosecution.

Mrs Gun didn't get off completely though. She was eventually taken to court by the RSPCA and heavily fined after Mr Gun found his beloved dog dead from an overdose of sleeping tablets.

20. Scum in badly fitting suits

You know, I quite enjoy going to court. I don't like getting nicked or nothing, that can spoil your whole week, but when it's necessary, and as long as it ain't for nothing too bad, it can make for quite a nice day out. I'll explain.

Court days are real surreal, if you know what I mean. It's like none of the usual rules apply. The police are there, so are the victims, the criminals, their families and friends, witnesses, lawyers, judges and social workers, all milling around in the same corridors, all drinking tea in the same cafes, and all cautiously staring each other out. It's really strange. The only way I can really describe it is like a truce, a temporary cease-fire, like in those old war films when both sides stop mowing each other down with machine guns for half an hour so that Dr Frank Sinatra can nip across to the other side and operate on the little sweaty Jap with appendix trouble. Everyone gets civilised, with the possible exception of the victims, who don't know how to play the game because they ain't in the trade. But I think I've already gone over all that.

Another reason I enjoy court days is that you get to meet up with a lot of the boys. In fact, in all the times I've been to court, I've never had an appearance where I've not bumped into someone I've known. It's a great place to catch up with old mates you haven't seen in ages, and make new ones.

I first met Animal at court. It was half a dozen or so years ago. I was up for criminal damage and he was starring in a case about a man going equipped. By the way, people call him Animal not because he's violent or wild or nothing (he's actually a bit of a rake if you look at him), but because he's a right old fucking messy eater. He got stuck with the name at school when some teacher comes up to him in the dinner hall, sees his peas, mash and custard all over the shop and tells him not to be such an animal. All the kids laughed and hey-presto, the poor bastard's still stuck with the tag more than twenty years later.

Mind you, she weren't wrong, the messy bastard.

I liked him straight away. We had a chat and a laugh over a couple of cups of tea and squash, swapped a few stories, and got tanked up at lunch-time. That afternoon, when it was my turn to go before the beak, the usher calls out my name and in I go.

'Blimey, don't go standing too near the bench,' the usher says, 'you'll get four weeks if he smells your breath. He's dead against the drink.' Which, in my opinion, tells me that he shouldn't be a magistrate in the first place if he's going to let his own personal preferences influence a sentence he is passing in the name of the Crown. Supposing he don't like short arses, or blue shirts, or fat birds with wet-look perms, or black people. What does that mean then, that if you fall into one of those categories and appear before him you ain't going to get the same impartial decision as a blonde-haired, blue-eyed child of Charles at the Lodge?

So what if I've had a drink at lunch-time, there isn't a law against that is there? I was sober when I was collared and so cunt-hooks should judge me on the events of that night, not on how my attitude to alcohol differs from his.

I was really working myself up into one thinking about that as my case was being heard. Looking across the court at that smug, pencil-thin, gormless-looking bastard and imagining the thrill he must get from holding power over all the dirty masses. I really wanted to walk over there and smack his snooty, wanky, tea-drinking face in and just keep smacking and smacking and smacking until he'd had enough, and then give him some more. Wanker! But then, that could've just been the beer talking. Twenty minutes later, I was walking off with little more than a slap on the wrist.

Poor old Animal, on the other hand, got two months for his trouble. Well, that's what he got initially, but Animal's mouth is just too big for his own good. The magistrate passed the sentence and the screw was taking him down when Animal shouted over at the bench – 'And a Merry fucking Christmas to you too, you cunt!' (see, it was just before Christmas – December 20th or thereabouts). The magistrate ordered him to be brought back up again and slapped on another month for contempt of court.

Animal's like – 'What? What? What the fuck's that for?' – but even I, as biased as I am in Animal's favour, don't think he had a leg to stand on. There's asking for it and there's asking for it, and Animal was asking for it.

The first couple of times I went up (Aggravated Burglary – Winchester Crown Court), I was only a nipper really and the old folks insisted on coming with me. The old lady only came along so that she could act the old martyr and cry with the shame of it all. The old man had a good day out though and spent most of it sitting in on cases that had nothing to do with him. Treated it like a day out at the Opera.

'I've just been watching a rape case,' he tells me, the old lady, Ollie and his old man in the cafe at recess. 'Really interesting it is,' he says and fills us all in about this hitch-hiker, this trucker and this lay-by, last October. 'Real shame it is, such a pretty girl she is too,' which was probably what the trucker was thinking as he was trucking along up the A6. Funny thing to say though, typical comment really. Would it have been less of a shame if she'd been an old boiler? Anyway, the morbid old ghoul misses my first community service order watching the old perv getting sent down for eight years (which was nowhere near long enough in my opinion).

Their attendance soon went for a Burton, once it became apparent that this was more than just a stage I was going through. They decided, after that, to opt for the easier approach of simply disowning me.

'You're scum, we want nothing to do with you.' Which is a bit rich when you think about it. If I'd been up for a Nobel Prize or an Oscar or something, they would've been the first ones to step forward and take a credit. Get nicked a few times and suddenly it's all my own fault. That's very fair that is.

Anyway, I didn't want them going along in the first place. How can you have the crack with the boys when your old lady's standing next to you, busting to wipe her spit all over your face?

I bumped into Terry while I was up another time. This was obviously before the job we did together – and I still can't believe I went along with it, what a cunt, what a cunt.

'What you both up for?' Terry asks me and Ollie.

'Affray, 100 hours probably.'

'What?'

'We're looking at getting about 100 hours' community service,' I repeat. 'What about you, what you here for?'

'Bald tyres.' I looked at Ollie in confusion.

'Bald tyres? You don't go to court for bald tyres, you just have to plead it through the post?'

'Ahh, yeah, but they said I had to come in because I was pleading not guilty.'

'Not guilty?' Ollie laughs. I swear this is true.

How can you plead not guilty to bald tyres? Either they're bald or they're not, there isn't any not guilty about it. What a cunt! What he would've got, if he had pleaded guilty by post, would've been three points (per tyre) and about a £40 fine, which is basically unavoidable once Plod's written out the ticket. What he got though, through trying to plead not guilty, was six points (two tyres) and a £120 fine, which was basically unavoidable once he got up in court and started wasting everyone's time denying he had bald tyres. I thought at least he'd have a strategy or something, but instead he just stood up and said 'No they weren't' every time someone asked him a question.

Still me and Ollie enjoyed it, it was one of the funniest things I think I've ever seen. Even the usher was pissing himself. Again, there's asking for it and there's asking for it, and Terry was fucking begging for it. What a cunt!

Oh yeah, I forgot, Ollie had a little bit of Charlie on him, so me and him did a couple of lines in the bog, you know, just to set us up for the afternoon. We don't do it regularly or nothing – at £60 a gram we can't afford to – we just have it every now and again for special occasions and the like.

Anyway, Terry had never had Charlie before and he really didn't want to know until we started calling him Zammo and singing 'Just Say No'. One line later he's giving it the large telling us to get him a £500 deal, to set up his own distribution network.

'Go on, straight up, I'll use it, no problem. Five hundred quid, I'll have the cash tomorrow. Get us the stuff.' Of course he won't, of course he didn't, and of course he is.

I can't believe I did that job with him, I just can't believe it.

Mel tries to straighten my tie when I'm not looking but I pull back and tell her to get off.

'I'm going to get a cup of squash, do you want one?' she says.

'Mumble, mumble, fucking squash, mumble, mumble.'

'Suit yourself,' she says and walks off towards a little old lady standing behind scores of plastic cups of green and orange.

I'm in a bad mood. I don't want to be here today. I shouldn't be here today. Fucking pigs! I look around at all the faces waiting to be called up, but don't recognise any of them. I know Charlie's in the building somewhere, greasing palms, oiling doors, licking arses and other such things, but I haven't seen him for the last hour of the hour and a half I've been sitting here. I doubt I'll see him again until five minutes before I'm up, but when that'll be is anyone's guess.

See that's the bastard of it all. They tell you to get here for 10 o'clock, then keep you hanging around all day with no idea of when it'll be your turn. It could be first thing, it could be after lunch, it could be halfway through the afternoon. It don't matter, you've just got to sit around and wait for the usher to appear and read your name out. Don't they realise that not everyone can afford to spend a whole day sitting around in a badly fitting suit, drinking orange squash and tea. Some of us have got more important things to be doing, places to go, people to see.

Besides, I don't normally get up before 12 o'clock, it puts me in a bad mood all day when I have to.

Like I say, it can be a good laugh, if there's a couple of you going up and you're in the right sort of mood, but not today. Not when it's just me, Mel and a lot of disapproval for company. No, this has all the makings of a fucking awful day. I, at least, thought Ollie would've come along to see how I got on, but no, fuck old Bex, who gives a toss about him in his hour of need. Got something better to do no doubt – telly and papers, pint with the lads, game of pool. Yeah, when it comes down to it, you certainly know who your mates are. More likely than that though, he's probably just trying to pay me back for not going to see him last month when he was in hospital with that rash all over his boat race. If that's the case, then he's just being a cunt. Makes me fucking glad I didn't go and visit the scabby bastard.

Mel comes back and hands me a cup of green.

'Here, I got you a cup of lime.'

'I don't want any,' I tell her.

'Just take it and stop being such a baby,' she says making one or two of the assembled villains turn and look our way. I take it to stop her making a scene and drink the lot down in one. I actually quite like lime juice and despite being a bit on the weak side, it was really quite refreshing, but I don't let on to this because I'm in a sulk.

'Stop sulking for god's sake,' Mel says. 'Otherwise you'll find yourself sitting here on your own.'

'Oh yeah, that would be terrible wouldn't it,' I say. 'Not having anyone here next to me to remind me what a stupid bastard I am and how everything's all my own fault. Oh please, don't go!'

'Well it is all your own fault, if you could, just for once, keep your mouth shut, I wouldn't have had to take a day off work and you wouldn't have had to get out of bed before *Neighbours*.'

'Talking of keeping your mouth shut . . .'

'Don't you dare try to quiet me, you ungrateful little sod. I'm the one who . . . [blah blah blah blah blah blah blah

blah blah blah blah blah blah blah blah blah blah blah blah blah blah blah blah blah blah blah blah blah blah blah blah blah blah blah blah blah]. Are you listening to me?'

'Yes!'

'Well so you bloody well should. For too long now you've . . . [blah blah blah blah blah blah blah blah blah blah blah blah blah blah blah blah blah blah] . . .'

'Adrian,' Charlie says, putting in a rare cameo appearance as my fucking legal representative. 'I've had a word with the Clerk of the Courts to see if we could get your case bumped forward at all, but it doesn't seem likely now that it'll be heard before lunch.'

'Oh for fuck's sake,' I tell him.

'For fuck's sake indeed. You might want to take the opportunity to phone your family. I don't want to alarm you but the charge against you is a very serious one. The courts take a very dim view of that sort of behaviour. I think it's only fair to warn you that you may not be walking away from this one today.'

What a load of bollocks. You know what I'm up for? Resisting arrest. One charge, that's it, resisting arrest. Arrest for what? Arrested for resisting arrest. Is it just me or does that all seem a bit pointless?

See, this is what happened. I was down the Lion, minding my own business, playing pool, when all of a sudden, crash bang wallop, the Old Bill comes in and raids the place for drugs. See, this is Rodney's pub, he's in the corner sorting everyone out and Rodney, being the indiscriminate cunt he is, has already sold PC Plain Clothes a quarter of skunk.

So they've got him on the deck in the cuffs and are really giving him, and his little mate Barry, some stick. Not being one of life's natural bystanders, I step forward and say something. I can't quite remember what because I'd had a few beers, but I think it was something like – 'Excuse me officer, but don't you think you're being a little excessive in the use of force?' I can do this because I'm clean, haven't got a thing on me. I can speak with the confidence of an Untouchable. So I put my point across and they tell me to fuck off and sit down. I tell them that they've got no right to tell me to fuck off and I'm just talking to them when, before I know it, I'm in the back of the van with Rodney and Barry.

For no reason at all!

I couldn't believe it. We get down the station, they charge me and here I am. What a bunch of cunts.

'Thank you Mr Taylor, we'll bear that in mind,' Mel tells Charlie. And with that, he picks up his briefcase and disappears again.

'Bex?' Mel starts.

'It's alright, don't worry, he always says that, cheerless bastard. So that when I get a fine or bound over or something, it looks like he's done a good job for me in keeping me out of nick with his legal brilliance. It's the fucking oldest trick in the book, everyone knows it. Tell them the worst and then anything less looks like a result.'

'You know one of these days, you're going to be wrong and someone's going to knock you off of that high horse of yours,' Mel tells me, I think in an effort not to cheer me up.

'Yeah, and like I've said before, when that day comes, I'll jack it in. But that day ain't today, and it ain't for a long time to come yet.' I pride myself with the fact that I've been in the business sixteen or eighteen odd years and I've never gone down, which, when I put it like that, reminds me of several birds I use to know. I never wanted to be like Roland or the sort, who spend half their fucking lives in the nick. I always told myself that after my first stretch, I'd pack in the game and do something else. And for sixteen or eighteen odd years, I've ridden my luck. Come close a couple of times, but not so close that I couldn't ride my luck a little bit more.

And it would take more than a piss poor little case like this to end my career.

'Blah blah blah blah blah,' Mel starts up again and doesn't stop for the next half-hour.

'Bex!' someone shouts from the other side of the room. 'Bex.' I look over grateful for any interruption. Praise the fucking Lord, it's Parky.

'Parky mate,' I shout back and leave Mel in mid-blah. 'How the fuck are you?'

He tells me he's doing alright.

'Come and meet the boys man,' Parky says and takes me over and introduces me to the boys.

We stand around for a good little while, smoking fags and chewing the fat, while we wait to get called in. One by one the names are read out, there's a flurry of – 'good luck mate, all the best mate' – and our group gets smaller. There's a real camaraderie about it all. Greasers, skinheads, hard cases, the lot. Blokes I wouldn't normally cross the road to help out if they were on fire are suddenly my best mates. I suppose it's because, to one extent or another, we're all in this boat together, and all blindly paddling towards a fucking great waterfall.

We're all scum, in badly fitting suits.

'I'll go then shall I?' I hear Mel say just behind me.

'What?' I turn around.

'I've been sat over there for three quarters of an hour while you enjoy yourself with this lot.'

Ron (actual bodily harm) tries to cool Mel down by going

– 'Ooooooooooohhhhh!' – and everyone laughs, including me.

Mel stays just long enough to call me a bastard then stomps out in a huff, which is a bit of a fucking relief actually. I didn't want her to come down in the first place – I never do – but she fucking has to, every time, just to have a dig at me and ruin my day. When other people have come down with us as well, I can usually lose her in the numbers. But not today, it was a fucking nightmare before Parky (obtaining money through deception) showed up.

'You manage to get rid of that dog, Bex?' he asks me.

'Yeah, no problem,' I say.

'Good stuff, because I could probably get you some more if you want.'

'Er no, you're alright there Parky.'

Andy (taking and driving away) re-emerges from the court room and we all ask him what he got and what the beak said and all the other usual questions. Next out's the usher, who tell us all that the court is in recess and we can all go down the pub and get pissed up if we want. I think that's what he said anyway.

You know, sometimes, I swear I only hear what I want to hear.

We round up a bit of a posse and head on down to this boozer in town and take over one corner of it. On the bar in big letters is a sign saying NO DRUGS ALLOWED, which is there for the local council's benefit rather than ours. The landlord – he knows the score – must see it every day. Some skinhead with a large spider's web tattooed over his neck and rings through his face, wearing an off-the-peg two-piece, ain't going to be something big in the City. Especially when the local court's just round the corner.

So anyway, we're all in there, a good dozen of us or

so, having a good laugh, comparing notes, swapping tips, planning jobs, talking tough, etc, when this lad comes in and a couple of the boys call over to him to join us.

Allan, I find out later, is his name and he's up for criminal damage.

'Allan, over here man.' 'Saved you a seat.' 'Get us a pint,' and that sort of thing. Allan gets a pint and comes over but stops in mid-stride.

'What the fuck is he doing here?' he shouts. We all look around at each other and wonder who he's talking about. We follow his stare down to this matey at the end of the table in the C&A whistle. 'What the fuck are you doing here?' he shouts again.

'I just ... I just came down for a drink ... that's all,' matey replies.

'Steady Allan,' several of the blokes are saying. 'Calm down, all friends here.'

'Friends?' Allan laughs. 'FRIENDS! Do you know who this is? Do you know what he's here for?' I didn't, I hadn't talked to him or even really noticed him up till Allan pointed him out.

'He's the fucking chief prosecution witness in my case,' he tells us. Allan couldn't have got a more stoney stunned reaction, had he come in and told us we were all drinking his piss.

'A witness?' Dennis (shoplifting) says.

'What the fuck are you doing here?' Ron asks the C&A. He's looking really fucking nervous now, like as if twenty Dobermans have just wandered in and started growling at him. He starts to stand up slowly.

'I just ... I just ...' he says shitting himself.

'Just what?' I demand getting swept away with the baying mob.

'I just heard someone say that they were going for a pint...'

'And you thought you'd tag along. What a fucking cheek!'

'We don't like fucking grasses here,' Parky tells him. 'We're very fussy about the sort of company we keep.'

'I didn't know. I just thought...'

'You thought wrong you cunt,' Allan screams at him. 'You want a fucking drink? Here, have one on me,' he says and throws his beer straight into matey's mush.

None of us needs a second invitation and we all do the same and drench the fucker with a 'Whahey!'

'Don't stand too near the judge,' I shout at him as he trudges out. 'The beak don't like the drink.' And we all collapse about laughing, blissfully ignorant of the fact that it was the last beer three of our number would be having for a good few months.

21. Crossing the line

'Give you £150 for the lot.'

'£150? Do us a fucking favour, we got some good gear here.'

'Old models, there's not much call for them.'

'What about the computer. That computer is almost brand new. It's got all that stuff on it too, what it called Oll'?'

'Modem.'

'A modem. We even nicked the phone with it. Really expensive these are. We'll chuck it in with everything else.'

'Computers. What am I going to do with computers? If people want a computer they go to a computer warehouse, they don't come here. No, what am I going to do with it, there's no demand.'

'We were thinking of about £350 for the lot,' Ollie tells him, for once remembering his lines.

'£350, huh. What do I look like, some kind of millionaire. No, you want £350 you've come to the wrong place. I'll give you £180 and I'm doing you a favour because I know you boys so long.'

'£300,' I say.

'You go out, you ask around, you see if anyone will give you more than £180. If you find somewhere you come back and tell me because I need an idiot I can offload my stock on to as well.'

'£220,' Ollie jumps in blindly, without waiting for Electric to up his bid.

'I will give you boys £200 for everything – in cash – and that's my last offer. If you don't want it, then you can take your stuff elsewhere and try and sell it. I won't be offended.'

I stare at Electric for a moment while he counts out £200, in tenners, in front of me. I'm pissed off with Ollie again, because I know we could've got the old cunt up to £220, maybe even £250, but big mouth blew it again.

'You're a tight old bastard,' I tell Electric. 'Give me the fucking money then.'

'I'm still not offended,' Electric smiles. 'Business is business.' Which is a fair point really but I'd still rather get an extra £50 than listen to people making fair points.

Electric hands me the notes and tells Ollie to stick the stuff down on the deck by the door. You can tell that he's already got a price in his head, and you can bet it's a damn sight higher than the one we've just received.

'You lads, how long have we done business with each other?' Electric asks us.

'I don't know,' says Ollie automatically, not even bothering to have a think about it. I say nothing. Every time I've ever heard anyone start up this way, it usually ends up in me having less money than I started with.

'You know, if you lads ever want anything, you know, if you ever *need* anything, you just have to come to me.'

'What do you mean?' I ask.

'You know. Anything you might need,' he says giving us both a wink. 'That you might not be able to get anywhere else. Just come and see me.'

'What you selling now then Grandad, drugs?' Ollie asks.

'Fucking drugs! No I'm not selling fucking drugs thank

you very much. What sort of person do you think I am? Hey? Scum of the earth sort of person eh, scum of the earth. Drugs? I want nothing to do with them, nothing at all. Kill you they will, fucking kill you. Drugs.'

'What are you selling then?' I ask.

'Guns,' he says with enthusiasm.

'What? Are you joking?' I say.

'Guns?' Ollie pipes up as the penny drops. 'You're selling guns?'

'Yes. You want to see?'

Electric shuffles off upstairs while me and Ollie stand around and look at each other.

'Fucking hell, hey,' Ollie says. 'Guns. I can't believe it.' I nod cautiously, already not liking this. 'Where do you reckon he gets them from?'

'Same place he gets his videos I should think. From blokes like us.' This is new ground for me. I don't think I've even seen a real gun before, let alone had the chance to buy one. I mean, an air rifle's one thing, but a real gun's another.

'Be quite smart though wouldn't it, having a gun,' Ollie says warming to the idea.

'No. It fucking wouldn't,' I tell him back. 'Use your loaf. Carry a gun around with you and you are just asking to do some serious time.'

'No. I wouldn't use it or anything.'

'Of course you would. What's the point in having it then?'

'Just to scare people, you know,' Ollie says, waving his fingers around like John Wayne.

'Scare, scare who? We don't do houses with people in. Who you going to be scaring?'

'If we'd had one when old Fireman Fred came home we wouldn't have had all that bother with him. And you wouldn't have got a pasting.'

'Yeah and Fred would've been dead and we'd both be doing life about now.' Ollie isn't getting it though.

'I'm not talking about killing him,' he says. 'Just scaring him.'

'Oh, and supposing he wasn't scared of you and your gun. Or suppose he didn't see it. Or suppose it went off accidentally when you were pointing it at him, or even worse, me. What then Rambo?'

'Hey, you don't have to get it if you don't want to, I'll fucking get it. You just fucking . . . don't, you know, if you don't want to.'

'You honestly think I come within ten miles of you and a gun, you've got to be fucking kidding. You get it, and you're on your own.'

Electric re-appears behind us at the door in a way that makes me think he's been standing there listening to us for the last minute or so.

'Here you are,' he says, putting them on the table. Both of them look pretty old. One of them's a Luger, the other one's some sort of revolver. They're both black and heavy and fucking frightening. 'Go on, you can pick them up if you want, they're not loaded.'

Ollie goes straight for the Luger and his eyes widen noticeably as his hand wraps around the grip.

'Fucking smart,' he says mesmerised. 'It ain't loaded?' he asks Electric, who gives him a shake. Before I can say a word, Ollie points the gun straight at me and starts clicking away like a maniac on the trigger.

'You stupid . . . don't fucking check it first, whatever you do.'

'What?' Ollie says. 'Electric said it ain't loaded.'

'Yeah and we all fucking really trust that old cunt with our lives don't we. You stupid wanker, that's just the sort of thing I was talking about. That's just the way accidents happen. Thick, brainless fucking idiots like you blowing holes in their mates playing silly fuckers. It ain't a fucking toy you know. It's fucking real. It's dangerous.'

'Shut up,' says Ollie pointing the Luger at my head. 'Or I'll shoot you again.'

Sometimes there's no talking to Ollie.

There's no way in the world I want anything to do with guns. I mean, it's just not the sort of shit I want to know about. Besides anything else and what damage we might do, we start getting guns, then the Old Bill has to get guns as well, and knowing some of the unstable nutters already pounding the beat, that ain't exactly a prospect that excites me.

See, at the moment, Plod has to earn his money and run after us, if we bump in to each other out on the job. But if he had a gun that wouldn't even give us a sporting chance of getting away. We'd be shooting him, he'd be shooting us, and before you know it, it wouldn't be safe to go out and rob people at night.

'How much for this one?' I hear Ollie ask.

'That one, £500,' Electric tells him.

'£500, fuck, are you sure?'

'Yes, I'm sure.' And that was that. Ollie needed no further convincing. It was one thing to be able to shoot people, it was quite another to have to fork out £500 for the privilege.

'Yes, but I will buy back the guns off of you after you have done the job,' Electric says.

'What job?' Ollie asks.

'You do a job. You want guns, then you come and buy the guns. After you do the job, I buy the guns back off you . . .'

'For how much?' I ask.

'£400 – providing you haven't killed anyone with them – and everyone's happy.'

'We ain't doing any jobs like that though,' I tell him.

'No, but if you ever were to, you can come and see me.'

'Well we're not. And Karel mate, you want to be careful who you have dealings with, there's some fucking idiots out there you don't want to be giving guns to.'

I was sharing a van ride home with one of them.

A couple of days later I get a call from Electric telling me to get down to his place right away. He sounds as if he's in trouble. My gut reaction is to hang up, unplug the phone and leave him to it, but he assures me it's not that sort of trouble. Reluctantly, I agree.

I call round for Ollie on the way down to Electric's and tell him what the old man told me, which weren't a lot. Ollie says 'Fuck him, it ain't our problem.' But by the little Electric told me on the blower, I don't even know what problem it is I'm considering running away from.

'Well then,' Ollie says. 'Again, fuck him, don't worry about it.'

'Look, just fucking get your coat,' I tell him.

'Bollocks.'

'Are you coming or what, make up your mind?'

'No. Look, you go and mix yourself up in all the trouble you want, I'm going back to bed.'

And with that, he shuts the door and climbs back underneath his jiz-streaked duvet. I jump in the van and make some tracks of my own hoping to avoid the evening rush hour.

It's a weekday and I'm not making a delivery so I go in by the front entrance like a regular customer rather than the back entrance like a regular mug. Electric's there, sat behind his till, biting his nails. I don't think he's doing it out of nerves, I think he's just a nail-biting bastard.

Electric spits out the little bits on to the floor, when he looks up, and tells me to bolt the door behind me and turn around the OPEN/CLOSED sign, which I do.

'Well, what's up?'

'Look at this, in the back,' he says and disappears through the back and upstairs. I follow him up to his living room and he shuts the door behind me. I've never been up here before. I always usually stay in the stockroom downstairs while he disappears and does things up here. I've always wondered what his place looked like, and now I know, I suddenly don't want to be here any more.

I know this'll sound a bit strange coming from me but this is his living area, his private area, where he comes to relax and unwind. We've always had a strictly business relationship and me being here, in his private area, goes beyond business, and leaves me feeling distinctly uncomfortable.

I hope he doesn't start undressing.

It's not my fault I feel like this, it's just the natural homophobe in me coming out. It's the same with every bloke. If some geezer you know a little suddenly starts to get all matey with you and lets you in to his confidence, you can't help but feel it's because he wants to shag you up the arse.

He steps past me and walks over to the telly.

'Where'd you get that stuff from?' he asks me.

'What stuff?'

'The stuff you brought round the other day, the video and all that. Where'd you get it from?'

'I don't know, a house. Why?' Electric looks strange, not like I've ever seen him before. He looks ... what is it ... pissed off, or fruity, or something.

And he's got a gun somewhere.

'What's up? What's the matter?' I keep asking.

'You not in to any funny business are you?' Electric asks.

'No I'm fucking not,' I say without even wanting to know what sort of funny business he's talking about.

'You sure?' he says crooking his neck *funnily*.

'Yes I'm sure.' It's about now I start to realise that he's probably fancied me for years. Now that I think about it, he always liked to hold the back door and stand in the way as me and Ollie squeezed past him in the narrow hallway. Urgh, the fucking old pervert. He's probably been waiting years for this, to get me on my own, building up the courage to offer me a load of money to let him do things to me. He wants a smack in the mouth doesn't he the fucking old poofta.

Just let him try it.

'Look at this,' he says, sticking a tape in to his video and turning on the telly.

It takes a moment for the penny to drop but when it does it takes half my guts with it. It's horrible. On a bed in a fuzzy back room, two blokes hold down this little nipper and . . . well, I don't think I have to say what really.

Without saying a word I turn and smack Electric in the side of the head with everything I've got, and the old man goes down like a sack of shit.

'What you doing? What you doing?' he screams as I pick him up by the tie for some more.

'You dirty old fucking bastard,' I shout back. 'You're a fucking dead man.'

'Wait, wait,' he shouts holding up his hands to defend himself. 'Take it, take it, I don't want it. You can have it.'

'I'm going to fucking kill you,' I shout. 'I'm going to fucking kill you, you sick bastard.' I shake him by the neck and drag him around the floor kicking him as I go. Electric tries to hang on for all he's worth, but doesn't do a very good job. He's still shouting and screaming, but I'm so angry I can hardly hear him. However, one sentence does make it in to my brain and stops me in my tracks.

'Please, please. I'm sorry I looked at your tape. I'm sorry . . .'

'What?' I say. 'What d'you say? My tape?'

'I'm sorry, please don't hurt me, please . . .'

'My tape? It's not my tape. What are you talking about?'

'What?' sobs Electric.

It's about now I think there's been a bit of a misunderstanding.

'What d'you mean "my tape"?' I say. Electric thinks for a moment, straightens his glasses and looks up at me.

'Isn't it your tape?'

'No it's fucking not, what sort of bloke d'you think I am?' I shout wanting to hit him again.

'Well why were you kicking me?'

'I thought it was your tape.'

'My tape? My tape? Oh and what sort of man do you think I am then?'

I let go of Electric's tie and offer him my hand. He hesitates at first and flinches nervously, but then accepts it.

'So where'd you get it then?' I ask as I pull him up.

'I got it off you,' he says. 'Out of that video you sold me.'

'Well it ain't mine is it. It's whoever owned that video's.'

'Yes. That's what I thought until you started hitting me.' Electric walks over to the sideboard and pours himself a large vodka. He wiggles the bottle at me and I say I'll have one as well. We drink for a moment and say how horrible the video is and how the bloke who owned it should be strung up and burnt alive and that sort of thing, then I ask him why he gave me a call.

'I wanted you to take it away.'

'Why didn't you just throw it in the bin?'

'Look, you brought it here, you take it away. I don't want anything to do with it. And I don't want to go leaving it in my bin for the dustmen to find and hand in to the police.' He drinks his vodka and waves his hand at me to leave.

'What do you want me to do about it?' I tell him.

'I don't care, just get it out of here. Go on, take it away.'

I eject it from the machine, slip it in to my pocket and go to leave.

'Oh and Karel, sorry about beating you up,' I say, looking back at him holding his face, which is all starting to swell.

Electric just waves a hand at me, which I take as 'yeah, no problem' although I suspect it probably wasn't.

I drive back to my gaff and think about chucking the horrible thing out the window. But I really don't want anyone to see me sling it and take down my number and report me and someone finds it and they think its mine and it's got my prints on it and . . . and . . . and, having this in the van just makes me paranoid. Besides, I don't want anyone else getting their hands on it, in case they're – as Electric might say – *funny*. And besides again, the geezer I nicked this off of ain't getting away with this.

I've already made up my mind what I'm going to do with the tape, I'm going to send it in to Weasel, anonymously of course, along with the address of where I found it.

Don't get me wrong, I ain't no grass, never have been and this don't count. I ain't grassing up a criminal, one of my own. I'm blowing the whistle on a sicko bastard who deserves to be strung up and burnt alive and everything else. By doing what I'm doing, I'm doing the world a favour, a service even. Any self-respecting burglar, robber or thief will tell you the same.

It ain't being a grass, it's just being a man.

See that's one of the things I hate about so-called 'law-abiding citizens'. They always lump the decent honest criminal like me in with the fucking nonces and perverts.

'They were a cut-throat lot, robbers, rapists and murderers,' as the expression goes. Now this to me is an insult to robbers. Stealing stuff is just stealing stuff. You ain't doing it because you're a sick bastard, you're just doing it to make a few quid, which, let's face it, is something everyone in the world is out to do. Raping and murdering women and kids – now that's basically evil, and people who do it should be strung up and burnt alive and have their hands cut off, etc.

Yet half the fucking judiciary are falling over themselves to give these evil fuckers an easy ride.

'It's an illness, they can be helped.'

Who gives a fuck, get the rope and the matches. As far as I'm concerned, the moment they've hurt some poor little kid, they've forfeited their right to life. Isn't it funny how none of these bleeding-heart liberals ever step forward and speak up for the poor bastard who's been caught nicking a pair of shoes because he can't afford to buy them. And curing thieves is easy. All you've got to do is give them enough money so they don't have to go out nicking again. That might sound like a lot of money but when you consider how much it costs to send nonces on these caring and sharing courses, and how much it costs the taxpayer to keep everyone in prison, it doesn't start looking so silly anymore.

So, string up the perverts and buy off the thieves. Makes sense to me.

Several weeks later, me and Ollie were going over to Electric's to drop some more stuff off when we found his shop had been closed down. I asked the bloke in the curry house next door, where he'd gone and the bloke told me he'd been arrested.

'Apparently, he was selling guns to people and someone got shot and died,' he said.

A couple of months later Electric was sent down for fifteen years for possessing illegal firearms, conspiracy to rob, handling stolen goods, and so on.

No one-to-one classes for old Electric. Just fifteen years of hard porridge. At his age. Poor bastard'll never make it. The only way he's coming out is in a wooden overcoat.

Justice? – Bollocks.

22. No show

It's pissing down with rain and I'm freezing and fucked off. Ollie was meant to be here and pick me up fifteen minutes ago and like an idiot I believed him.

He does this all the time. We agree to meet at a certain time, he's late, and I end up hanging about on street corners for fucking hours on end. I mean, how difficult is it to turn up on time? What's so fucking impossible about meeting up with someone at the time agreed?

I don't get it, I just don't get it. I ain't uptight or anything but what's the fucking point of agreeing a time if you're not going to stick to it? I reckon I've probably wasted some-where in the region of a day, a day and a quarter, something like that, waiting around for that cunt, if I add it all up together. A day and a quarter, leaning against lampposts, staring down the street like a lost puppy, looking at my watch and working myself up in to one. I could accept it if it had only been once, I mean – we're all late from time to time – but every-fucking-time, that's got to be deliberate.

I've been with him before, when we were meeting someone else and I've watched him in action. He'll sit around, watch telly, smoke fags, practise juggling oranges, anything, except actually get ready to leave on time. No matter how much you nag on at him, no matter how many times you tell him you're both going to be late, he just won't get up and move his lazy arse. And finally, at the last minute, just when you think he's had a wash, put on his boots, found his keys and is set to walk out the door, he'll turn round and have a bowl of cereal in his hands.

It's like it's got to be a point of principle with him or something, you know, keep 'em waiting and they'll appreciate you more.

I tried giving him a taste of his own medicine once and arranged to meet him outside the fish and chip shop in town. Knowing he'd be about fifteen or twenty minutes late himself, I thought I'd err on the side of caution and turned up well over half an hour late. And you know what, I got there exactly the same time as Ollie. I looked round and there he is, strolling down the street with a big, dumb, couldn't-give-a-fuck smile on his face.

And that annoyed me more than anything.

He's more than twenty minutes late now and the rain's really coming down. The pub shut fifteen minutes ago so I can't even nip across the road and get out of it. I'm stuck, in this fucking bus shelter, waiting for the cunt.

We've got a job on tonight – nice house over in Claremont Street – and he should've been here at quarter-past eleven to pick me up. It's the only reason I let him have the van. He was taking out some old bird tonight, Belinda, or 'Bell-end-her' as he likes to call her, and I was meeting my brother for a couple of drinks, so I let him use the van for his 'fish supper and fish dessert' date, on the condition that he came and got me at chucking-out time.

Cunt!

I give it another ten minutes and when he doesn't show I jump on the last bus across town and head over to his place to go and get the bastard.

*

The bus drops me on the main road, half a mile away from Ollie's. I run most of the rest of the way, through the rain, skipping between puddles and running through the bigger ones, until I'm fucking well and truly soaking. I get to the point where I decide I can't get any wetter, so I stop and walk the rest of the way.

I get to Ollie's at just after midnight and, sure enough, the van's there, parked outside. I feel the bonnet and it's stone cold.

The bastard hasn't even been out this evening.

I slop up several flights of stairs up to his flat and go to ring the bell, but decide, instead, to let myself in. Ollie and me, we've both checked out each other's gaffs and know exactly how to break in without much fuss. I tickle the catch on the kitchen window open and clamber, as quietly as I can, over the mountain of washing up and take-away tins and lower myself down in to the plate of cat food on the deck below.

I walk through the hall and up to the bedroom, where I know the lazy bastard'll be. I peer round the woodwork and, sure enough, there he is snoring away with Bell-end-her next to him.

I'm about to wake them up with a scream, but, at the last moment, have second thoughts. I decide to, while I'm here, I might as well check out his bird's tits and beaver first. Very gently, I pull the covers back and peer down inside, but I can't see very well because it's too dark. So just for a second, I switch the bedside light on, to have a better look, only to get the fright of my life when she wakes up and screams the place down.

'Help, help, help,' she's screaming, as well as other things like 'Ollie' and 'Oh my god, no no no,' and 'Please don't hurt us' and stuff like that, and pulling the covers up to her chin. She only stops when Ollie rolls over, opens his eyes and says hello.

'Oh alright Bex, what time is it?'

'What time is it? Fucking ten past twelve you cunt. I waited there half a fucking hour for you. I'm fucking soaking.'

'Do you know each other?' Bell-end-her asks.

'Yeah, that's my mate Bex. Bex this is Bell- . . . Belinda. Belinda, this is Bex.'

'Half a fucking hour. And I'd still be there if I wasn't here. You fucking wanker.'

'He was lifting the covers off me and looking at me,' she goes.

'Half a fucking hour.'

'Ollie?'

'And I've had to walk all the way from the bus stop in the pissing down rain, look at me.'

'Ollie,' Bell-end-her keeps interrupting. 'Ollie!'

'What?'

'He was looking at me under the cover,' she says all outraged.

Ollie looks at me and then back at her.

'So? What d'you want me to do about it?'

'What do I want you to do? He's a bloody pervert, he's been looking at me while I've been asleep . . . in your bed . . . next to you. Aren't you even going to say something?'

I spark one up while Ollie searches his brain for something to say to me. I chuck the fags over to Ollie and he does likewise.

'Well,' he looks up at me. 'What d'you reckon?'

'Very nice,' I say just to be polite, but to be honest I've seen better. Still there's no point in hurting the poor girl's feelings. 'Right, come on then, get dressed, we've got work to do.'

'Ollie!' Bell-end-her says but Ollie's largely ignoring her by now, being that he's suddenly far too busy trying to wriggle his way out of doing this job with me tonight.

'Oh Bex, come on. I'm fucked, let's not bother, do it tomorrow or something.'

'They're back from holiday tomorrow, we have to do it tonight, it's our last chance,' I say stripping out of my wet clothes. 'You got a T-shirt and a pair of jeans I can borrow?'

'Yeah in the drawer over there. Oh no, actually no they're not, they're on the floor over there.'

'Ollie?' Bell-end-her says again. 'Where you going?'

'Nowhere.'

'You fucking are,' I tell him. 'Now put you fucking clothes on and let's go.'

'Ollie?' Bell-end-her's really starting to get on my tits. 'Ollie, Ollie, Ollie?' she keeps asking and when Ollie fails to answer, she simply says 'Ollie?' some more.

'Bex man, it's fucking cats and dogs outside.'

'I know, you fucking left me out in it for long enough,' I say, pulling one of Ollie's 'I Hate Man Utd' T-shirts over my head. 'Urgh, have you washed this?'

'When?' was his reply.

'Lately,' I say, pulling off my jeans for a pair less clean than the ones at the bottom of my laundry basket.

'Yeah,' he says all indignantly, which just goes to prove he's a liar as well as a smelly bastard.

'Come on Ollie, get dressed,' I say looking at him still in bed.

'Oh Bex, I've got me bird here. I don't want to fucking go out and do a job now.'

'What job?' Bell-end-her asks. 'What are you doing?'

I chuck his jeans at him and then his sweatshirt.

'Ollie?' she goes again. 'Ollie?'

'WHAT?' Ollie finally answers.

'Where are you going?'

'To do a job,' I tell her.

'Are you a robber?'

'Look, it isn't how it sounds. Bex you fucking big-mouthed wanker, what's the matter with you?'

'What did I fucking say?' I fucking say.

'Ollie? Tell me. What is it?' she asks.

'Nothing,' he says, trying to shut the door after the cat's out of the bag, or whatever. 'I ain't doing nothing. Don't listen to him, he's just . . .'

'Ollie?' This time it's me. 'Are you going to get dressed or what?'

'No.'

'Can I come?' Bell-end-her asks.

'What?' I say.

'Can I come, do a job with you?'

'Bell-end . . . Belinda?' Ollie says but Bell-end-her's got the devil in her eye.

'Can I?'

'Yeah, why not,' I tell her. 'You stay in bed mate, I'll do the job with your bird. Looks like she's got bigger balls than you as it is. Come on then.'

'Belinda?' Ollie says.

'Oh come on Ollie, let's do it, please?' she says sounding like someone in need of a bit of excitement, which – not to read too much in to it – reflects badly on Ollie.

Ollie ain't up for it at all, but all of a sudden he's got even more pressure on him and doesn't want to look bad in front of his bird, so he has to go along with it.

'Okay,' he tells her and she gets all whoopidy-do like we've just given her the vote or something.

'Er, do you mind?' she says to me nodding at the door.

'What?'

'I want to get dressed?'

'Oh don't worry about that, I've seen it all before.' Ollie doesn't give a fuck and is already stepping in to his pants at this point.

'Then you don't need to see it again,' she says.

'Oh don't be so fucking daft. If we're going to work together, we've got to be able to trust each other. Look, I don't give a fuck, I've seen women naked hundreds of times before, so stop being so silly. Now hurry up and get dressed.' After a little pause she jumps out from beneath the covers and climbs in to her knickers and bra as I stare at her unblinkingly.

On the drive over there she insists on telling me how she and Ollie met. But seeing as Ollie doesn't really want me to know and I don't care, I think she was just going on more for her own benefit; nerves and all that, you know.

' . . . and then he said, I bet you £10 I will have sex with you tonight,' she rabbits on. 'I thought, £10, for *not* sleeping with this . . . this Ogre. Okay, it's a bet.'

I take a fag from the packet and hand one to Ollie who takes it without a word.

'But then he said, oh no, but if I win this bet and do have sex with you, you're not allowed to call the police and tell them about it. And I thought, what? I'm not going to pay you £10 to force yourself on to me! And we both laughed, didn't we?'

Just like I am at the moment. I'm laughing so hard that it looks as if I'm really bored.

'Ollie? Didn't we?'

'Yeah,' says Ollie who's busting up as much as me. It certainly sounded like the sort of thing Ollie would do, though I think it said more about her than about him. But then, I really don't care. I don't care if he pulled her from a burning building or made her out of parts of dead bodies or met her in a spaceship or anything. I just don't care.

So then, why did she insist on telling me that story?

I'll tell you why, because I haven't got it together with Mel in over a month and she knows it. Don't ask me how she knows – women, they just know. That's the thing about women, they do love to rub a bloke's nose in it when he isn't getting any. It's the cruel streak in them. They all have it. She'll start nibbling at his ear in a minute, thrusting her tits around the cab and saying things like – 'Oooh, when we get back home, remind me to empty your bollocks for you,' – not because she's really in to Ollie or anything, it's because she can sense that I haven't had it in ages and I feel like I'm sitting on a small spacehopper.

'Ollie?' Bell-end-her says. 'Tell him what you said to me that first night.'

'Oh please don't,' I say to Ollie. 'I really don't want to know.'

'Suit yourself Mr Grumpy Face, be like that then.'

I feel sorry for Ollie in this situation, he's in the middle of it, vested interests in both corners. There's me, a mate, he's known for fifteen odd years, or Bell-end-her, some old fucking boiler he's been stoking for a couple or three weeks. What a choice!

He doesn't want to say anything that'll upset me because I'm his mate, but he also doesn't want to say anything that upsets Bell-end-her, because she might not let him come on her tits any more. Solution – sit quietly, say nothing and stare out of the window at the rain, until we get there. Which is just what he does.

'Did you get the tenner?' I ask Ollie.

'What?' he says.

'That night, did you get the tenner?'

'No. That's a point.'

We pull up outside the house and Ollie tells Bell-end-her to stay in the van, but she's having none of it. 'I didn't come all this way to blah blah blah . . .' and all that. In the end, we agree to let her come up to the house and stand look-out. Once we're in, we give her a shout and let her come in and get out of the rain.

She's all excited and giggling like some fucking old St Trinian, picking up ornaments, going through drawers, rifling through cupboards and so on. It's her natural, all powerful, female nosiness, suddenly let loose, and it's really quite frightening. While me and Ollie are looking through stuff to nick, she's looking through stuff to see what they've got, which if you ask me, is a bit more disturbing than good old-fashioned, honest-to-god nicking.

'Can I have this?' she says holding up a small china windmill.

'Ain't mine is it,' I say. 'Take it.'

'Oh look, look at this little tiny picture of a river,' she says pulling a frame off of the wall. 'Can I have this as well?'

'Look, don't fill your pockets with too much shit other-wise you won't be able to carry the stuff that we do want you to nick, alright,' I tell her then turn round and see Ollie grabbing handfuls of miniature bottles of booze out of the mini-bar and stashing them all over his body. 'Oh, do what you like,' I say. 'Just, I don't know, go and have a look upstairs. Don't take too long though. Quick check and we're gone.'

'And don't go trying on any of her clothes,' Ollie tells her as she skips past, finally taking my side. 'Birds hey!' he tuts.

'Ow shut up.'

I finish stacking up the telly, video, hi-fi and so on by the French windows, bring the van up on to the drive and go to tell Ollie to give me a hand loading up, but he's gone. I have a quick scout about in the kitchen and dining room but can't find him anywhere and figure he must be upstairs giving Bell-end-her a hand. I go upstairs and have a look in several rooms before hearing sounds coming from the main bedroom. Before I even open the door I know what's going on. The way she was acting downstairs, it was so obvious. She was like a bitch on heat with all the excitement of doing something naughty. And sure enough, when I push open the door, there she is, bent forward over the bed, her trousers round her ankles, taking all that Ollie could throw up her.

She looks round at me standing in the doorway.

'Oh yeah. Come in and join us.'

'Er hang on . . .' Ollie starts to say but there ain't no need, I'm already halfway down the stairs and heading for the French windows. It takes me less than a minute to load the gear in to the van and fuck off. Now it's Ollie's turn to walk home.

And as for Bell-end-her? I think that proves that Ollie's not the only bloke who can get her wet.

Bell-end-her weren't the only tag-along I've ever done a job with, but not all of them were as useless and as annoying as her. I don't know if I ever mentioned this but Animal's got a little kid – Paul I think his name is – and he brought him along on a job once to help us out. He's only about eleven or twelve or so, but Animal tells me he's showing him the ropes, teaching him a career.

So we do this job right – little end-terrace in Worcester Gardens – with me and Animal downstairs nicking the grown-up stuff, while little Paul's upstairs filling his little bag with toys.

And I'll tell you what, he was a fucking diamond, a real little burglar. A credit to his old man. I've done jobs with blokes before that were three times his age but not even half as professional. I go up to see how he's getting along and he's all loaded up and ready to go quicker than me and Animal.

'Come on Uncle Bex, look in here, I'll show you where they keep their jewellery. And I found a wallet with credit cards in it.' Oh yeah, he was brilliant. A fucking natural.

I'll do a job, any day of the week, with little Paul over all those wankers in the pub.

What a smashing kid!

23. The wedding ring

I hate Norris, he's a cunt.

'Alright Bex, you working?'

'What do you want?'

Norris sits down opposite me without waiting for the invite, which he wasn't going to get. He plonks his pint on the table, his fags, the *Daily Sport* and a huge bunch of keys fixed together by a hard porn key ring he picked up in Amsterdam (actually, I wouldn't mind one of those).

'Nothing, just saw you in here, thought I'd come over and say hello. Can I nick a fag?'

'You'll fucking have to, because I ain't giving you one.'

Norris smiles weakly as if we're mates having a laugh.

'Ah, that's alright, I was gonna buy some anyway,' and off he wanders to the vending machine.

'You got two fifty pence pieces Bex?'

'No,' I answer without checking. 'Try the garage down the road.'

'Ah it's alright, don't worry, I've got a couple.'

'Oh! Cushty!' I try not to look up from my paper at all, in the hope that Norris might take the hint and fuck off.

'Fag?' offers Norris.

'Yeah, alright,' I say taking one and shoving it in my almost full packet. This might seem a bit hypocritical of me, accepting a fag from someone I don't like. Well that's because it probably is. I don't care, I've been called worse things. And besides, the way I see it, the more fags I take from Norris, the less he's got for himself. He can dish out fags and buy me pints all night if he likes, he ain't getting anything back.

'One for Ron?' I say, taking another and slipping it behind my ear.

Norris reaches over towards my side of the table but I grab what he's reaching for first.

'Here, what you doing? those are my matches.'

'What, I just wanted a light.'

'Well then fuck off and buy some then, I've only got . . .' – I open the box and have a quick count up – ' . . . twenty-eight left. Buy your own you tight bastard.'

Norris fucks off to the bar to get some matches while I flick through his *Daily Sport*.

'Bex,' Norris says as he sits back down finally, smoking. 'Are you working at the moment?'

'What's it to you?'

'Oh nothing, nothing. I was just wondering because I heard that you and Ollie had . . .'

'Heard what?'

'Nothing, I just heard you weren't working together any more that's all,' Norris says all innocent-like. 'I couldn't believe it myself. You and Ollie, split up? Nah, I thought someone was pulling my pisser. Bex and Ollie? It's like fucking Canon and Ball or Chalk and Cheese or whatever.'

'What d'you want?' I ask him again.

'I just wondered if you were working, that's all. Wondered if you had anything lined up.'

'No, I haven't,' which was true. Me and Ollie hadn't spoken in over a week and neither of us were about to be the one to make the first move. This stalemate is standard

procedure for blokes and usually goes on for a couple of
years until we bump in to each other by accident, get drunk,
make up and then try and remember what it was we fell
out over in the first place.

In the meantime, I hadn't got round to pulling any jobs.
Like I've said before, I don't really like knocking over places
on my jack, it's double the risk and half the crack. I hadn't
even really been looking, which has left me starting to feel
it in the pockets.

'You want a beer?' Norris offers. I drain what's left of
the pint in front of me and pass him the glass.

'Get us some crisps while you're up there.'

'What flavour?'

'Salt and vinegar and cheese and onion.'

And you ain't getting any of them, I think to myself as
he queues up waiting to get served.

'I've got a job for you Bex,' Norris says. 'If you're
interested.'

'I'm not,' I tell him, but a spark of curiosity is ignited in
my bonce. Norris goes in to his hard sell pitch and tells me
what a cunt I'd be to pass this one up, and what a doddle
it is and all the usual shit I tell Ollie whenever I need his
help on some particularly risky job.

'It's like taking candy from a baby,' Norris tells me with
such conviction it makes me suspect he's actually got experience in this area.

I hate Norris, he's a cunt – which I may have mentioned
earlier – but I'm skint, I've got nothing on the cards myself
and I need the wedge. Personal feelings don't come in to it
when you can't afford to go out at the weekend. It's business. He's a cunt, he's a weasel and I don't fucking like him
– but then I imagine most people in the world find they
have to work with someone they can't stand. So fuck it!

I let him buy me a couple more pints before biting.

'Watch yourself, there's grease all over the floor where I knocked the chip pan over climbing through,' Norris says opening the back door. I step in and carefully walk over the thin film of oil that covers the tiles. I look round to see Norris following up behind me in the same fashion and almost laugh. We both look daft, sort of funny, like we're moving in slow motion or shit our pants or something.

We leave the kitchen and head through to the living room. Norris wipes his feet on the carpet and tells me he doesn't want to get any grease in my van, which I suppose is fairly considerate of him.

The house in a mess; plates, cups, newspapers and rubbish; the whole place is a fucking tip.

'What a fucking tip,' I say.

'Is it?' he looks round. 'Yeah, I guess. Come on then, let's get on with it.'

We round up the usual stuff, telly, video, etc, plus a large collection of CDs and videos I notice matey has, or rather, had. These are always good to nick because I can get rid of them at my car boot sales. I like to go to car boot sales at least once every couple of months, just to offload all the little bits and bobs, like CDs, videos, vinyl, computer games and suchlike, non-traceable goods. I always go over to ones in the next county. Even if you price them at silly low prices, couple of quid each, you can still walk away with a pocket full of money, with nothing to pay to a middle man – which is just as well really.

What with Electric being banged up, I've had a bit of trouble getting rid of some of the stuff I've lifted. This is probably another reason why I haven't done a job since my barnie with Ollie.

I don't know, with Electric it was just too easy. I nicked

it, he bought it. He might have shafted us every time we went round to see him, but you've got to give him his due, he was always ready to take the gear off your hands. I guess I just got a bit lazy, didn't bother sussing out new outlets because . . . well, I didn't need to. Or at least I didn't think I needed to. I always thought if ever we got in lumber with the Old Bill, it would be me who went down. It never even occurred to me that Electric might go inside, and leave me out here all on my jack.

Which is why car boot sales are such a blessing. You can go along, tell everyone you're moving house and getting rid of your old excess, and then sell them a load of nicked gear. I can see myself becoming more and more reliant on car boot sales if I don't find another Electric.

I get a couple of bin liners from the kitchen and fill them up, while Norris has a look upstairs.

'Here Bex, Bex, come up here a minute.'

I put the stuff in the hall by the front door and head upstairs. When I get there, Norris hands me a little 35mm camera he's found in the bedroom.

'Here, take a picture of this,' he says turning round to show me three toothbrushes sticking out of his arse. 'A mate of mine told me about these bikers who did this. What you do is, you leave the camera where it was and when matey gets the film back from Boots, he sees what he's been brushing his teeth with. Go on, take it. For a laugh.' I take the picture, but I ain't that happy doing it. If you ask me, it isn't a very nice thing to do.

'What d'you want to do now, spunk in his Head and Shoulders?' I ask him.

'Nah, come on, let's clear out and fuck off. Just got to check out a couple more rooms.' Norris carefully puts back the toothbrushes in the mug on the bathroom shelf and rubs his hand with glee.

'Have a look at this,' he says from one of the kiddies' bedrooms a moment later. I go in and see him unhooking a computer – a good one by the looks of it – and then spot all the computer games by the side of it. They go in my pockets while Norris looks around the rest of the room.

'Whahey, look at this,' he says grabbing a big pink china piggie bank off the window sill.

'Oh don't be a cunt,' I tell him. 'Put it down, leave him his pocket money at least.'

'There's notes in here,' says Norris giving it a shake.

'Give me that here,' I say snatching it off him and quickly smashing it with my crowbar on the bed. '£20. Tenner each alright,' I say shifting through the pieces.

I leave Norris to take the computer downstairs and go and have a quick look through the main bedroom. This is also a tip; clothes, papers and so on, all over the shop. I go through the drawers and the cupboards, but there's nothing but clothes, and a little bit of jewellery, nothing really worth having away. Norris joins me and pulls the camera out of his pocket and sets it down on the side.

'Almost forgot,' he says. 'We ready then?'

'Yeah, I suppose.'

We're just about to leave when Norris backtracks his torch over the make-up table.

'Here, look at this,' he says picking something off the table.

'What is it?' I ask.

'Look, it's a ring; gold. Wedding ring it looks like.'

'Put it back,' I tell him. 'Don't take that.'

'Hey? Why not?'

'Not a wedding ring, I never touch wedding rings. It's too cuntish.'

'What?'

I never take wedding rings, it's one of my rules. And

seeing as how I don't have that many rules, the ones I do
have, I stick to. A wedding ring isn't just another thing to
nick and hock, it means something to people. It's fucking
precious. It might be gold, which is always nice, but it's
worth more to whoever owns it than fifty times its weight.
It doesn't matter how many tellies and videos you have
nicked, you can always get another one, but a wedding ring,
that's a one-off – that goes, you'll never get it back. I think
I probably got this off my old lady. She lost her wedding
ring when I was twelve and I never heard the end of it.
Broke her fucking heart it did.

I explain all this to Norris.

'But it's fucking gold man,' he says.

'Put it back.'

'Fuck off!'

'Look, I ain't . . . wait a minute,' I suddenly realise. I go
back to the wardrobe and look through. It's full of dresses.
I look round at all of the mess and think of all the mess
downstairs. Then I look back at the picture on the make-
up table – the only uncluttered surface in the house – where
Norris found the ring.

Why would she go out without her ring? I think to
myself. The penny finally drops.

'Do you know who lives here?' I ask Norris.

'Well, not really. Sort of,' he says.

'The wife, where is she?'

'Eh? What d'you mean?'

'She's dead isn't she?' I say. 'That's it, isn't it? She's
dead.'

'Yeah, so?' Norris shrugs.

'And the family, where are they?'

'Gone to stay with relatives, I heard.'

This is so low I can't believe it.

'You are a cunt aren't you. You are a fucking cunt.'

'What's wrong with you then?' he says as I snatch the ring out of his hand.

'Come on, we're leaving.'

'Alright then, give us a hand with the stuff, loading it up in the van.'

'We ain't taking the stuff, we're leaving,' I say walking for the door.

'What? What do you mean?'

'Come on we're going. We ain't doing this place.'

'Hey fuck off, we've got some good stuff here . . . fucking not doing it, what are you fucking on about?'

'The bloke's wife's just died. The kiddies just lost their mum, we ain't doing this to them.'

'Oh well boo-fucking-hoo, I'm all fucking gutted for them, but I need the dosh. You don't want any, then fine, fuck off, I'll do it all myself. I don't need you.'

'You are a cunt.'

'Yeah, and sticks and stones will break my bones.'

Now there's an idea.

'You ain't using my van to put the stuff in,' I tell him.

'Oh come on Bex, don't be a cunt, what's up with you?' Norris goes in to one telling me how I'm being stupid, how we've practically done it now, and how, next to something big like their mum dying, they probably won't even notice something little like being burgled, but I ain't buying it.

'Fine, I go back and get my motor and pick the stuff up later.'

'I'm fucking warning you . . .' I say but Norris is easily as big as me and much as I don't like the cunt, I wouldn't like to tangle with him.

'Oh yeah, what you gonna do, call the Old Bill?'

'Cunt,' I say.

*

I leave via the front door and walk round the back to the van. I get in and start the engine, but I can't leave just like that. Norris is still up there routing around while the poor old bird ain't even cold yet. He would've had the fillings out of her teeth if she was in there laying in state.

It ain't right, even by my standards, it ain't right.

I drive round the front and stop outside the house. I climb out, leaving the engine running, pick up a big stone off of the rockery and throw it through the living room window.

A dozen curtains twitch in surrounding windows as I jump back in the van and speed off down the road.

In my pocket is the only thing I took from the house – the wedding ring. I took it to make sure Norris couldn't. I've got no intention of keeping it though. I'll stick it in the post first thing tomorrow.

And while I'm at it, I think I'll stick in a 'sorry' note as well.

24. Sorry

This reminds me of a story I read in the paper a couple or three years back. I can't quite remember all of the details, but I think what happened was something along these lines.

Back in the 1960s Ronnie and Reggie Kray, as you probably know, ruled London, or at least the East End of it. They used to beat people up, take money from them, break mad axemen out of Dartmoor and generally scare the shit out of people.

Naturally, everyone loved them. Particularly the rich and famous.

They were the in-thing around town. Anyone who was anyone had a snap taken of them shaking hands with the boys at their club – pop stars, films stars, celebrities, Barbara Windsor – they were all at it. They had their picture taken by David Bailey and their portrait painted by that old idiot who was big in those days, can't remember his name. Everyone loved them, they were local heroes, icons of the community, everybody admired them.

Anyway, to cut a long story short, the boys horribly murdered a couple of blokes and got sentenced to life in prison, where they commanded enormous affection in the hearts of the nation for some thirty years.

That's the background, this is the story.

A few years ago, this art gallery was turned over and a shit-load of paintings were half-inched. One of these paintings was the original Ronnie and Reggie portrait painted by matey.

Ronnie and Reggie heard about this from their prison cells and let it be known that they weren't too happy about this.

And this is the part I find fascinating, within a couple of days the picture was posted back to them with a note telling the boys how sorry they were for taking it and how it had all just been a big misunderstanding.

This was to two ageing (no offence, please honest) gangsters who had been behind bars for more than thirty years. Now that's what you call commanding respect. Awesome hey?

By the way, just for the record, it wasn't me who took the picture.

25. Sorry II

Here's one I should've said sorry about but never got round to.

I'm an Arsenal fan. Have been since I can remember. As a boy, while the other kids were talking about becoming firemen, train drivers and other such glamorous public sector jobs, I was dreaming about stepping out on to the pitch at Highbury in the famous red and white.

I'm still as nutty about them today as I ever was, even though I don't wear the pyjamas or swap stickers any more. So then, a couple of years ago, when I see one of my all-time Arsenal heroes sat in my local boozer, I couldn't believe my eyes.

I go over, sit down, have a bit of a chat and tell him all about how he was one of my favourites when I was a kid and all the rest of it. It was great, sat there talking to him, it brought back all the old memories – where I was when I saw him score this goal, what it was like the first time I went to Highbury, how old I was when I could remember and recite the entire Arsenal squad going back to the year I was born (and I can still remember a fair few today).

He thought I was really interesting. He even said so.

'You're really interesting you are,' he says.

It was brilliant talking to him and his wife all night like

that. And, at the end of the evening, I walk away with a handshake, an autograph and his old lady's purse.

Just as a souvenir, you understand.

Anyway, it turns out the geezer (who I ain't going to name, by the way, for reasons that'll become obvious) had just bought a big house over in the posh part of town and, thanks to me liberating his good lady wife's purse, I had his address.

I goes over there a couple of days later and have a look round – you know, just out of curiosity – and end up coming away with his doorstep milk bottle caddy and his front door mat. I didn't mean to nick them, I just couldn't help myself from helping myself.

I mean, think about it, that caddy was the one he actually used to bring the milk in with. And even more so, the mat, which now sits proudly outside my front door, has probably actually had that sweet left foot of his wiped across it after a kick-about in the front garden with the kids.

Smart eh!

In a little over three weeks, his garden hoe, wheelbarrow, stone heron and bird table all made their way over to my place so I could pay daily tribute to the man.

I finally decide that garden tools and accessories can only get a man so far, what I really wanted was a proper souvenir, something I could really treasure. So, I get my screwdriver, jump in the van and collect Ollie on the way round.

For a posh house it was remarkably easy to break in to. The garage door was practically hanging off its hinges and the connecting door inside wasn't locked. This is something you don't expect from someone who spent most of his playing career with such a defence-minded team. Stacked up against the fridge in the kitchen is a collection of garden tools he's obviously decided not to leave out any more. I make a mental note to have the hedge trimmer away when we leave.

'Now there's something I wouldn't mind,' I say picking a mug up off the draining board. 'That's his mug, that is. Look at it.'

'It's just a mug,' says Ollie not getting it. Ollie's not really a football fan. He's watched a few England games but doesn't really give a monkey's about any of it. I don't know about you, but I always think there's something a bit ... funny, about blokes who don't like football.

I'm not saying anything against him, don't get me wrong, but, in my experience, blokes who don't like football almost always seem to fall into one of three categories – trainspotters, public school types and poofs. And seeing as Ollie went to the same comprehensive as me, and he ain't got a train set, I can't help but feel a little worried.

'This ain't just a mug, it's *his* mug,' I say, but he still ain't with me.

'Are you having it then?'

'Fucking right, and while I'm at it, I think I'll get a plate and a knife and fork and all, to eat my dinner off.'

'You do that, and I'll have the microwave,' says Ollie. '*His* microwave.'

'Wait,' I say. 'Wait a minute. We can't do the place over.'

'Why not?'

'Why not? Because, because ... it's, you know, *his* place.'

'We're already doing *his* place over, whether you like it or not. What do you think we're doing here? It's just a question of what we drive away with tonight; the TV, video and stereo, or a load of fucking crockery.'

I think about this for a moment and realise Ollie's right. I knew what I was getting in to when I left the house tonight. I must've been kidding myself to think I was going to come all the way over here for just a mug.

'Alright,' I say reluctantly. 'Let just take it nice and easy okay, don't go wrecking the place. The bloke's a hero of mine, alright.'

'Yeah, yeah, yeah,' says Ollie and heads off for the main bedroom. I get out a couple of bin liners and fill them up with cups, plates, cutlery, signed photographs, videos and everything.

In all my years as a burglar, I don't think I've ever done over a house so completely before in my life. We took fucking everything; lampshades, clothes, photographs, everything. We even took the toothpaste and soap out of his bathroom.

I say we, I do of course mean me. Ollie busied himself getting the usual stuff while I spent almost a full hour scouring the house for more and more personal souvenirs. And not just for me either. Plenty of my mates are Arsenal fans as well and were only too happy to stump up the cash to buy the very glasses he watches the telly with.

As for me, I found my souvenir. Sod the pot plants, the mugs, the Deep Heat and everything else we had away. I got his FA Cup Winners' medal.

Not a copy, not a fake, but the *very* medal that was presented to him at Wembley for his part in Arsenal's trouncing of Manchester United in the 1979 Cup Final.

And now I've got it.

It's my most treasured possession.

26. Clever plans: number 5

Here's an old ploy that's so well known it was once used as a plot on an episode of *Terry and June*. It's fairly simple, but it does involve a few blokes and a fair bit of front.

From what I can remember, it goes something like this –

Terry comes home from work all in a fluster as usual, after another long hard day of spilling his coffee down Sir Cedric's secretary's tits and having his trousers fall down at awkward moments. June, as usual, says – 'Never mind dear, let's have a nice cup of tea' – and they both get on with the business of being a nice, non-sexual, suburban couple.

A bit later, Terry hears a noise outside and goes out to investigate only to end up hilariously bumping in to a prowler and shitting his pants. June spends the rest of the night comforting Terry, while he goes in to his full range of 'man scared of own shadow' routine. The next day a CID and uniform come round to patronise the pair of them for a bit. CID tells them that the prowler Terry chased away has been spotted on several nights running in the area, and how a couple of houses have already been turned over in the next street.

Terry again shits his pants.

The CID tells them not to chicken curry, he's got the perfect solution, a Neighbourhood Watch scheme. Terry's all for it and rushes round and badgers all his neighbours in to attending the meeting, set up by DS Plod, at the local scout hut. June lays on teas, coffees and cakes while Terry spends the evening arguing with one of his cardigan-wearing neighbours over who's going to be in charge of the gavel; loses and sulks.

When DS Plod fails to turn up to address the assembled neighbourhood, everyone gets restless, realises *Coronation Street*'s on and heads off home, only to discover that while they've been at the Neighbourhood Watch meeting, their houses have been robbed. DS Plod and the uniform turn out, in fact, not to be policemen, but the burglars themselves, and Terry the unwitting fool tricked by their cunning stunt.

June says 'Never mind dear, let's have a nice cup of tea,' only to discover they can't because the fucking kettle's been nicked.

Now this might seem like a bit of a far-fetched plot, unlikely to work outside of *Terry and June* and *Bless This House*, but that's where you're wrong. This very same ploy was used a year or two ago to do over ten houses in one street in one night in a leafy suburb of south London. Which just goes to prove, there really are buffoons like Terry Metcalfe out there. Quite comforting that, isn't it.

Another ploy along similar lines is the subject of one of these urban myths that blokes in the pub love so much.

Geezer comes out in the morning to find that his car has been nicked. Bit pissed off, he reports it to the police and goes to work on the bus. The next day he comes out and finds that his car has been returned, along with a full tank of petrol and a sorry note. The note says something like sorry for taking your car, but it was an emergency, my wife went in to labour, had to get her to hospital, but my car was in the shop, please accept my apologies and these tickets to go and see *Blankety Blank* being recorded at the BBC.

The geezer is touched, feels genuinely heart-warmed and tells the police he's got his car back and doesn't want them to take any further action over this matter. That night, he takes his wife down to London for the night and when he comes home, you've guessed it, he's been completely cleaned out.

Happened to a mate of a mate of mine. Or it might have been a mate of a mate's dad. I don't know, can't remember, someone down the pub told us.

While we're on the subject of telly, Roland came up with a pretty good plan recently, though of course, Roland being Roland, he fucked it all up by the end.

It all had to do with Channel Five, that new telly channel that came out in 1997, I think it was. If you remember, when it was first launched, practically everyone in the country had to have their videos retuned for some unknown reason. Well, this gave Roland the idea of posing as a Channel Five retuner after some little bloke came round and retuned his own video.

So, what he did was he got himself a clipboard, a few different coloured biros, a tool bag, and went from door to door asking whether or not they'd had their videos done. When he found someone who hadn't, he would go in, fuck about with their video and telly for a bit, Umm and Arh, and tell the poor unsuspecting bastard that they had the old-style machine and that he would have to take it, and the telly, back to the shop for a proper retuning. The houseowner would ask what about *EastEnders* tonight and Roland would tell them not to worry, he'd be back with a replacement 32in wide-screen surround-sound TV and video system within the hour, and sorry for the inconvenience.

Of course, Roland never did return with either the 32in or their old telly and video, but then, being a burglar, I don't suppose anyone except the houseowner expected him to.

Roland was doing alright and got away with this same trick more than ten times before finally being caught after trying it on with a proper Channel Five retuner and his already retuned TV and video.

No matter how good the plan, Roland was never going to get away with it. But then, Roland being Roland, I don't suppose anyone except Roland expected him to.

27. In the line of duty

Animal looks awful.

Both eyes are purple, his lip is split, his nose ain't nose-shaped any more and the rest of his face is ... well ... all over the place. It's painful on my eyes just looking at the poor bastard, and all of it was a good five days old.

'Does it hurt?' Ollie asks for reasons best known to himself.

'Have a guess,' Animal winces and lifts the pint to the side of his mouth and pours most of it down his chin. People who don't know Animal would put this down to his injuries, but me and Ollie have seen him eat and drink before when there was nothing wrong with him and so know better.

'What did the doctor say?' I ask.

'He said I'd been beaten up,' Animal tells us.

'Really? Must've come as a bit of a shock,' I say with a half-hearted laugh.

'Yeah. I was thinking it was tonsillitis, stupid cunt!' he says with a roll of the eyes and spills some more lager down his chin.

'You want to fucking do the cunt, I tell ya,' Ollie tells him. 'I fucking would.' Animal simply looks at Ollie and spills what's left of his pint down his shirt and on to the table.

I knew exactly what he meant, it wasn't even worth answering. Ollie's a bit of a hothead, always has been. He's sitting here, looking at Animal and working himself up in to one, not taking in to consideration that Animal wasn't about to fucking do any cunt, because the cunt had already fucking done Animal, leaving him unable to fucking do or do fucking to anything or anyone.

Animal looks at us and then his pint, all pathetic like.

'Bex, will you do us a favour, go up to the bar and get us a pint will ya?'

'Fuck off,' I say looking at the queue at the bar. 'Get it your-fucking-self, there's nothing wrong with your legs.'

'I feel a bit dizzy though.'

'That's 'cause you've had four pints and two chasers already, most of which I might add, me and Ollie bought, so there, you've had your full quota of sympathy, don't go taking the piss out of us. Go on go yourself.'

'Ollie, do us a favour?'

'Bollocks,' says Ollie.

Animal looks sorry for himself a bit longer then gets up, pushes his way past us and heads off to the bar.

'Oi Animal,' I shout after him, 'Get me and Ollie one while you're up there,' then laugh a bit with Ollie.

Animal had got what all burglars fear the most; a fucking good hiding from the householder who had caught him in the act.

He'd been working this house over in Mallard Street, behind the High Street, when he got collared. A mate of ours, Devlin, put him on to it. Devlin works on the door at *Glitzy's* and we all got to know him through Ollie when he worked there. Anyway, Devlin tells Animal about this wedding party that's booked the club for the night and gives him the geezer's address.

Animal's thinking, nice easy score, the couple will be away all night in a hotel somewhere, and there'll be a shit load of wedding presents up for grabs back at his place. He does the maths in his head and decides the best time to do it is in the early morning. So him and his mate Snowy (who I don't know) go to work around three.

The only problem is that Devlin's information is a little inaccurate. It wasn't a wedding party that had booked the club, it was a Stag Party, a dozen of which had stumbled and crashed back at the house in Mallard Street at around two in the morning and were rudely awoken by the sounds of Animal dropping in through the kitchen window.

Animal comes back balancing three pints on a tray on his plaster cast and sets them down on the table.

'So, when you in court?' I ask.

'For what?' he asks back.

'Your case, burglary, when you up?' Animal has a think.

'Later this month, 21st I think.'

'What you reckon you'll get?'

'Hard to say. Seeing as I didn't get a chance to nick anything, it's only breaking and entering, and what with mitigating circumstances and all, the beak might think to go light on me.'

'Seen Charlie yet?'

'Yeah, saw him yesterday. Says it doesn't look good. But that don't mean anything in Charlie-speak. Knowing him, he'll say it'll be something like death by hanging argued down to a caution.' Sip, spill, wipe. 'Nah, I'll probably only get another lot of community service. That sort of thing.'

'And what about old matey's case, when's he up?'

'The next month, ABH. Cunt. Hope him and all his mates go down.'

'You know, you're lucky we're not in America. In America they can beat you up and fucking do whatever they fucking-well like and you can't do a thing about it. Got no come-back at all in America.'

'They can shoot you if they like,' Ollie says. 'And it's all legal. Kill you, bang you're dead, even if you're trying to surrender at the time and it's totally allowed.'

'Yeah,' I agree. 'That's why all the burglars out in America have to carry guns. It ain't safe to go out breaking in to places over there without people killing you and getting away with it.'

'They wouldn't get away with it though would they,' Animal says. 'They'd get done for manslaughter or something wouldn't they?'

'No,' I tell him. 'If you're breaking in to a Yank's house, they can kill you and you can't do nothing about it.'

'Nah, I can't believe that,' Animal says not believing it.

'Straight up,' Ollie tells him. 'It was on the telly, remember it Bex? *Panorama* or one of them. If you're in their house, they can shoot you and kill you and call it self defence.'

'That's not right,' Animal goes. 'That shouldn't be allowed.'

'Tell me about it,' I say.

I think it's outrageous personally. I mean, we've all been there. Bloke comes home, gets annoyed that you're turning him over and has a go. Fair enough, I can appreciate that, I can see how a bloke can lose it like that. But in this country, the bloke'll only start if he's tasty enough, and even then, he won't do you in because he knows if he does and he does you bad, he'll go to prison. All you've got to do then in that situation is get away. The sensible ones let you, the idiots try and stop you.

Everyone knows where they stand. That's how it should be.

But can you imagine if we lived in a country where, if you went and broke in to someone's house, any old fucking streak of piss could not only blow you away, but suffer absolutely no come-back for it whatsoever.

Where's the deterrent to not pull the trigger?

What's to stop the geezer taking the law in to his own hands and teaching you a lesson you'll never remember?

And while we're at it, what's to stop someone inviting you round for tea, shooting you dead and then telling everyone that you broke in and came at them with a knife?

Fuck living there!

'If I lived there, I'd have a gun,' Ollie says.

'Yeah I'm sure,' I say back. 'And I'm sure it wouldn't be long either before you got to sit down in a chair with a plug on it.'

'You know, talking of Americans,' Animal says, 'you reminded me of this story Snowy told us once about Americans. See Snowy, he used to live round one of them American Air Force Bases, not a nuclear one or nothing, well I don't think so. Anyway that's not important to the story.' Animal takes a big deep slurp, wipes his chin and reaches for my fags. I let him take one because I'm nice like that.

'What happened was, a couple of mates of his used to go up to the air force base and have a drink with the Yanks in the bar, cheap booze it was, all subsidised by the air force. One day though, they got a bit pissed up and started giving it the large and all that, and so these Yank MPs took them outside and gave them a good working over with their truncheons. Really fucking laid in to them they did.'

'Cunts,' says Ollie getting caught up in the story.

'Yeah really,' Animal agrees. It makes me laugh it does.

Neither of these two know the blokes in the story but automatically they're taking their side just because they're a couple of Brits. For all they know, they could've been threatening to glass a load of babies and the only way to stop them was to overpower them with the truncheons. But don't let that get in the way of a good story.

'So what they did was, they got a couple of their mates to go up to the base and get all matey with the MPs, buy them a couple of drinks, chat about sport and that's what they did. After couple of visits by Snowy's mates' mates, one of them says to these Yanks that they're both part of this amateur baseball team and that they're looking for another team to have a game with. The Yanks bite like a good'un and tell them that they'll get a team together out of the MPs and take them on. Snowy's mates' mates give them the name and address of this pub and tell them to come along Sunday lunch-time.

'Sunday lunch-time comes round and a dozen or so Yanks all turn up in shorts and Hawaiian shirts and all that, with their wives and kids and picnic baskets, hoping to make a day of it, right. What they don't know is, waiting for them inside this boozer, are twelve of the fucking hardest and nastiest animals you've ever seen in your whole life. All of them have got motorbike chains and knuckle dusters and, of course, baseball bats.

'Well they absolutely beat the fucking shit out of these poor unsuspecting bastards. The first Yank through the door, they just fucking fell on him like he didn't know what. Fucking half-killed them they did.'

'What about the wives and kids, didn't they do anything to stop them, call the police or nothing?' I ask.

'Nah, they couldn't could they. Blokes beat them up as well.'

'What, the wives and kids?' Ollie asks.

'Yeah,' laughs Animal. 'They didn't care, done the lot of them they did. After that, the locals never got any more trouble when they went up to the air force base for a drink.'

'Didn't they get done?' Ollie asks.

'I don't know, that's all the story I heard.'

'Well what about the wives and kids?' Ollie asks again.

'What about them?'

'What happened to them?'

'I don't know, they all went back to America when the base shut down I suppose. I don't know.' Animal shrugs his shoulders but I've seen Ollie like this before and can tell by his expression that another stupid question is on the way.

'What, they shut the base down?' Ollie asks.

'Yeah, but not because of that,' Animal says. 'They closed it because the fucking Cold War ended didn't it, not because a load of fucking carrot crunchers smashed their heads in at a picnic.'

'Yeah, but the General of the base, he must've said something?'

'Well maybe he did, but he didn't tell me about it did he.'

'How comes the police didn't go after them?'

'I don't know, Ollie. Maybe they didn't call the police, maybe they just called it quits.'

'Yeah, but the General, he's not going to just call it quits is he. A load of his blokes get a fucking good hiding from the locals and he just calls it quits because a couple of his blokes was a bit rough on one of them?'

'Well, I don't know. I suppose not, but I just don't know.'

'Why didn't they just shoot them then? The Americans I mean.'

'I don't know,' Animal tells Ollie. 'Maybe they didn't have their guns with them. I don't know.'

'I thought they had to carry their guns with them all the time.'

'Did you? Well, I don't know,' Animal insists. 'I don't fucking know.'

'Oh,' says Ollie looking a little disappointed. 'Sounds like a load of bollocks to me.'

'Well it probably is then isn't it,' Animal finally says.

He looks at me and I smile. There's nothing Ollie loves more than ruining a good story with a load of stupid fucking questions that just ain't important. Personally, I find it quite funny. But only because for once they weren't aimed at me. He does it with jokes as well.

I change the subject before Ollie asks Animal why Russia lost the Cold War.

'Is it just the one geezer who's getting done for ABH on you then?'

'What? Yeah, just the one. The groom. The rest of them scarpered before the Old Bill turned up and he never gave them any names.'

'They should throw the fucking book at him,' I say.

'Yeah, the cunt. I was on the floor screaming at them to stop but they just kept on fucking laying in to me.' Animal rubs the side of his face with his plaster cast, even the memory hurting.

'That's so out of order,' I say. 'Restrain a bloke yeah, but no need to fuck him up.'

'He's apparently acting all outraged,' Animal tells us. 'He was in the local paper saying it was a disgrace he should have to go to court, and fucking half his fucking street all wrote in supporting him, with letters about how they'd like to birch me. Cunts.'

'He's broken the law, simple as that,' I say. 'He wants to live by the law then he should be prepared to die by the law as well.'

'He says in the paper "I'm not a criminal", which is bollocks, because if he's convicted of ABH on me, then he is a fucking criminal. And that's a fact. Which makes him a liar as well.'

'Not a criminal,' Ollie says. 'Like that's some sort of bad thing!'

'You know, just because you were going in to nick his stuff that's no excuse,' I say. 'If I went off to the bogs now and came back and found my fags gone, would that then give me the right to go and smash old Albert's head in over there if I saw them on the table in front of him? Would it? Don't think so.'

'And I don't suppose you'd get too many people writing in to the papers going on about how you was a fucking hero either,' Animal says.

'Yeah, cunt,' I agree. 'It's only a bit of business. Why get carried away.'

'Yeah, I mean, why take it so personally,' Ollie agrees this time. 'The amount of times we've been stitched up taking that fucking van in to the garage for its MOT and that. What would everyone think if we beat the cunts up every time they give us the bill?'

'I think that's a bit different Ollie,' I say.

'No it's not.'

'Well it is,' Animal says. 'It's a bit different.'

'Ow, well whatever,' Ollie says and slumps back in his chair in a boo, after having his point shot down in flames.

'So what you reckon? Reckon he'll go down?' I say.

'No, doubt it. You know what these old beaks are like, probably try and give him a fucking medal instead.'

'Nah, don't you worry, he'll get done. He'll get a taste of his own fucking medicine, you watch.'

'I hope so, I fucking hope so. It ain't right if he gets away with it,' Animal says and takes a big spill of his pint. 'Mind you, it'll help us in a way if he don't go down.'

'How's that?' I ask.

'Well, then me and me brothers won't have to hang around for so long waiting for him to get out.'

28. Downright dishonest

You want to know what the perfect crime is?

Well I'll tell you, there isn't one. The perfect crime is like the perfect woman – they don't exist outside the pages of airport novels or late night fantasies. You can get close with both, but never spot on.

You want to know then what the closest thing to a perfect crime is?

Nicking stuff that can't be reported as nicked. In other words, nicking nicked stuff. This is a lot more common than you might think; the only reason you probably haven't heard about it before is for precisely the reason it goes on – i.e., it can't be reported.

There was a story in the paper, you might have read, last year, where a gang of robbers came running out of a bank, only then to be held up by another gang of robbers who shot the first robbers, grabbed the money and ran. Good idea – robbing four blokes on a pavement is easier than robbing a heavily protected bank. Animals (not my mate Animal, but animals) are always doing it too. I think I've already mentioned how hyenas and lions are always ripping each other off. It's the first law of nature; do the least for the most return.

Well, my nature anyway.

Not that I've ever, for an instant, thought I was up for pulling off the perfect crime. Perfect crimes are again like perfect women, a bit out of my league, although don't tell Mel I said that. No, my level is probably around about the stealing from my mates sort of mark.

I know I said I don't do that sort of thing, but fuck, what can I say, I'm a liar as well as a thief – lock me up and throw away the key.

And besides, it's not as if it hasn't happened to me before. Only six months ago me and Ollie did a job, pulled in to the pub on the way home for a couple of beers and had all the booty nicked out of the back of the van. That's why I can be so philosophical about what I do, because I've had it done to me. I know what it's like, but you don't hear me ranting and raving, calling for the lynch mob do you? That's because I ain't a hypocrite.

I might be a liar and I might be a thief, but one thing I ain't, and that's a hypocrite.

Another time we was ripped off was by this friend of Ollie's – Clive his name was, goes to the same gym as Ollie – when he bought a telly and video off us a few months back. Only trouble was, he didn't have the cash with him when we give him the goods, but being one of his mates, Ollie lets him have the stuff on account.

A week goes by, and then a fortnight, and still he don't come up with the cash; it was only £150, not exactly a down payment on a mortgage. Every time we phone him it's a different excuse – I lost my wallet, I don't get paid for another week, all my money's in a ninety day account. I was getting right fucked off with this, I don't mind telling you. I was all up for having a go, but Ollie didn't want to say nothing because it was 'his mate'. Some mate.

What finally did it was seeing him out on the piss at the flashest club in town, while me and Ollie could hardly scrape together enough coppers for a couple of pints and a game of darts at the Pheasant and Goose.

Although even then, Ollie still didn't want to have a stand-up fight with him, because he was his mate. So what we did instead was we took him out for the evening a week or three later, once we had a bit of bunce. We bought him a few pints, had a couple of games of pool and took him for a dance up *Glitzy's*, where halfway through the night, we got Devlin to chuck him down the stairs and give him a kicking on the pavement outside.

He told Clive it was for passing dodgy tenners over the bar, but by the way we stood back and watched as Devlin gave him a good going over, Clive must've known it was for something else. Still, what could he say, after all, Ollie's a mate.

Life's funny like that.

Ollie slows the van down and clicks off the lights as we pull up to the garages.

'Which number is it again?' I ask, straining my eyes in the dark. There are no street lights back here and both blocks of flats are a good fifty yards away. Ollie stops the van and turns off the engine.

'Sixteen,' he says. 'Sixteen or seventeen.'

'Which one is it?'

'Sixteen,' he tells me. ' . . . or seventeen.'

We get out of the van and close the doors quietly. Ollie unlocks the side door and pushes the spare tyre to the back to make room for the gear.

'Alright, come on,' I tell him.

We tip-toe over to the garages as quietly as possible and keep to the shadows. The place might've been pitch dark anyway and yards from the nearest window, but people have a way of being everywhere – and this was a notoriously dodgy area. There was a lot of crime that went on around here, and there was about to be some more.

Makes me glad I don't live on this estate.

We get to garage number sixteen and try and peer inside, but all we can see is more darkness. Ollie shines the torch through the crack in the doors but it doesn't help.

'You sure this is the one?' I ask.

'No.'

'Yeah, but you're pretty sure aren't you?'

'I don't know, could be.'

'This was your fucking idea,' I say.

'It's the one,' he tells us.

'You sure?' I ask again.

'No.'

'Oh fuck it,' I say and lever off the padlock with my crowbar. The doors are wooden and the hinges squeaky and I make too much noise for my own liking, but once we're in, it's just a case of loading up and fucking off. The lock falls to the floor and Ollie pulls back the door to reveal a red Cortina, which ain't what we're looking for.

'It's seventeen,' he says.

'You cunt,' I say. Guess what, it wasn't seventeen either. It wasn't even eighteen. No, it finally turned out to be nineteen, the garage we were looking for. Number nineteen.

This was Parky's uncle's garage. Parky's uncle didn't have a car and so Parky used it to store stuff he couldn't get rid of right away. Me and Ollie have a similar sort of place. We call it the lock-up, but really it's a shed on his grandad's allotment.

Parky had some smashing stuff – videos, tellies, stereos – at least three jobs' worth. This was a good score. Parky, unfortunately, weren't around to enjoy it. He was nicked three days ago, after his last job, and got remand instead of bail. It was quite funny actually, from what I heard. He was in this house, turning it over, when he looks over his shoulder and sees this geezer standing behind him, filming him with a video camera. The bloke's been done over about four times already in the last two months and, from what I can gather, was doing what some other geezer on the telly did, by confronting his burglar in the course of the break-in and catching him on camera.

Of course, Parky just smacks him in the mouth and takes the video camera as well, but then, that's just Parky.

The bloke picks Parky out of an ID parade two days later, and the magistrate sends him down pending trial. Poor bastard.

Anyway, Ollie figured he wouldn't be needing his stash where he was going, so we should have it. Besides, the Old Bill would only find it after a little while, and that would tie Parky in to a few more jobs and lengthen his final sentence. So in a way, nicking his gear was doing him a favour really.

The stuff is stacked in a big pile at the back of the garage, under an old mildewed duvet cover. Ollie whips the cover off and we take a look at what Parky's got. A mini-stereo system, three hairdryers, a tropical fish tank pump, two black and white tellies, a vacuum cleaner, a junior tricycle – hang on a minute!

'Show me that vacuum cleaner,' I tell Ollie. He picks it out and shines it under my torch. 'That fucking cunt!' I say.

'What?' Ollie asks.

'This is our fucking vacuum cleaner.'

'Ours?'

'Yes ours. You remember, we nicked it from that bungalow in Haskin Gardens. Someone had it away out of the back of the van with all that other gear while we were in the Lion.'

'You sure?'

'Fucking right I'm sure. Look at the scratch down the side where you dropped the crowbar on it. It's the same one.'

'You reckon Parky nicked it?'

'Dhur, I don't know, what do you reckon? Of course he fucking nicked it, and the telly, and the exercise bike, and all the other stuff we had. What a cunt! What a cunt! Imagine doing that to one of your mates.' Ollie looks at me a little awkwardly.

'Well, we are, sort of.'

'He stole off us first,' I tell him.

'Yeah, but we didn't know that did we?'

'And your point here is?'

'Nothing.'

Yeah, as usual.

'Don't say anything though, about the hoover, when you see him next,' Ollie says. 'Otherwise he'll know it was us who cleaned him out.'

'Don't worry, I won't,' I tell him, although I do want him to know that I know it was him who nicked off me, and me who nicked off him. That way, we both know where we stand and don't need to say anything more on the subject.

Life's funny like that.

We carry the stuff to the van and load it all in the back. Ollie has a quick look through the other three garages we opened up in the course of finding Parky's, just in case there's anything worth nicking, and comes back with a car battery charger and a tool kit.

We jump in, Ollie starts her up and we drive off back to our lock-up. Ollie reaches over to stick in a tape while I spark up. 'The cunts!' he says.

'What? What is it?'

'Someone's had the stereo away.'

'What?' I look, but there's only a couple of wires hanging from where the BlauPunkt used to be. 'Oh those little bastards. If I ever get my fucking hands on them, I'll ... [etc].'

Okay, okay. So I'm a liar, a thief and a hypocrite.

Call the police why don't you!

29. Well, it weren't me

Mel's not around. I've called at her place three times already this week, but she hasn't been home at all. Her flatmate says she hasn't seen her all week, which could be true or it could be otherwise, you just can't tell with her. Her track record in telling me the truth ain't something that would stand up in court if it came to it. Birds are like that when they get together.

Chances are, she's gone back to her mum and dad's. She always goes running back there whenever we have a row, to cry on their shoulders, tell them what a bastard I am and eat cake. Only, we haven't had a row. At least, I don't think we have. Again, you just can't tell. Sometimes we have rows without me even realising it. The first thing I know about it is when she slams the door behind her, stomps off upstairs or starts to cry.

God, I really don't fancy going round there; they always take her side and I'm the one that gets to be made out to be the villain. But I really want a shag.

So I have a wash, put on a shirt and jump in the van.

Tony answers the door. Mel and her old lady keep out of sight, but I know they're in the back stuffing chocolate pie down each other's throats.

'Why, you've got one hell of a nerve showing your face around here.'

'Can I speak to Mel?' I say.

'Clear off,' he says stepping out of the porch towards me. 'Keep your nasty little arse away from my family, otherwise I'll kill you.'

'Hang on a minute, hang on,' I say as I back away from him. 'What the fuck's . . . I mean, what the hell's brought all this on? I haven't done anything.' I don't think.

'I mean it,' he says still coming for me. 'I'll break every bone in your body you little bastard.' I get in the van and back out of his front gate and close it behind me. Tony continues to shout more abuse at me from the safety of his front garden, but he doesn't come out after me. 'Bastard this and bastard that, I'll do you, you should be hanged,' and that sort of thing. All the neighbours start twitching the curtains to try and get a clearer view.

'Just tell me what I'm supposed to have done for fuck's sake, you stupid old duffer.' At this, Tony rushes back inside the house and comes back out with a cricket bat. I think about going for the crowbar in my van, but decide fucking her dad up won't help my chances of patching things up with Mel.

So I leave it. I jump in the van, give Tony the wanker sign, and beat a tactical retreat.

Fuck knows what I've done, but whatever it is, it's bad.

I go to the pub for a couple of hours and bump in to a few of the boys, who give me some great advice, all of which I chose to ignore. I drive round to Ollie's, but he's not in, I drive round a bit more and finally end up back at Mel's flat.

I know she's not in, but maybe her flatmate, River Dog,

or whatever she calls herself, can shed some light on what I've done. I ring the bell and she comes to the door.

River Dog, or whatever she calls herself, thinks she's some sort of hippy chick. She wears beads in her hair, walks around in skirts tied at the waist and says 'man', 'groovy' and 'babe' a lot. She also calls herself a stupid name, like River Dog, Mountain Goat or something like that, which I can never remember. Although, even if I could, I think I'd still pretend I couldn't.

'She's still not here,' River Dog says.

'Yeah, I know. I came to see you.'

'Me? What do you want to see me for?'

River Dog's standing there in the doorway wearing a silky red dressing gown which is flapping very slightly in the breeze. I'm immediately distracted.

'I just want to talk to someone,' I say staring at her legs.

'I'm busy,' she says going to close the door.

'Please,' I stop her, although I still don't lift my eyes from her legs. 'Look, I'm desperate. I know you don't like me but please, come on, just give me five minutes. Mel won't speak to me and I just want to know what it is I've done. I just want to make it up to her.' Oohh, I saw a bit of *fur* then!

'Alright,' she says, standing aside. 'Just for five minutes.'

I go on through to the living room and sit on the sofa. River Dog asks me if I want a cup of tea and I say yes. She comes back a couple of minutes later with a cup of that weak perfumey tea she and Mel like. I don't know whether to drink it or splash it all over – as Henry Cooper used to say.

She sits, cross-legged, on the floor opposite me next to the fire and carries on with her half-eaten bowl of Cocopops. Her slippery silk gown parts at the waist and for the briefest of moments while she readjusts it, I see her dark furry beaver growling at me. I sip my tea silently while she casually pulls the gown back over her knees and thighs.

'What do you want to know?' she asks as if nothing has happened.

What I really want to know is can I fuck you without my girlfriend finding out, I think to myself.

'I want to know why Mel isn't talking to me and why her old man came at me with a cricket bat.'

'A cricket bat,' she sniggers. 'Maybe she just finally woke up to the fact that you're a no good bastard. Maybe she just decided she doesn't need the hassle or the bother any more.'

'It's not that, it's something specific. Something's upset her and I just want to know what.' I sip my tea and keep my eyes peeled, but try not to make it too obvious.

'Have you any idea how much she likes you? And have you any idea how much you hurt her? I mean, how would you like it if ... [blah blah blah] ...' Her dressing gown was slipping open again and this time she didn't realise.

As she's talking, the cord around the middle is loosening up, until suddenly – there it was – one of her nipples popping out to give me a little wink. I look down between her legs and see hair. I sip my tea and nod and agree, but to be honest, I can't hear a word she's saying. My mind's got much better things to concentrate on than what's up with Mel. I haven't had sex in two weeks, and I haven't had sex with someone new in more than five months.

I'm stiff as a board and having trouble hiding it.

' ... better off without you,' I hear her say, but can't tell you what came before that.

'Yeah, yeah, you're right,' I say, transfixed by her bush. She must know. She has to know. And if she does, then she must be doing it on purpose. And if she's doing it on purpose ...?

I decide to take this nice and easy.

'Shall I skin up then?' I say. 'I've got some gear on me.'

'No,' she says. 'I've got to go out in a little while. Actually, look, you better go, I've got to get ready.'

'Where are you going?' is all I can think to say.

'To meet a friend.'

'Well why don't you blow them out, give them a call. We can stay here and get stoned instead.'

'No, I've got to go,' she says rising to her feet and giving me a full second of free-hanging knocker.

'You don't have to go,' I say, moving towards the edge of the sofa. She swishes back her long brown hair and ties it in a knot at the back of her head. Isn't that supposed to mean she wants to fuck me or something?

I have to rearrange my jeans before I can stand.

'Come on,' I say. 'Come on, don't go. Let's stay here and talk.' She stops and looks at me, which I see as my cue to move forward and stick my hand inside her gown, but she's got other ideas.

'What are you doing?' she says drawing away quickly, almost knocking over the bookcase. She pulls her dressing gown tight around herself and backs away from me further. 'What do you think you're doing?'

'I thought that you . . .'

'Look, I think you ought to go,' she tells me with a scowl. Something tells me I've badly misread the signals.

I hesitate for a moment trying to think of something I can say that'll make all this go away but all I can think of is – 'You won't tell Mel about this will you?'

'Get out Bex. Now!'

I slam the front door behind me as I leave and look back to see Moon Wolf – that's it, that's what she calls herself – giving me the evil from the window.

What a day!

You know, I can't help thinking I've made things worse.

I drive round to see Ollie, but he still ain't there. I go back down the pub and see a whole lot of new boys who all tell me that they would've shagged her and I must be gay for blowing a chance like that. Only Norris pitches in on my side and says that the same thing happened to him once. Once?

I go home and recreate the event in my mind over a wank.

Ollie phones me later and asks where I've been all day, so I tell him. He says he'll come over and we'll go out for a beer. But to be honest, I've had enough crap advice for one day, so I tell him not to bother, reach for the scotch and stick on the box.

You know, now that I come to think of it, Wolf Breath is always mooning about in her dressing gown. She sits around the place half naked in front of everyone, like she's got no modesty. Bare-foot, nature-communing, josh-stick smoking, free spirit, who 'lives beyond the constraints of society' (her words) in every way except for her fortnightly UB40 cheque, housing allowance, disability benefit and Coco-pops.

Fucking hippy chicks hey!

Still . . .

The banging on the front door wakes me up and causes me to knock the ashtray off the arm of the chair.

'I know you're in there,' someone is shouting through my letter box.

Fuck this, I think, zip up my flies, and go for the back door. I'm just about to leave, when it occurs to me that I don't even know who I'm running from. I close the back door, lock it, and edge my way up to the front window and peer out through a gap in the curtains.

It's Philip, Mel's brother – fuck, they're all at it today. I open the door, safe in the knowledge that I could have the bastard any day.

'What's all this then?' I shout at him and he immediately backs off down the path. I thought so.

'You bastard,' he says suddenly unsure of himself. It's obvious he's come round to give me a kicking, but Philip hasn't been involved in a kicking since he was at school, and even then, he was usually on the wrong end of it. One look from me and he's choked it.

'You've gone too far this time, Bex. If I wasn't such a . . .'

'Wanker?'

'No. Such a restrained bloke I'd come over there and . . .'

'Oh shut up Philip and come in and have a drink,' I say lighting up a cigarette. 'Then perhaps you can tell me what I'm suppose to have done.' Philip looks at me cautiously.

'I'm not going to do anything to you Phil, I just want to know what it is I'm suppose to have done. Come on, don't be like everyone else and automatically jump to the wrong conclusion. Don't you want to hear what I've got to say?'

'Alright, but just don't start anything.'

'Philip, you're the one that came to start something. Personally, I can't be arsed with all this nonsense today. Come on.' Philip follows me in and I half-think about punching him in the back of the head while I've got the chance, but I don't. My need to get to the bottom of all this hysteria is greater than my need to lump one on old wank streak here. Maybe later?

'So,' I say as I pour him a scotch in to one of my Arsenal mugs, 'tell me what everyone is upset about.'

'You're not fooling anyone Bex, everyone knows it was you.'

'I'm not fooling anyone about what?'

'You think we're all stupid or something? How did you think we wouldn't think it was you?' he says taking a sip.

'What was me?'

'Will you cut the crap for just once in your life and do the decent thing?' That's it, I'm through playing guessing games. I raise the bottle, as if to club him with it and bark as loud as I can at him.

'Philip. If you don't tell me what I'm supposed to have done, I will smash this over your nut!' Philip shits himself with fear and pointlessly lifts his arms up to defend himself, knocking my mug over on to the floor and snapping off the handle. 'Now Philip, now! I'm losing patience.'

'You burgled mum and dad's house,' he splutters.

'I what?'

'You burgled mum and dad's.' Philip had that annoying habit of referring to his mum and dad as just plain mum and dad to people other than his immediate family.

It suddenly all made sense though, all the shit I'd been getting off everyone today.

'So that's what it's all about,' I say. 'Your old folks have been turned over and you all think it's me.'

'It was you,' Philip says.

'Oh don't be daft. Why would I want to do that?'

'Because that's the sort of thing you'd do.' I stoop down, pick up my broken mug and offer it to Philip, who flinches at first, like a dog who's been shown the stick too much, before accepting it. I pour him a scotch and set the bottle down behind me.

'Thanks! Stealing from my girlfriend's parents? Thank you very much. Fuck, you've all got me down as some sort of cunt haven't you.'

'We all know it was you Bex.'

'Do you. All certain are you? Know that for a fact eh?

Love to have you on my jury.' I take a sip and think for a moment. Philip starts to tell me about how much it upset his mum, and how she cried for three days, and how his old man wanted to kill me and blah blah blah etc.

'It wasn't me,' I keep saying but he's having none of it. 'Alright then, when did this happen?' I ask him.

'Oh Bex, just don't even bother . . .'

'No, when Philip, when?' Philip looks at me a while and shakes his head. He puts his drink down and heads for the door.

'You know when it happened, and I'm not going to play this game. You're a wanker Bex, a fucking wanker.' And with that he leaves.

Has ever a man been so wronged?

I try phoning Mel a couple of times, in a variety of different voices but can't get past her old man. According to Philip, Mel's practically spent all week around there comforting her mum, who's been milking it for all it's worth. Though from the little Phil told me, I gather it was a bit worse than a mere burglary. Someone messed up the house really bad; clothes ripped, the taps upstairs left on, the word 'SHIT' spelt out on the living room carpet in Domestos and someone had had a piss in the fridge.

Didn't exactly sound like the work of a professional.

I put the word out that there's a good drink in it for whoever gets the little bastards who done that to Joan and Tony's. I know a lot of blokes in this town, someone in every boozer. If the culprits were local, I'd hear about it.

That sort of damage is only ever done by kids or wankers, and neither are very good at keeping their mouths shut. It wouldn't take much, you know how fast rumours and gossip spread around a small town.

I'd hear. Sooner of later, I'd hear.

*

Chris squealed and curled up in to a ball as Ollie gave him another boot in the ribs.

'Sorry, sorry, I didn't ... ooouhff.' That one was from me.

'You little bastard,' I shout at him. 'You dirty little bastard.'

'Please wait,' he shouts back as Ollie rolls him over to stamp on his bollocks. 'No, nooiiiiii!!!!'

People crowd by the windows to watch us give little Chris his kicking, and some even spill out of the pub on to the pavement, but no one tries to stop us, not even his mates.

'Please Bex, please. I didn't know, I didn't know. Please I'm sorry, I'm sorry.' Ollie grabs him and picks him up by the hair.

'You're a little shit,' he says. 'What are you?'

'I'm a little shit.' Ollie drags him round and gets him to repeat it over and over again in front of his mates. 'I'm a little shit, I'm a little shit.' It's a sorry state of affairs when young kids can't even take their kickings with a bit of dignity. Almost makes you feel guilty about giving it to them.

'Please Bex, I'm sorry, I'm a little shit,' he says as I smack him in the mouth.

'You little WANKER. You've put me to a lot of trouble you have. Now, we're going to go and get the stuff and you're going to say sorry to the nice people you fucked over, and tell them it wasn't me. Understand?'

'Please Bex,' is all he says.

'Come on, let's get him in the van.' Ollie and me pick Chris up by an arm each and shove him in the back of the van. He struggles a bit, but not so that we noticed. The people on the pavement look at me and Ollie all nervous like as we get in the van, but no one says boo.

'Fuck off,' Ollie shouts at them and we drive off.

I ring the doorbell and Tony answers again.

'I told you . . .'

'Oh put a sock in it for a second will you Tony. I've brought your stuff back.' Tony looks at the pile of his belongings Ollie and Chris are unloading at the top of his garden.

'I knew it,' he says not knowing anything. 'I bloody knew it. Joan,' he shouts down the hallway.

'You didn't know anything, you fucking half-wit. We didn't nick this lot. Well, at least not me and Ollie. He's the one that turned your place over, that one there, with the black eyes.' Chris looks up from the telly he's carrying and gives a little wave.

'Get off of my property,' Tony says as Joan and Mel appear behind him.

'Tony?' Joan says. 'What's all this?'

'He's admitted it at last.'

'Hold your fucking horses Lord Justice Taylor, I didn't admit nothing, I just fucking told you it wasn't me, it was the panda over there.'

'You're scum,' Joan shouts at me. 'Scum, bloody scum. Go on, clear off.'

'I'll get my cricket bat on you,' Tony says again, walking after me as I turn and fuck off back to the van.

'Oh I've had enough of this,' I say as I close the gate behind me. 'Go and get your cricket bat then you big wanker, see if I care.'

'I will,' he says.

'Well go on then.'

'I mean it.'

'Go on.' I turn around and walk back through the gate towards him. Tony stands his ground and just stares at me not moving. Hmm, thought so, like father like son. A lot of the old flannel but fuck all to back it up with.

Mel gets in between us.

'Dad, go back in to the house.'

'Mel, this is between me and . . .'

'Oh shut up Tony and fuck off,' I tell him.

'Please dad, it's not worth it, please.' Joan grabs his arm and tugs him towards the front door. Tony eventually moves, relieved that someone has finally decided to pull him back. Being a bloke, he couldn't very well retreat on his own. And being all front, he couldn't very well step forward and have a go. If Joan hadn't of stepped in, we could've been here all night.

Mel looks at me and shakes her head slowly.

'Go away Bex, I don't want to see you again.'

'But, it wasn't me. I didn't do it, it was Chris over there.'

'I don't care,' she says. 'It doesn't make any difference.'

'Doesn't make any difference? What are you talking about? Of course it makes a difference. I would never do over friends or someone we know, especially not your parents.' I thought about maybe trying to explain about Parky, but I doubt she would've understood.

'It doesn't matter. If it's not us, it's someone else. How many people have you made feel the way you made my mum and dad feel?'

'Mel?'

'I don't want to see you again, not ever.' She picks up the telly and carries it to the door.

'But Mel, wait a minute. Let's talk about it at least.'

'There's nothing to talk about,' she says as she pushes the porch door open and drops the telly in the hall. She cocks her head and turns to me. 'My dad's phoning the police. You'd better go – and don't come back.'

'Bex!' Ollie shouts. 'Come on man. Bex.' Chris runs off

down the road and out of sight and Ollie starts up the van. He gives the horn a couple of blasts and shouts at me to come on through the window again. 'Bex, move it, I'm going.'

I turn, close the gate behind me, and climb in the van as Ollie hits the accelerator.

30. The chase

'Come on Ollie, faster,' I shout at lard-arse beside me. 'Down there.' We smack in to each other like dodgems as we turn to the right and dive in to the alleyway.

I don't look back, I've been caught like that before. Turning around to catch a glimpse of Plod closing in on you only slows you down.

Never look back.

You don't need to, you ain't going that way.

Just look forward.

Forward – that's all you need to see. Concentrate on forward, and then run at it as fast as you can.

'Come on,' Ollie shouts. 'Come on.' Plod's size twelves pound the ground behind me and keep in step with my heart, which is just about to go. 'Over the fence, come on.'

Shit! What a way to spend a Saturday night.

It had started out so promisingly as well. Nice house, pucker gear, cash in the drawer, and someone went and ruined it by phoning the Old Bill. Next house probably. I told Ollie we were making too much noise and should've given it a half-hour, but oh no, Ollie knows best. 'Oh come on Bex,' he goes. 'Let's not fuck about. We'll get this one done and get down the pub.' Cunt.

'Come on Bex, don't fuck about,' he shouts at me as I

squash my nuts on the top of the fence. 'Come on.' One of the coppers reaches up to grab my leg, but I manage to get it out of the way and drop down the other side before he gets a hand to it. My nuts breathe a sigh of relief.

Ollie whacks the top of the fences with an old half a brick, every time either of the coppers get a grip, buying me enough time to get to my feet and find my wind. 'Okay, go,' he shouts and tosses the brick over. We run across the waste ground, climb over another fence – a wire one this time – and charge off across the park.

It's dark. In fact it's very dark. There's street lights on the main path over the other side of the park, but where me and Ollie are running, there's just darkness. Plod's still behind us, and I get the idea that maybe we can lose them in the shadows.

'Ollie,' I gasp. 'Split up. Lose the bastards and hide.' Ollie steers right and heads off to the edge of the park. I steer left and run for the black. Behind me I listen as both sets of plates turn in my direction and power on after me. This is fucking typical, the deaf bastards haven't heard that we've just split up. I feel like shouting back to tell them which way Ollie ran off in, but that would mean one less breath, and at the moment, I need all the air I can get.

Something clips my thigh as I run blind through the pitch black. Fuck knows what it was, a bench or a concrete bin, or something, but the shock nearly knocks me off my stride and on to my arse. 'Oooohh, fucking hell,' I swear to myself. I carry on running with my hand clasped over my leg and feel blood through the rip in my jeans. £50 that's going to cost me for a new pair.

Behind me I hear the sudden thud and painful moans of one of the coppers running full pelt in to whatever I just missed.

'You alright Alan?' I hear the other say and smile to myself as Plod's groans fade in to the distance.

Ten minutes later I'm out on the main road and heading towards town. My leg's really starting to throb now, but this is nothing compared to how it's going to feel in the morning. For the moment though, it's still serviceable and able to take my weight. All I've got to do is get to a pub and get a lift off one of the boys. I look up and see Ollie coming towards me.

'Ollie,' I shout. 'Come on, I've lost them.'

Ollie gasps frantically for breath and clutches at the huge stitch in his side. 'I haven't,' he shouts and sways to one side enough for me to see two fucked-looking coppers wobbling after him.

I turn and try and crank up the old engine again but Ollie's soon catching me. 'Run Bex, run,' he says as he passes by. Being overtaken by Ollie doesn't exactly bode well for me showing Plod a clean pair of heels. I step it up a gear to put the pressure back on fat boy. 'Come on,' I tell him, wishing I was at home and in bed.

My chest screams with every burning lungful of air and my leg feels like it's bumping in to a concrete bin with every step. The only consolation was Plod behind; they were having just as hard a time of it as me and Ollie. The poor old fucking pie-eaters were sweating on their tea break, while the rest of their relief was tied up cleaning the puke out of the back of their jam jars and dealing with the Saturday night trouble-makers.

Thank fuck for small town boredom.

We get off the main road and head down a leafy side street. As ever, Plod turn in after us and pant our course change in to their radios.

'Oh fuck off,' Ollie shouts back. Well, if that doesn't do it, I don't know what will.

'Stop where you are,' one of them shouts back, the first time since we all first met up. 'It's useless. You can't get away,' gasp, splutter, cough.

'No. Fuck off,' Ollie repeats optimistically. 'Please,' I hear him mutter.

Of course, it would've been a different story if we'd made it to the van. We could've been home, dry and in the pub by now, but again, Ollie knew better.

'Not the van,' he goes. 'They chase you forever on the road. Leg it on foot and they give up after a couple of hundred yards.' What a cunt, and this time I think I mean me for listening to him. I haven't run this far since I did cross country at school; and even then, we could always slow down for a smoke. No, I'm fucked and I don't think I've got much left inside me.

But I can't stop, I can't. This one's burglary. I've got too many convictions in this field already. Get collared for this and I'm going down. Much as I can hack a few nights in the cells, I really don't fancy straight porridge. Oh no, that's not for me, no thanks.

Maybe if I can outrun Ollie and they get him, they might be so happy that they got one of us, they might let me get away?

I step up the pace and start to pull away from Ollie.

'Oi hold up,' he's panting. 'Hold up Bex.'

Ollie finds it in him somehow to give it a bit more and suddenly he's, not only back level with me, he's starting to pull away, which wasn't in the plan. This urges me on to make an even greater effort. There's no way he's leaving me behind to get feltched in the showers at Parkhurst. Ollie sees me going for the line and starts slapping his plates against the ground faster still. This signals the last lap bell for both of us and we streak down Wilson Gardens like speeding bullets, desperately trying to leave the other behind. We're a fucking blur to on-lookers. Driveways, joggers, junctions and pavement seating outside a pub, the only thing to slow us down is the occasional hand on the jackets as we both try and claw each other back.

By the time we get in to Oppus Crescent, we're both well and truly fucked.

Ollie catches his boots on an uneven paving slab and falls flat on his kisser. I stop and turn ten yards on. 'Get up you fat cunt,' I shout at him, but Ollie's shot his bolt. He lies, face down, in the middle of the pavement panting like a, like a . . . like a lard-arse who's out of breath, and gives up the ghost.

'I can't make it Bex. You go, leave me.'

I don't need telling twice and leg it towards town. A little further on I hear a siren coming my way. I look back just in time to catch the flashing blue coming round the bend, and dive in to the nearest front garden. The danger passes with a wail, but when I try to move, I find that I'm so total shagged I can't get up off my arse. I take the decision to give it another couple of minutes and stay where I am a while longer.

After a couple of minutes, I manage to struggle to my feet and peer around the corner. Way off, a hundred yards or so back, I see two little old ladies helping Ollie to his feet. I look around but the Old Bill are nowhere to be seen. They must've given up as soon as we started giving it a bit of the old Roger Bannister. I limp off towards them.

'You sure you don't want to come in for a cup of tea love. It's only around the corner,' one of them is saying.

'Yes, come on, come back for five minutes and we can ring your mum for you, come and collect you.'

'No thank you ladies,' Ollie says. 'Really, I've got to get going.'

I sidle up to Ollie and whisper in his ear that it might be a good idea; lie low, get our breath back, have a cup of tea, bit of Battenberg Cake.

'Fuck that,' he says. 'I'd rather take my chances. Anyway, I don't fancy yours much.'

At that moment, the flashing light comes zipping round the corner and we're off again, sprinting down the road. We've got less than half a mile in either of us, and all that asides, there's no way we're going to outrun a police car.

'Follow me,' I shout and run up someone's drive and in to their back garden. I hear the panda mount the kerb and screech to a halt on the drive. Two new coppers jump out of the car and take up the chase with fresh legs.

That can't be fair can it?

Me and Ollie are already scrambling over the garage roof, at the back of the garden, when Pinky and Perky leap at the wall. They're climbing fast but stop dead when there's the sound of a big crash from out of the front. Both drop down and charge round to investigate and I just hear one shouting something at the other about not putting the fucking handbrake on again.

Ollie and me run across a dozen garage roofs, while police cars speed, unseen, all around us. Behind terraces and hedgerows and garden fences and shops. The bastards are suddenly out in force and they want us bad.

We stop at the edge of the row of garages and are just about to jump down in to the dark, when I hear something. I look up and shit myself.

'What is it Bex?'

'Fucking helicopter.'

'You're joking.'

'See me laughing.'

Ollie squints in the darkness. 'I can't see it.'

'Neither can I, but you can bet they can see us. Infrared gear they've got.'

'I don't want to be the poor cunts who gets nicked on *Police Camera Action*, Bex,' Ollie says.

'Neither do I. Come on, let's get moving, and quick.'

Ollie and me jump in to the garden below and run through to the front. The Old Bill are already screeching in to the street, at the end of the road me and Ollie are running across.

'Shopping centre,' I shout at Ollie as we run. 'Saturday night it'll be chocka.'

There are sirens all around us. The pork pie in the sky is directing the whole shooting match, giving away our position to Plod on the deck, while we try to dodge the bastards, with mazey runs through the front and back gardens of half a dozen different houses. We make it to the main road, but no sooner are we there than the fuckers descend on us like flies at a picnic. Ollie ain't hanging about; he's through the doors of the Metcalfe Centre (Britain's seventeenth-largest indoor shopping complex apparently) and leaving me for dead, as the bastards leap out of their jam jars and after us.

The centre's pretty busy. Not Saturday afternoon busy, but busy enough. There are wine bars and restaurants, fast food and all-night supermarkets here for people to spend their lives in. There's also plenty of walls and benches for kids, who can't get served in pubs yet, to hang about on, drink alcoholic Um Bongo and swear at old ladies.

Me and Ollie bomb it through the centre while the Old Bill swarm in from every entrance. Metcalfe security guards suddenly see their chance for glory too and get on after us.

'Police! Stop where you are,' shout a dozen voices behind us.

'Fuck off,' Ollie shouts back.

Late-night shoppers and drunken delinquents stop what they're doing and turn to watch the show. Some shout at us as we leg it past them, but most just stare. There was one bird in particular, really saucy; blonde bob, short lycra skirt, tight white T-shirt and nipples you could hang your coat on. Nothing to do with the story, she just stood out – if you know what I mean. Funny, the things you remember.

'Alright Ollie?' says Norris as we run past him.

'You don't know me,' Ollie shouts back at him.

'Or me,' I yell as I dodge round the other side.

Things aren't exactly going to plan. The further we get in to the centre and the more the coppers surround the centre, the fewer our exits get. I count a good half dozen or so coppers and security guards when I look over my shoulder. People in front are ducking to one side to give us room, but it doesn't matter. All too quickly, we're running out of shopping centre.

'This way!' Ollie shouts. 'Look.'

I look up and, fifty yards away, see Devlin on the door of *Glitzy's*, waving frantically at us to get inside. 'Come on,' he's urging us. 'Come on.'

I dig in and give it one last effort. I'm puffing and panting and I can't breathe and I ache all over, but if we can just make it inside? If Devlin can just hold the filth up long enough? If we can just get through the dancers and get to the fire exit out the back?

I needn't of bothered. Twenty yards from the door, some cunt in glasses and cardigan earns himself a have-a-go-hero caption in the local paper by tripping me up on my arse and falling on top of me.

'Don't try and struggle,' he's shouting in my ear as he pulls my arm up in to an arm lock. 'I've got you. You ain't going nowhere.' I've just done the fucking eight thousand metre sprint, I'm laying face down on hard, cold tiles, with a fourteen-stone librarian on my back and I'm three seconds away from being jumped on by every copper in town and he says don't struggle. The only thing I'm struggling against is vomiting. The bastard's being really rough, pushing my arm up further and kneeling on the back of my leg. I try to say something but I'm too fucked. It's almost a relief when Plod arrives to lift him off and slap me in the cuffs.

'Sergeant Atwell,' I say as he picks me up off the ground. 'How nice to see you.'

'Nice to see you Bex,' Atwell grins. 'Alright, let's go.' Behind us somewhere, I hear Ollie complaining about the cuffs being on too tight and being told to shut up. Atwell leads us off in the direction of the main entrance, while old four-eyes gets a pat on the back and asked how to spell his name.

'Banks, Ian Banks. That's I-A-N, not I-A-I-N,' he says. Funny, I know that name from somewhere.

The saucy bird's still there on the way out and me, Ollie, Atwell and the rest of the boys in blue, give her a smile and a wink as we all go past.

31. It's a fair cop guv'

Why didn't I run faster?

Why didn't we go home with those old ladies? Why didn't we give it half an hour before going through the window? Why do I listen to Ollie? And why do they keep taking my fucking boots?

These are just some of the questions they've left me alone to torture myself in the dark with.

Other questions, such as – I wonder how long I'll get? I wonder what prison's like? and, I wonder what Mel will say when she hears? – will all get their turn tonight.

I tuck my knees up underneath my chin and pull the little tan blanket over my feet and legs to try to keep them warm. It doesn't really work.

I wonder how Ollie's getting on? I wonder what's keeping Charlie?

I wonder what Mel will say when she hears?

I've thought about prison a lot. In my line of work, I suppose, you can't help but think about it. But until now, until this very moment, I've never really stared it in the face. I can't help but feel a bit scared. I wonder if Ollie feels the same way? Of course, when I see him, we'll both give it the large and talk a load of bollocks about how we'll do it standing on our heads. But here, alone in the dark, I'm scared.

I hope we end up in the same nick together. I hope I don't blub when they lead me down the steps. I hope Mel will think of me while I'm away.

Why didn't I run faster?

Charlie'll be here soon. He'll give me the low-down as to what I'm facing. Six months probably; maybe even a year.

A year? Fuck.

A year of being stuck in a little cell like this. A year of being told what to do. A year without a drink. I hope it's only six months, I could do six months, I couldn't do a year.

What if it's more? I can't even think about that, no way. A year and a half. Two football seasons. No way, I'd top myself, I know I would. A year – max – that's all I could do.

My feet are cold.

What am I going to do about my house? I'm going to lose that. And all my stuff? Maybe they'll let me out on bail, sort out my affairs, as they say. I could do a runner, fuck off to France for a few years, you don't even need a passport to get over there these days. I could get a job picking grapes or working in a bar or something, bit of cash work, no one would know. Learn the lingo, get a suntan. Ollie'd come with us. Maybe even Mel. She likes France, she can even speak a bit of it. France, that's not a bad idea, not a bad idea at all.

Of course, it might mean my old lady losing a few quid on the bail money, but I can pay her that back, she won't mind. I wonder if she'll put it up? I wonder if she would if she knew I was going to do a bunk?

What if I only get three months? I could do that, I could

do that easy. If I do a bunk though and they was only going to give me three months, they might then put it up to a year or even a year and a half for me doing the bunk. Fuck. I wonder if there's any way they can let me know before I go to court? Maybe it would be better to take my chances with the judge. If I was facing life then I'd definitely do a bunk, but doing a bunk for just three months, it's not really worth it.

I wonder what prison's like?

Nothing like Roland says it's like, that's for sure. If I believe him, it's like one long fucking tea break, but I bet it's not. I bet it's horrible. Three to a cell, shitting in front of blokes you don't know, handing over half your snout to the landing nutters and watching your back in the shower. I bet it's horrible.

Why didn't we go home with those old ladies? We would've been safe with them. Got off the street, cup of tea, phone a taxi. Why do I always listen to Ollie?

I wonder how he's doing? Asleep probably. I wish I was asleep. I wish I wasn't here. I wish I was tucked up in bed with Mel.

Oh Mel. I wish you was here. I wish I could turn back the clock. I wish I could make it up with you. Oh Mel, my sweet lovely Mel, I'm so sorry.

Charlie arrives a little after two. Atwell lets him in and leaves us alone for a moment.

'Hello Charlie.'

'Hello Adrian. How are you holding up?'

'My feet are cold,' I tell him for now.

'Well don't worry, we're going to have a bit of a chat with Sergeant Haynes in a minute. I'll have Sergeant Atwell give you your boots back, then we'll go in.' He gives Atwell a shout and gets my boots brought in. While I'm pulling them on he sits down and starts to talk. This is unusual because normally, it would be me doing the talking while he just asks a few questions. Not this time. In a low hushed whisper, he starts to talk to me in a way I've never heard him talk before.

'I want you to do exactly what I tell you to do. I want you to say nothing unless I tell you to say it. And I want you, for once in your life, to keep your big bloody mouth shut. Do you understand?'

'What's going on Charlie?' I ask him.

'That is exactly the sort of thing I'm talking about. You are going to prison Adrian. You are looking at a year, or maybe even two. But – and this is a very big but – there may be a way out of it if you are interested. Are you interested?'

'A way out, how?' Two years? Fuck.

'Adrian, stop asking questions and start answering them. Are you interested in avoiding going to prison, yes or no?' I look at Charlie and wonder what he's got up his sleeve. I wonder if he wants me to grass up everyone I know and become a police informant. I wonder how it is he can wangle it so I don't go inside.

Two years, there's no way I could do two years. Fuck!

'Yes or no, Adrian? Yes or no?'

'Yes.'

'You must do exactly what I tell you and nothing more. Is that clear?'

'Yes,' I say.

'Good. We find ourselves in an interesting position here Adrian. Unique even. Sergeant Haynes has a proposition for you.'

'I'm not being a grass,' I tell him straight.

'Adrian, you're interrupting again. If you keep doing that the whole deal will fall through. Just to put your mind at rest though, it's alright, he doesn't want you to grass on anyone. What he wants from you is quite the opposite in fact. What he wants from you is your sworn silence. You mustn't breathe a word of this when you get out of here to anyone. Anyone. Not even your own mother.'

'That's alright, I never tell her anything anyway.'

'Adrian.'

'Sorry. Go on.'

'Haynes has a deal for you. You say nothing, you do nothing, and you walk. It's that simple. You can take it or leave it, it's up to you.'

I don't understand what Charlie is saying. Why would Weasel just want to let me off. Why, after all these years, would he want to do that? And why is Charlie so cosy with Weasel all of a sudden? I don't understand any of this. I'm not being told something and I don't know what.

But, I'm frightened to ask. I'm frightened to ask because if I do, I might blow it. It might all go away. And I don't want it to go away.

I might not go to prison. I might walk away. But why?

'Ollie?' I ask.

'Ollie too. All you have to do is say nothing, do you agree?'

I look at Charlie and I don't get any of this, but I do agree. I nod my head almost fearing to speak.

'Trust me on this one Adrian. Right, come on.'

Weasel sits across the table from me and looks down at the evidence bags with the crowbar I dropped in the chase in it. He says nothing for ages. No one does. Not me, Charlie, Weasel or DC Ross. We just sit there. I look at Charlie, who gives me a nod and mouths for me to stay shtum.

After a while, Weasel opens the bag, takes out the crowbar and gives it a good wipe with a tissue. I look again at

Charlie, but this time he says nothing. Weasel puts the crowbar in to a new bag and seals it up. He starts up the tape recorder, does the introductions and looks across the table at me.

'I'm showing the suspect a crowbar recovered near the scene of the burglary and marked exhibit 1. Mr Beckinsale, is this your crowbar?' Before I can say anything, I look in amazement as Weasel shakes his head at me. I turn around to look at Charlie and he's also shaking his head. Ross starts doing the same and I don't understand why.

'No?' I ask. Weasel nods.

'Mr Beckinsale, did you break in to the house at number fourteen Bladen Park Road?' Again he starts to shake his head. I do the same and shake my head.

'For the tape please Mr Beckinsale.'

'No,' I say.

'Can you explain, then, why you ran from our officers when you were spotted near the scene of the burglary, and indeed, what you were doing there in the first place?' I'm just about to blurt out some badly worded lie when he pushes a bit of paper under my nose and mouths for me to 'read that out'. I quickly scan the page then start to read.

'My friend, Mr Harrington, and I, were driving to the Rose and Crown to meet another friend, a *Mr Norris*?' I screw up my face at Weasel but he urges me to read on. 'For a few drinks and a laugh. On our way to the pub, our vehicle developed engine problems and broke down, so we decided to walk. When the officers approached me, I feared that they might look at my vehicle and see that I had two *bald tyres*?' This is pathetic. 'So, Mr Harrington and I ran, as a decoy measure to draw them away from the van. PTO.'

PTO? What's PTO? I look up and see Weasel drop his face in to his hands and shake his head. Ross snatches the piece of paper from me, turns it over and hands it back.

'Sorry,' I say and start to read again. 'It was a stupid thing to do, and I am very sorry for wasting your time and not stopping when asked to.'

Weasel takes his hands away from his face and asks me if Mr Norris'll back up my alibi. I tell him yes, as I stare at all three of them nodding their heads.

'Of course, we'll have to examine your vehicle and check for these bald tyres, but if it all checks out then we'll leave it at that. Interview terminated at 2.29 a.m.,' Weasel says and turns off the tape recorder. 'PTO. You really are a fucking idiot aren't you Bex!' He hands over a tape, which I sign for and Charlie pockets, then he gets up to leave. I still don't get any of this, but I say nothing.

'We owed you that one alright,' he says waving a finger at me. 'Next time, we'll throw the fucking book at you, you got it?'

'Yes, I've got it, but I don't get it,' I tell him. 'Why?' Charlie grabs at my arm, but Weasel just pulls open the door and leaves.

'Let's just say, we like blokes who hurt little boys even less than we like sodding burglars like you,' Ross says. I look at him in confusion. 'Mr Taylor will explain it to you, no doubt. After you leave the station. And remember, any word of this to anyone and you'll be back in here and looking at a serious stretch before you can sneeze. Right gentlemen, this way if you please.'

We like blokes who hurt little boys even less than we like sodding burglars like you? Charlie told me and Ollie all about it on the way home. The house we'd done over, six months back, and the video Electric had found. Over twenty people – no, not people, sickos – over twenty sickos were rounded up and nicked on the strength of that evidence. My evidence. No one would ever have known if it hadn't been for me and Ollie doing that job. More sick films would've been made, more little boys abused . . . or worse.

I guess Weasel and Ross and Atwell and co, as much as it galled them, felt they owed us one. As unbelievable as it sounds, the fuckers let us off. For once in my life, it felt like we were all on the same side. And it didn't feel too bad. For once in my life, I'd done the right thing and people had appreciated it. Fuck knows how they'd known it was me, fingerprints probably. Got to remember to be more careful in future.

In future. I have a future. No nick, no lock-downs, no barbed-wire fences, no slopping out. I get to go home this morning. I get to wake up in my own bed and go to the pub and walk down the road and . . . maybe see Mel.

I don't want that taken away from me again. I don't want to go to prison. I've seen what it's like and I didn't like it one bit. I can't go to prison. I can't do the time.

And 'if you can't do the time, don't do the crime,' as the expression goes.

Maybe this is the only clever plan there is. Maybe all the rest of it is just bullshit. I'm already talking it with Ollie, about how I was never worried and how I could do a year easy, and this, that and the other. But deep down, I know I'm talking shit.

I'm not prison hard, I'm not like Roland, and I can't go through that again.

Here, in the front seat of Charlie's Jag, I make a decision to quit the life and fall in line with the rest of the world.

Here, in the front seat of Charlie's Jag, I know what it is I've got to do.

First thing in the morning, I'll go round and see Mel. I'll tell her what I've decided and make it up to her, make it up to her before it's too late. Then I'll settle down with her and get a job, a proper one. No more nicking, no more house-breaking, no more fucking about like I was still seventeen. I'm out for good. Retired. End of story.

From now on, I'm going straight.

But then, that's what I always say while I've still got money in my pocket.